RED SHOES

Carmel Bird grew up in Tasmania and lives in Melbourne. *Red Shoes* is her fifth novel. Her earlier novels are *The White Garden*; *The Bluebird Café*; *Cherry Ripe* and, under the name of Jack Power, *Crisis*. She has written four collections of short fiction, *The Common Rat*; *The Woodpecker Toy Fact*; *Automatic Teller* and *Births, Deaths and Marriages*; and two books of inspiration for writers, *Dear Writer* and *Not Now Jack—I'm Writing a Novel.* She is the editor of three anthologies of Australian writing, *Relations*; *Red Hot Notes* and *Daughters and Fathers*. Her home page is at <http://www.carmelbird.com>

Also by Carmel Bird

As author:
Births, Deaths and Marriages
Cherry Ripe
The Woodpecker Toy Fact
Dear Writer
The Bluebird Café
The Common Rat
Not Now Jack—I'm Writing a Novel
The White Garden
Crisis (as Jack Power)
Automatic Teller

As editor:
Relations: Australian Short Stories
Red Hot Notes
Daughters and Fathers

RED SHOES

CARMEL BIRD

VINTAGE

A Vintage Book
published by
Random House Australia Pty Ltd
20 Alfred Street, Milsons Point, NSW 2061
http://www.randomhouse.com.au

Sydney New York Toronto
London Auckland Johannesburg
and agencies throughout the world

First published by Random House Australia in 1998

National Library of Australia
Cataloguing-in-Publication Data:
Bird, Carmel, 1940– .
Red shoes.
ISBN 0 09 1834015.
I. Title.
A823.3

Cover design by Yolande Gray
Typeset in 10.5/14pt Sabon by J&M Typesetting
Printed by Griffin Press Pty Ltd

10 9 8 7 6 5 4 3 2 1

For Jack

How beautiful are the feet of
them that preach the gospel of peace

Romans 10:15

He fitted inside her like a little
prince's foot inside a scarlet slipper

CARILLO MEAN, *Sex and Shoe*

The svelte stilettos of a frozen stillicide

VLADIMIR NABOKOV, *Pale Fire*

CONTENTS

THE NARRATIVE

ACKNOWLEDGEMENTS

The author thanks the publishers of the following works for permission to quote: *To the Wedding* by John Berger (Bloomsbury, 1995), *Without Sin* by Spencer Klaw (Penguin, 1993), *Speak Memory* by Vladimir Nabokov (Weidenfeld and Nicolson, 1967), *From the Beast to the Blonde* by Marina Warner (Chatto and Windus, 1994).

The author expresses gratitude to her editor Meredith Rose for her sensitive and elegant work on *Red Shoes*, and also to Dr Susan Schwartz, to Philip Harvey at the Joint Theological Library, Ormond College, and to Brian Johnson at the Church of Scientology for generous assistance with research material.

THE NARRATIVE

What shall we do before eternity?
Take our time
Dance without shoes

JOHN BERGER, *To the Wedding*

The Central Blood-red Chamber of the Kingdom of the Heart

This story concerns three women: Petra, Sylvie and Colette. To avoid any chance of mystification, I want to explain that Sylvie was Colette's mother, and that Petra adopted Colette and renamed her Celeste. Petra was the leader of a religious community of which Celeste was a member from birth. The group marked its singularity by the wearing of red shoes or sandals, like fairyfolk. Sylvie did not belong to the community.

When Petra was a child in the forties living with her large family in a decaying old house in a small town in Tasmania, she liked to spend her time in a room at the back of the house. This was a large dark room where there were old books and magazines left behind by people who had lived in the house before. Petra liked to read and dream and imagine. In one of the magazines Petra found a tinted photograph of a very small and fragile girl. The girl was sitting on a nimble rattan chair which was placed on the leaf of a giant lily pad in the middle of a pool in southern India. The edges of the leaf, which was six feet across, were turned up like the rim of a platter. It was a miracle the way the girl could sit there in a chair on the surface of the water, as if the liquid had turned to ice. Perhaps there was a thin sheet of glass below the surface? Perhaps it was just what it seemed, a marvellous trick of nature where lily leaves were so strong that they could support the weight of a child on a chair. The name of the plant, *Victoria regia*, was supplied with the picture; the child was anonymous. The wonderful image of the child lodged in Petra's heart. Petra carried with her forever a belief that in some way she was that child, that princess in the frothy white dress, the white stockings, the button boots made from the soft skins of young goats, dyed red. The colours were subtle, faded.

That child, Petra told herself, is me.

Petra imagined herself stepping down from the chair, tripping and skipping and dancing and pirouetting and somersaulting across the lily leaf and leaping like light, moving like air, sailing like a bubble onto the next leaf and the next. Until she had reached into the far distance of the photograph. And was gone.

Day after day, year after year, Petra crept into the dark room where she worked her way through the books and magazines, absorbing in a trance the images and information in the encyclopaedias. She became addicted to the smell of the room, the smell of the books, the stillness, the darkness. The feeling of past time, of no time. The world she entered in that room was separate from everything else she knew; it became the world of her imagination. The princess in the white dress on the lily pad read steadily on subjects from Alchemy to Zoroaster. She loved history and fairytales, loved to feel her heart range from beauty and ecstasy to bitterness, danger, cruelty and despair. She read Dickens, Tolstoy, Defoe, Sir Walter Scott. Tennyson, Keats and Shelley. The thought of a magic

---

Tolstoy

carpet captivated her, a rich red square of silken carpet with strange symbolic patterns woven into it, magic shapes with occult meaning and the power to fly. She imagined the broken-down old room (where the boxes of books shared the space with crooked bicycles and pieces of rusty farm machinery jumbled up with tattered armchairs and bits of beds) to be the secret room in a palace, a room where the walls were lined with gold and scarlet silk and where the couches were draped in velvet, the tables made from glass. Vast mirrors reflected the glitter of cascades of crystal chandeliers, and over everything there glowed an aureole of crimson rays. It was the central blood-red chamber of the kingdom of the heart. And above her in this kingdom I was always hovering. I am her guardian. I don't mean this in the sense of someone who has been appointed by a court to assume responsibility for Petra's health and financial well-being; I am spirit; I am her guardian angel.

Be not afraid.

There exists a dramatic tension between what is aerial and what is terrestrial.

I exist on a line that defines that tension.

Think lightning.

I am actually more like pure thought than anything else, a kind of pure idea, sometimes represented by light itself and generally invisible to the naked human eye. Angels are sometimes visible to people, clothed in the bodies the human imagination has been programmed to supply, and we usually appear or manifest at times of stress, terror, or ecstasy. Most people have never seen an angel.

The story I tell is best read as a kind of dream, as a mirage, perhaps. If you could read it with your eyes shut, I would strongly suggest you do so, but I know this is not possible. A state of intense relaxation, if you can achieve that, is desirable. I do not present you with what is known as virtual reality, but with virtual dream, virtual imagination, the virtual unconscious mind. All humans dream; see this tale I tell you, if you can, as a dream. Perhaps I am frightening you again. In your dreams you have known terror.

Be not afraid.

I must warn you that I exist—that I think—in the present tense. Time with its past and its future has no real meaning for me, although I have attempted, in the telling of this story, to accommodate the concept of a range of tenses in a bid to come down to earth, to trace a narrative through the lives of Petra (b. 1940), Sylvie (b. 1952) and Colette (b. 1968). Dreams, you know, are tenseless in the way that my view is tenseless. Dreams can give what are seen as timely warnings, but the narrative itself is careless, carefree about the sequences of history.

> I confess I do not believe in time. I like to fold
> my magic carpet, after use, in such a way as to
> superimpose one part of the pattern on another.
> Let visitors trip.
>
> VLADIMIR NABOKOV, *Speak Memory*

The group of people who made up Petra's following were sometimes known as the Red Shoe Cult, for Petra developed a rule that footwear was to be red, or that the bare feet of adults were to be decorated with designs in henna, the feet of children dyed with mercurichrome. The group's real name was the Hill House Brethren, first formed by Dr Irving Clay, of whom more later. Uniform of some kind is nearly always important to distinct groups of people, whether the people are together for religious, sporting, military or other reasons, and Petra decreed that her people would be marked by their red feet. The shoemaker's shop in the grounds of Hill House was always busy making shoes, sandals and ballet slippers. The principal item made was the scarlet ecclesiastical slipper, as worn by Catholic priests in Latin countries. I was interested in the fact that although Petra went to great lengths to escape from her origins, at Hill House she replicated her father's shoemaking shop.

> Of all forms of erotic symbolism the most frequent is that which idealizes the foot and the shoe.
>
> HAVELOCK ELLIS

The importance and meaning of shoes had gone so deeply into Petra's spirit, into her heart, that she could not, would not, leave them behind. If you look at the stories of Hans Christian Andersen you will see also that

---

Hans Christian Andersen

this son of a poor shoemaker in Odense is fascinated by feet and shoes, not least in 'The Little Mermaid' and in 'The Red Shoes'. The evil, nightmarish pain and loss brought to the realm of the foot in these stories is of the darkest, most sadistic, masochistic kind. The sudden castration of the foot with an axe, the sensation of walking on hot knives.

You will notice, from time to time, that I have listed the odd word at the foot of a page. By this I mean to suggest to you that you may wish to turn to the section called The Footnote, where I have expanded on these key words in The Narrative. You could try looking up Hans Christian Andersen now.

You get cults that wear flowing robes of only a certain colour—black or red or orange or white or silver—cults that shave their heads; cults that never cut their hair; cults that always cover their heads; cults that wear feather cloaks; cults that dress like flowers or animals. And these are only the uniforms, the clothes that set the cults aside from other people, mark them as special and different and blessed and superior; followers of great and holy leaders by whose word the cult members live or die.

Not so crazy was Petra's fascination with feet, and with dance, for all religious ritual began as dance. And not so mad, either, her use of the title Queen of Sheba, one of the most celebrated foot-queens of history.

Feet are ascribed telltale marks of identity and origin, perhaps through the literal-minded word-play of the imagination, since they are the

lowest part of the body and in touch with the
earth as opposed to the heavens.

MARINA WARNER, *From the Beast to the Blonde*

The planet is seeded with groups of people who are trying to live according to rules of their own making, who are using the bits of civilisation that appeal to them and inventing the rest. Such people usually come to the attention of the world only when they self-destruct in some way—like at Jonestown or Waco. It takes a charismatic leader with a weirdly strange idea. Petra was charismatic, I can see that, and from my position I have been able to follow the development of her nutty ideas and her power over other people. It's no use a leader giving the faithful a sane and rational idea to follow—the point is you dream up something crackpot and then sell it to them. And of course when I say 'sell', I mean the leader usually gets rich. I have heard Petra preaching to her followers—who were by no means stupid people—and I tell you, nothing she said made any sense. Now and again I will give you little tastes of this kind of thing. Of course, half the time she and the Brethren were away with the fairies on LSD or mushrooms.

We will enter from time to time (you see how eager I am in my efforts to follow the clock) a series of hallucinations, of swift-shifting kaleidoscope-scapes. The hallucinatory juices of a mushroom may be poisonous or deliciously benign; and the shape of the mushroom is mimicked in the cloud arising from nuclear explosions. It is instructive to compare the shapes things take. (Think, for instance, of how many things in nature resemble the human eye.) Human beings attain visions of timeless ecstasy and bliss when the chemicals from mushrooms, those umbrellas of the fairies, invade their mushroom-shaped brains. And I hear that a vision of the god-of-all has recently appeared to a woman in the form of a great white umbrella surrounded by dazzling flocks of multi-coloured butterflies.

I notice how much language seems to depend on words that acknowledge the presence of time. I, of course, actually have no language to call my own. Angels must borrow what they can where they will.

> The highest enjoyment of timelessness—in a landscape selected at random—is when I stand among rare butterflies and their food plants. This is ecstasy, and behind the ecstasy is something else, which is hard to explain. It is like a momentary vacuum into which rushes all that I love. A sense of oneness with the sun and stone. A thrill of gratitude to whom it may concern—to the contrapuntal genius of human fate or to the tender ghosts humoring a lucky mortal.
>
> VLADIMIR NABOKOV, *Speak Memory*

The sky, especially the starry sky, opens its umbrella, arches its ribs, over this planet. Petra sometimes preached a doctrine explaining that the Brethren were made from

---

butterflies

what she called star-stuff, had been chosen by some grand universal selection process to get the really good material for their bodies. I was always amazed that the great minds of the city fell for this—don't they know that *everybody* is made from the same elements as the stars? Star-stuff. Sounds good, doesn't it?

Multi-coloured butterflies clouding round the great white umbrella became the visionary woman's personal metaphor for god-of-all-with-angels. Rather nice, in its way. Difficult to sustain and develop as a great myth, but somehow a delicate marrying of natural and domestic things in an attempt to express what is sublime. Think umbrella, think butterfly. I also think of the giant umbrella of the lily leaf on the pond in southern India, the leaf with the Petra-like child in her red boots sitting on a little chair, floating on the surface of the water, staring at the camera.

Think back to that image of strange floating innocence.

Think float, think flight, think wing, think hand.

Think foot.

Think fire, passion. Think red. (Sometimes at this point I say something like: think Massacre of the Innocents; think Saint Bartholomew, Catherine de' Medici.) Red shoes, ruby slippers. Think shoe, think foot.

The Shoe Story

So this is the shoe story, the foot story. If the shoe fits, wear it, as the prince said to Cinderella—but more of Cinderella later. Forget about romance and think sex.

> Of all fetish objects sexy shoes are among the oldest and probably most common. They taper the toes. They arch the instep. They lift the calves. They tilt the fanny and bow the back and oil the hips and sashay the gait. Their leathery, animal scents and textures evoke the jungle blood sports braided in our genes.

There you are, a strange mosaic of images—jungle blood sports braided in your genes.

> Shoes make the foot look shorter and more precious, and yet add the formidableness of extra height, and often a sort of stiletto menace. A sexy shoe is a masterpiece of concealment and disclosure and so defines the dynamic of lust itself.

This is all from *Esquire* magazine—and as I said, forget about romance, think stiletto menace.

I've been in charge of the shoe story for as far back

as anybody can remember. You get people like the Master of the Queen's Stables, Master of the Mirrors, Post Master, Guardian of the Lungs and Heart—well, I'm Guardian of the Foot (and by implication, the Shoe).

I feel that I should acknowledge the sexist nature of the language here—everybody seems to be a master of some kind or other, don't they? Well, those are their titles from way back, and I am at a bit of a loss what to do about it. 'Guardian' is a nice word, I think, and I'm glad I fall into that category. The other night on television (I should warn you that I rather like these modern inventions) I saw a man who writes novels talking about books and writers in general, and the only writers he talked about were men. I thought that was pretty daring, in this day and age, and I must say I would never do that. But he's a man who offended some people so much with one of his books that they have sworn to kill him, so I daresay getting up the noses of a bunch of feminists is small beer to him. Maybe he is challenging them to come after him, I can't say. I have heard he does his best work under pressure. People often do.

Angels write in blue ink, in a lovely kind of copperplate that flows like the sea on a Japanese beach. Sometimes people remark that the nuns must have taught us how to write, but it's the other way round—it was we who taught the nuns to do it, and they passed it on to all the children in their care. One of my brothers, if you could call him that, is actually in charge of fountain pens, and that's a very big thing which also takes in cigars. Yes, in case you're wondering, he was appointed guardian to Sigmund Freud—a hell of a job, what with one thing and another.

If Petra knew I was telling you this story she would kill me (well, that's really nothing but a figure of speech; it is not possible for Petra to kill me because of the nature of my existence, but she would be furious and would make life very difficult). She has the vilest temper of anyone I know, and that's saying something. I have seen her beat a child around the face with a shoe—a red stiletto. I said this was the shoe story. I have seen her order another woman to tie a child to a chair and apply hot coals to its bare feet to teach the child to walk quietly. That's just a couple of things. If you thought this was a pretty story, think again. I issued a kind of warning when I said Massacre of the Innocents and drew your attention to Catherine de' Medici—incredible woman. Petra proudly claimed to be related to Catherine, and expressed great interest in her so-called ancestor.

There's a book Petra had, a small book with a red cover that she pinched from the library one night at King's College right under the nose of the Master. Under my nose as well, but of course it isn't my affair if she takes other people's property. It's a book about the massacre on Saint Bartholomew's Day, and she enjoyed it so much she used to read it to people, particularly children, at dinner. She was carried away with the fact that the first modern ballet, *Le Ballet Comique de la Reine*, was staged in Paris on the eve of the massacre, and was written for the occasion by Catherine de' Medici. A light would come into Petra's eyes and she would read out terrible details about the massacre. I used to wonder that her audience didn't

---

Catherine de' Medici; Saint Bartholomew

realise she was mad, but they accepted everything she said, everything she did. I daresay she is a kind of witch, a fascinating, mesmerising, charismatic witch-woman.

Thirteen little girls with long golden hair, black dresses, black stockings and red shoes sat up to the table, damask napkins tucked under their chins, and while they drank their soup from thick white bowls Petra read to them from the red book. She embellished the text, inventing her own narratives from slender and horrible details, and encouraged the children to illustrate the stories in their drawing books, and to act out sequences in costume. Petra had no particular political or religious line to promote with the stories; her motive in telling them was to thrill and terrify and horrify the little girls, and to reinforce the notion that life outside the walls of their home was very ugly and dangerous. The stories were, in a sense, cautionary tales. And it was not at all clear that these things happened far away and long ago. The massacre on Saint Bartholomew's Day might have been just down the road, just last week, for all the children knew. Although Petra had a grip on time such as I have not, she found it useful to confuse and blur the past-present-future in the minds of the girls.

Massacre of the Innocents

There was the story of the Huguenot who died in the massacre, strangled by his own necklace made from the ears of priests. Petra told the children how Queen Marguerite retired from the sounds and terrors of the massacre behind the curtains of her four-poster bed, only to be startled by a wounded man pursued by four archers. The wounded man dived into bed with her, and to escape from him she slipped into the space between the bed and the wall, her snow-white linen nightgown drenched in the man's blood. Petra made it clear that this became a sexual encounter and was the beginning of a passionate affair. She enjoyed telling the girls about love, romance, sex.

There was the noble Huguenot woman who tried to escape disguised as a peasant in coarse woollen clothing, and who was recognised when her fashionable coloured silk petticoat showed beneath her skirt. The button maker and the king's dealer in feathers were hacked to pieces along with their wives and children, Petra revelling in her own descriptions of all the different kinds of buttons in a soup of blood and excrement, of all the bundles of wonderful and shimmering feathers splashed scarlet and floating down the Seine like grotesque, misshapen swans.

---

scarlet

A man, covered in the blood of his victims up to his dark and bushy beard, carried to the river a laughing baby. Then on the bridge the man plunged a dagger into the baby's heart and tossed the body into the water. Children themselves tied belts around the necks of babies and dragged them screaming round the streets like dolls, until they fell silent in death.

One of Petra's favourite characters was the Maker of Gold Thread, whose house was built on a bridge. He kept some of his victims prisoner and then cut their throats and dropped them into the Seine through a trapdoor in his kitchen. He took delight in the months after the massacre in drawing back his sleeve to display the arm that had killed, he said, more than four hundred Huguenots.

The children at the table listened in silence, drinking their soup, as the spellbinding voice of Petra wove the stories deep into their hearts. She liked to end with the Miracle of the Mayflower. The day after the massacre, Paris was a silent city. But at noon in the churchyard of the Holy Innocents a dead and withered hawthorn bush burst into white blossoms and green leaves. Although the red book pointed out that the miracle was organised by the Franciscan who looked after the graves, Petra never said so.

She told the children about the hysterical joy of the people who saw the miracle as a vindication of the massacre, as a sign of God's pleasure, and as a licence to go out killing again. And more miracles followed as a statue of the Virgin Mary wept and a new star appeared in the heavens. A little boy, who would grow up to be the Marshal of France, had lain motionless for hours beneath the bleeding, writhing, dying bodies of his father and brother. He was found by the umpire of a nearby tennis-court who had come to rob the bodies, and his life was spared. Petra might add this story as an exemplary and moral lesson in fortitude.

And sometimes, if the fancy took her, after telling one of these stories, Petra would select a child who had transgressed in some way, who had perhaps folded her dinner napkin wrongly, and she would summon one of the women from the kitchen and order the woman to hold the child by the ankles, naked over the pit of excrement in the cellar. This pit was where they emptied the chamber pots, and it was known as The Truth, in a gesture towards Aldous Huxley who said that truth lies at the bottom of a very dirty well.

I should tell you that Petra, the great and glorious and shining Petra, is fascinated to the point of obsession by shit. I mean that literally. Shit. This is a little-known fact about her, and I hope I am not putting you off by mentioning it so soon. Perhaps it is natural for a woman whose life is dedicated to things of the spirit to be deeply interested in her own bowels and those of other people, and the products thereof. The great Carl Gustav Jung, after all, had a vision of God depositing a great heap of shit onto the roof of the cathedral in Basle. I think that was how it went. Wrecked the roof. These people and their visions! And on the subject of shit—Petra, who is obsessed by ballet, delights in the way the dancers call cheerfully to each other before a performance, '*Merde!*'

That idea rather appeals to me, as many French ideas do. There you have the whitest, airiest, most virginal, pure creatures in satin and tulle, looking as if they are about to take off into the ether, nothing further from a piece of shit was ever seen. And as the orchestra tunes up, what are they saying to each other? Shit, shit, shit. Petra was only a mediocre dancer herself, but she employed a Russian ballet master to teach the children in her care, and saw to it that everyone regularly greeted each other with '*Merde!*' It was as if she wanted to reinforce to the girls that they might give the appearance of beauty and goodness on the outside, but inwardly they were corrupt little bags of tripe and shit. This gave her control over them, but she also believed it to be true. Petra believed wholeheartedly in her own teachings, and this belief, added to the natural light in her lovely eyes, was part of her fascination.

I was appointed Petra's guardian when she was born, and I know her inside out. She is dead now, but because she made such an impression on me I am inclined to think of her as living, and this false belief can play havoc with my tenses, which are, as I have explained, unstable at the best of times. Bear with me. I was, in a strange way, afraid of Petra. She died by her own hand at the age of fifty-five. (By some curious and swift trick, somewhere along the way, she added ten years to her age, officially dying at sixty-five or sixty-six. Consequently, she appeared to be miraculously younger-looking than her age.) And don't ask me where she has gone, because it is not my business to know that kind of thing. You may be surprised to learn that it was also none of my business to save her from herself; if there is one thing a guardian angel can't do, it's intervene in the event of suicide. We hover round saving our charges from accidents and so forth, but if they get into their heads the idea that they want to kill themselves, there's nothing we can do.

She caught on very early to the fact that I was there, and was able to use me to make her way in the world. I recall the first incident.

At the Fountain

Petra was three years old, a strawberry blonde with a high-domed forehead and pale blue eyes. Her eyes, I thought, were actually like Terence Stamp's. She imagined they looked like the eyes of the Grand Duchess Anastasia. A kind of celestial aquamarine, as Petra sometimes described them. There were times, I must say, when I thought they resembled aluminium.

We were in the park. She was sitting on the edge of an ornamental pond, where coloured fish wove about beneath the lily leaves and where the ripples from a central fountain faded out, and she was releasing the petals of a rose onto the surface of the water, petal by petal like little scarlet boats, when a boy of about five came up and swished the flotilla with a stick so that the petals were scattered as if by a violent wind. Petra sat very still, her back to the boy, then she lifted her head, turned her face towards where I was standing and, as if she could see me, she looked straight into my eyes and said, 'Why don't you kill him?'

I can tell you I was completely taken by surprise. It is not my business to go round killing people; all I am supposed to do is keep Petra out of harm's way. But the boy heard her and lost his footing and fell off the rim of the pond into the water. (It seems nobody was really looking after him.) And of course it was none of my concern to try to save him. He sat up, bawling in the shallow water, covered in green slime and weed, with the mud containing the accumulated shit of generations of bright fish, unable to understand what had happened. Petra's dress was splashed, but she simply continued to sit, silent now, on the edge of the pond, her silence backed by the rush of the water from the fountain.

First the boy's mother, and then Petra's mother, came dashing from different corners of the park, scooped their children up and bore them off. From behind a tree a shamefaced guardian appeared and followed the boy. Across her mother's shoulder Petra looked again into my eyes and smiled. She said nothing at all; she was known for being a quiet child with a strong will and the famous temper I have already mentioned. From a little church across the park the angelus was ringing. I recall that at the sound of the pretty bell Petra swung round in her mother's arms to face the source of the carillon and broke into a truly dazzling smile.

The lifetime bond between Petra and myself, forged at her birth, was changed and strengthened that day, charged with a special kind of electricity and emotion. Petra grew up to be an unusual adult who retained a close relationship with her guardian. And of course she didn't only have me working for her, she was one of those children born with the Halo Effect, the children everybody loves and prefers, the ones who don't seem to have to do anything to get their way. The ones with beauty and charm and talent—call it charisma. Petra was always able to generate an atmosphere favourable to herself, just with—what—her personality I suppose.

As a baby she was so pretty, with large eyes wide apart, broad cheekbones, neat little chin, dazzling smile, and not only did her grandmother and grandfather (she believed they were her parents) dote on her, the whole world wanted to pick her up and cuddle her and run its fingers through her red–gold ringlets. Light, I swear it, emanated from that baby. She was like the sun glistening on fresh honey. People were drawn into the field of the halo that softly radiated from her. I have theories about these things, and I think that before Petra was born, when her real mother tried to abort her with a long steel knitting needle and half a bottle of gin and a hot bath, Petra got the message that she was desperately not wanted and responded to the murderous attack with a super, extra-tenacious hold on life. Having won against the killer knitting needle, she was going to continue to win and win and win.

Petra always called me Beau, addressing me thus on Christmas cards and suchlike, although she later began to spell it 'Beaux', when she discovered Ernest Beaux, the creator of Chanel No. 5. The name, to me, is neither here nor there. And that's an interesting little phrase—neither here nor there. I don't wish to bore you with theology, but I just note in passing that Thomas Aquinas said that angels move in discontinuous time. We can be now here, now there, with no interval of time in between. Neither here nor there; both here *and* there. When we move there are not two instants separated by time; between the beginning and the end of the movement there is no time at all. We are in the perpetual present, the eternal now. *We* might be, but of course people can't grasp that so well. Michael the Archangel (who is made, by the way, from snow) can be in three of the seven heavens at once. And there's a woman in Switzerland who is quite well known for entertaining angels and writing down the music they bring her, and she says they take four or five days to come from wherever they live. I'm not sure how she figures that—maybe they have had to tell her that so she will give them some peace. We can move faster than the speed of light if we want to, and this plays up with time and space—it's an Einstein thing.

Return, now, to the park and you will see that although we are in rural Australia in the forties, the design of the park is European, some compromise between English and French. A high fence of fancy iron pickets surrounds a rectangle which is cut diagonally from each corner by gravel paths, between which are planted lawns and flower beds and European trees.

Green wooden benches beneath the trees; in the centre of it all a wide and shallow pond, circular, with water lilies and goldfish, and in the very heart a piece of large bronze statuary complete with nymphs, mermen, trumpets, vigorous acanthus leaves and gushing fountains. The semi-nakedness of the figures is both welcomed and ignored, it seems, by adults; whereas alert and knowing children such as Petra are fascinated, entranced by breasts and other suggestive bulges in the group. Larger than life these people, these creatures, recline, entwined, gesturing, waving, smiling, promising loud ecstasies from the middle of the pond.

The fountain is the most elaborate public object in the town, and there is a legend that it was sent here by mistake, that a factory in France muddled its orders, and this little town ended up with a fountain destined for somewhere very grand. The people of the town were so impressed, quite overwhelmed by the sight of such a glorious bronze scene of lust, desire and sexual frolic that they raised the funds to keep it. I don't know how much truth there is in the story.

The boy twisted his ankle when he fell in the water. I've hurt my foot! he yelled. I've hurt my foot!

I said the mothers came running to the pond and gathered up the children, and that is certainly how it looked at that moment. I have no reason to suppose that the woman who claimed the boy was not his mother. And I know for a fact that Wanda, the young woman, you might almost say *girl*, who collected Petra, was Petra's mother. However, Petra did not know this. To all intents and purposes, Wanda was Petra's sister, and Lydia was the mother of both of them, as well as of a number of other children.

In the part of this story that I call The Footnote you will find my comments about some of this stuff, if you're interested. The universe is full of things to think about, if one can find the time. You will also get a fair bit of information about many a thing under the sun—try the story of 'The Snow Queen' for starters. I figure that if I want you to think of Petra as some sort of Snow Queen, you will need to have a look at the text of that story, and I want to save you the time of running about like a frantic rodent from one library to another only to be told by tired, bored or arrogant librarians that the book is out, lost, untraceable, being repaired, being processed. (When they say 'processed, being processed', I imagine they are turning books into cheese.) This library run would drive you mad, and the thought of it brings me out in a rash. Fortunately they have invented hypertext and interactivity just in the nick of time and so you can load the CD-ROM and click on 'The Snow Queen' and go for your life if that's what you want to do. Make links. Go-go-go. Hot spot!

Years ago, between jobs, I was staying at the beach and I read *Sons and Lovers*, and I kept wishing there was a way I could get a picture and some information every time there was a reference to a flower. That book has more flowers than Kew Gardens. If only, I thought, I could look over at the wall and see some sort of coloured projection of crimson roses or dahlias sodden with rain—'wet-black crimson balls'. I imagined how it would be if I could gradually add the pictures of the flowers, one after another, until the whole room—walls, ceiling, floor—was covered with them. Just a space in one wall for a window onto the sky, and a space in another for the door. And there I am, lost in the conservatory, one off-duty guardian angel reclining on some oriental sofa arrangement, reading a book. I first became interested in D.H. Lawrence because of all the stockings in the text, even elastic stockings and wooden legs, and then I discovered the flowers as well. Tall white lilies reeling in the moonlight—I liked that. Anyhow, my point is that these days you can switch to the image of the flower and back again with just a nibble of the mouse.

I think The Footnote is rather nice in its own way, by that I mean the good old-fashioned print version of The Footnote. If you don't want to use the CD-ROM, don't want to sit down at the PC and choof around the screen with a mouse, you don't have to worry. I've organised things so you can lie on the couch propped on silken cushions and idly move around in the book itself, choosing a hot spot and flicking over to the references in The Footnote. Not so 21st-century an approach as the CD-ROM—probably closer to Scheherazade, depending a bit on the nature of your cushions.

You will probably have your own mental version of 'The Snow Queen' and the other stories in The Footnote, but I want you to have the chance to read my versions. Here you have my Narrative, and if all you have time to do is read The Narrative, that's okay. But you will discover that certain words in The Narrative have long entries in The Footnote, and at any time you can wander off into The Footnote and back again.

I imagine The Footnote as if it were the mud and slush at the bottom of a pond. On the surface of the water are the leaves and blooms of the lilies, in the form of The Narrative. Try going to water lilies or lotus in The Footnote.

And don't forget that you can always get into your gladrags and park the car in the basement of the theatre and go see whole performances of ballets about Snow White and Cinderella and so forth, some time. Or park the car in the car park next to the video shop and take out the video—well, there are plenty of things you can do. If you

---

couch; Scheherazade

do go to the theatre, you might look up to the ceiling and catch a glimpse of me, or at least some of my colleagues. We like to get out. There are usually dozens of us drifting around the ceiling of the Paris Opera. And another place we like to go—we sing in the choirs of all the great cathedrals, in major basilicas and in minor basilicas. I actually enjoy going off to tiny country churches and joining in the singing. Once I started singing at the Windmill Hill Methodist Church, but Petra was so embarrassed I had to stop.

I think it is worth setting down some of the bare, plain facts about Petra's past, as Petra herself had a habit of offering only what can charitably be called romantic versions of these things. Since she died I have been looking for work and so I have had the perfect opportunity to write all this up, get straight some of the facts (insofar as I know them). Petra was not in truth the youngest child of Lydia and Stephen Penfold, bootmakers, but their grandchild, offspring of red-haired Wanda and a mysterious stranger. Petra gets the mysterious stranger part right, conjuring up for herself a fabulous heritage. I have heard her tell people she was adopted by Lydia and Stephen, that she was the child of, for example, a Russian nobleman, a Spanish count, a wandering musician, a Swedish scientist, a gypsy dancer, according to her mood and her audience. The story that was current for about the last thirty years of her life was that she was descended from French royalty, in a line from Catherine de' Medici, a nasty piece of work to choose for an ancestor.

Wanda died young, without ever revealing the identity of Petra's father; perhaps it's just as well. It has crossed my mind that Wanda's father was also Petra's father, but then I have seen so much of that kind of thing in my time that I have an over-suspicious mind. And I believe Petra died without ever knowing for sure that the people she thought were her parents were in fact her grandparents, and that Wanda was not her mad sister, but her mother. It was not my job to tell Petra these things.

Mad Wanda

On that day in the park, after the incident at the pond, Wanda put Petra in the pusher—this was a striped canvas affair and was actually designed for a doll, so that it was a bit on the small side for a three-year-old girl. Petra accepted it, knowing no better, and she enjoyed being pushed around the streets by Wanda. She adored Wanda. Wanda didn't think much of Petra, believe me. When Wanda would have liked to loiter on street corners talking to young men on bicycles, she had to be Petra's nursemaid instead. She was very angry and frustrated, and on more than one occasion she took her hand off the pusher and let it roll down the hill. Of course I was there to intervene and so the child came to no real harm. Then Wanda started to turn her rage upon herself; she became fixated on her hair, which was a long, shining, red–gold mane. First she chopped at it with blunt scissors; then she took to tearing it out; then she had a phase of striking a match and seeing how close she could get to it without setting it on fire—and it did catch alight a few times. Wanda would scream and grab a towel or a blanket or rush to the nearest tap.

You may wonder where her guardian had got to: Wanda's guardian was one of those careless ones who leave at the first sign of trouble and hang out with others of their kind in disused factories and warehouses and so forth, sitting around playing cards and smoking and waiting for their person to die so they can get on with some other more cushy and interesting assignment. I have even heard rumours of guardian angels who have gone feral and who inhabit the wild extremities of the planet, snarling and spitting and generally behaving in a most uncharacteristic and unbecoming way. And I have known guardians who, instead of pulling children back from the edges of cliffs, will quietly tip them over. If you look carefully at paintings of children with their guardians, you can sometimes tell that the angel is about to push the baby into the river. Personally I prefer to work; the harder the job, the better, perhaps. I never abandoned Petra, even though she was the most difficult case I have ever had, and that's saying something.

The Family

Petra Alma Penfold was born in 1940 when Wanda was sixteen and working at the woollen mill. Not long after the incident at the pool in the park, Wanda was killed in a motor bike accident. What a sad life. Wanda was the sixth child of a cobbler, the second youngest in a family of seven. Her mother and father, Lydia and Stephen (known always as Cobbler), worked from dawn to dusk in the bootmending shop in the front of the house. They were never without food or clothing, but they would have been classed as poor. Everything was homemade, second-hand or third-hand, patched, darned. The red brick house had no front garden, but out the back there were a dozen fruit trees and a vegetable garden. They kept a cow and some chooks, and Lydia took in washing, so there was a perpetual double line of sheets and towels strung across the grass and a constant need to chop wood and stoke the copper. Jam and preserves were made, the dark kitchen filling up with sweet clouds of sticky steam. There were always cats and dogs, and Petra loved kittens above all. They sometimes allowed her to dress them up and wheel them about in a wicker pram with a long willow handle.

Wanda's brothers and sisters, Joseph, Arthur, Felix, Iris, Nancy and Greta, made a pet of Petra even before

---

Alma

Wanda's death, and when Wanda was gone, Petra grew into her potential, which was to be the family's Christ Child. She never chopped wood or dug vegetables, but she would happily take a basket and pick the raspberries from the canes, or collect the eggs. Her bed, spread with a spotless white counterpane, was in a corner of a room she shared with Nancy and Greta, who initiated her into what it meant to be a girl. Photographs of men hidden in the underwear drawer. Lipstick and powder and stockings, and sanitary cloths which had to be boiled and used over and over again. Iris and Joseph and Arthur had all left home to be married, and when they came round with their children, Petra was the acknowledged leader.

The children somehow sensed deep down that Petra was dangerous, but they were unable to put their finger on what it was about her that disturbed them, and they followed their beautiful little queen wherever she led them. And no harm came of this, except, of course, to Petra's own character. She learned to assume she would always lead, would always be right. Occasionally (less often than you would think), a teacher or some other adult would try to take her down a peg or two, would call her Miss Know-all or refer to her as your majesty, but this was all water off a duck's back to Petra. I love expressions like that—water off a duck's back.

Petra was very quick to learn, and she would learn anything she saw would put her at an advantage. But she also did things for pleasure, such as knitting and sewing.

When she was old enough she learned to sew on the treadle sewing machine which was kept in the big room with the books and all the other lost and broken paraphernalia, and she loved to cut the cloth and pin and baste and sit up to the machine and push with her foot, guiding the material with her fingers. And when she sat in the armchair reading she would often be knitting.

The Halo Effect

At the local school Petra exerted the power of her Halo Effect, manipulating with great ease the lives of the other children.

Boy: Don't go near the woodpile, little girl. There's a snake in there.

Petra: If there is a snake in the woodpile, little boy, you will kill it for me.

And the truth is that she grew tired of the smallness of her world. She listened to the radio and looked at the newspapers and watched her sisters knit bandages and balaclavas for Australian soldiers at war, and she longed to go to the battlefields and fight. Wear a uniform, fly an aircraft, carry a rifle, march knee deep in mud and blood and kill the enemy. Felix had been killed in France, and a photograph of him in his uniform was placed in the centre of the mantelpiece over the kitchen stove. Petra liked to sit in the apple trees and dream of being a man among men in the life-and-death moments of war—on the sea, in the clouds, in the desert. She could rock herself into ecstasy on the branch of a tree, feel a delicious heat prickling all through her and exploding in her belly and in her head.

What are you doing up there, Pet?

Nothing.

Well, be careful.

She hangs upside down from one of the branches so that her skirt falls over her head and her pants are visible. She does handstands on the grass, and she cartwheels along between the trees. On a swing hanging from a tree on a windy, barren hilltop not far from the house, Petra goes high, higher than anyone else, courting danger, tempting death, liable to go flying over the very top of the hill and crash onto the trees and rocks below. Actually, the bushes beside the swing could be the bushes where Petra was conceived. Petra sometimes goes about without her underpants. Nancy makes all Petra's underwear from special soft white material, and Nancy also makes satin slips for herself and Greta, spending hours at night in poor light doing rouleaux and insertions and grub roses by the dozen.

Petra revels in sniffing the bottles of scent that Nancy and Greta keep on the dressing-table, but she is also drawn to the smell of kerosene mixed with shit and urine in the outdoor lavatory in its little house that is covered in morning glory vine. Other girls are afraid to go down the yard to the lavatory at night, afraid of spiders, rats, men with axes, nameless monsters, the dark; but Petra is not afraid. She sits there by candlelight looking at the advertisements on the squares of newspaper hanging from a string.

The last square must come off your bottom as clean as a whistle, her father tells her. It's the polisher, you see.

One of Petra's aunts, Clytie, was so obsessed with excrement that she kept small suitcases of her own shit underneath her bed. She ended up in the loony bin at New Norfolk and was never spoken of, although Lydia sent her a parcel of cake and shortbread every Christmas until she died.

Petra was the family's little Christ Child, but by that I do not mean to imply this was a religious family. Petra was their star, the light of their lives. Lydia saw to it, however, that Nancy took Petra to the Sunday School, which happened to be Methodist, every once in a while. Petra liked it, the best dress, the clean socks, the straw or felt hat, the hymns and prayers and bible study, the pictures of flowers and Jesus to take home and keep. Best of all she liked the way the small stone church nestled on the side of a hill, hidden by dark, unruly trees. It was, with its slender, pointed windows and air of mystery and otherness, a place of fairytale. Would the good people of the congregation have been surprised to learn that Petra found there was something exciting, something a bit sexy about the whole Sunday morning thing at the Methodist church? Perhaps they all felt this anyway, to a degree. The teaching was bleakly anti-sex, and yet to Petra there was a faint erotic charge. The musty smell was a turn-on, for one thing. And the clear message of denial of the flesh was exciting in its way. The Windmill Hill Methodist Church.

And this next sounds like too much of a coincidence, but it's perfectly true.

To reach the clean and holy and sexy little church, Nancy and Petra had to walk past a place called the Snakepit. Go past the snakepit on your path to paradise. It was a square brick building where snakes were bred in order to be milked for their venom, which was used in medicines. Nancy hated the Snakepit, but Petra, while pretending to have a scientific interest in it, found it incredibly thrilling and fantastic.

Petra: I might go and work there when I grow up.

Nancy: Don't make jokes like that. It's a terriblc place.

Petra: I'd love it. And afterwards I might be a snake-charmer. Go to India and be a snake-charmer.

Nancy: Don't say things like that either. It's ridiculous.

Nancy would sometimes remember that poor loopy Wanda was the mother of this strange child, and then she would try to imagine who was the father. It couldn't be a local, but you didn't get too many strangers around here. Perhaps a sailor? How could it be a sailor? Maybe it was some madman who was already locked up. There was something very unsettling about Petra, some foreign, unknown strain.

The Flower is Always in the Almond

One of Petra's habits that troubled Nancy was her way of separating out, wherever possible, from any piece of fruit she ate, the seeds or kernel. She would then, holding a seed between her thumb and forefinger and using her incisors in the manner of a rodent, slowly grind the germ of the plant, and swallow the paste she had made. From time to time she took a moment to stare closely at the seed she was eating. She smashed the stones of apricots with a hammer in order to discover the jellied kernel in its soft brown envelope. From apples she removed the shiny fibrous cases of the seeds, and made patterns on her arm by licking the little shards and sticking them to her flesh.

Petra was always staring into space, her eyes not blank but swimming with some weird kind of knowledge and information, brimming with light.

Somerset, Love and Gwendolin Jones

At the Methodist Sunday School Petra became friends with Gwendolin, the daughter of the minister, Mr Jones. Gwendolin was the only and adored child of Somerset and Love Jones, and the family welcomed Petra into their circle. Nancy could safely leave Petra with the Joneses and go off with her own girlfriends, so it was a good arrangement all round. From the time she was about five until she was fifteen, Petra had a home away from home at the Joneses'. And Gwendolin, to tell the truth, loved to hang out in the cobbler's shop inhaling the tang of the leather and getting a little kick out of the *tap-tap-tap* of the hammer. She rejoiced also in the freedom and smells of the back yard with its fruit trees and chooks and cow. She was, however, nervous of the lavatory, and her fear gave Petra an added power over her. As if Petra needed that. She and Petra lounged in the dust and decay of the back room, making up stories and plays in which Gwendolin was the girl and Petra was the man. That's how it went. Petra had an instinct about just how much darkness, ugliness and smut Gwendolin could take, and she would stop short of truly frightening or disgusting her. Petra needed Gwendolin, who was like a ticket into a world that was otherwise out of reach. And Petra enjoyed Gwendolin's company, apart from the advantages it bestowed.

Petra and Gwendolin would wander together in the graveyard behind the church, reading out to each other ancient sad inscriptions, and sighing over the long-lost dead. They made little pilgrimages with flowers to the grave of Wanda, where there was a small white marble statue of an angel. It made Petra even more special, in Gwendolin's eyes, to have a sister in the graveyard.

The Joneses lived in the manse next to the church, and ladies came to clean and men came to garden and there were lawns and flowers and antiques and silver and crystal and looking-glasses and bookcases with glass-panelled doors. Vases of flowers in just about every room. Chinese, Japanese and Indian knick-knacks. The walls of the kitchen were tiled white, with a checkered band of black and white running round at the level of Love's elbow. In the electric oven Love baked heavenly sponges and scones of incredible fluffiness, and on special occasions she would whirl from the cupboard a gleaming sifter and would set about the lengthy process of making an angel cake. At the table everyone had a silver serviette ring scrolled with filagree flowers. There was a toilet in the bathroom with a roll of soft toilet paper. The floor of the bathroom was tiled with black and white marble squares, and there was a large gleaming white bath and a shower as well. In the pantry there was a refrigerator called a Silent Knight. Petra was amazed by the Silent Knight, by its quiet production of ice and cold, by the mystery of opening the door to find a gleaming, chilly cupboard lined with airy shelves. She and Gwendolin made metal trays of

---

angel cake

ice-cubes, and mixed lemonade and raspberry juice and poured it over glasses of ice which rattled and chinked and froze their tongues. Petra would run her fingers over the shining silver figurehead of the knight in armour that decorated the door of the fridge. She would even kiss it.

I should note here Petra's teenage admiration for Kim Novak, another girl with the Halo Effect. When Kim was very young she won a beauty contest that was sponsored by a freezer company, and she toured the United States under the title of Miss Deepfreeze.

Mr Jones drove a small grey car, and the girls would sit in the back when the family motored to the country for picnics by the river. A passion-fruit vine grew in the garden and Mr Jones showed Petra and Gwendolin how the parts of the flower resembled the instruments of the Passion of Jesus. Fish swam in a small pond where water lilies floated on the surface. The girls brought chairs from Gwendolin's doll house, placed them on the leaves and installed the dolls on them, and lo and behold, if the chairs and the dolls were light enough, the leaves supported them and did not sink or dip beneath the surface.

Gwendolin had a bedroom all to herself with two white beds and pink silk coverlets. The window was set with leadlight diamonds and looked out onto a rose garden. In the mornings Mrs Jones always brought Gwendolin a glass of orange juice to drink in bed before she got up for breakfast. The contrast between Lydia Penfold and Love Jones could scarcely have been greater. Lydia was skinny and grey-haired, with gnarled hands and

---

water lilies

a face filled with lines of anxiety. If you looked closely you could see a hint of Petra's lovely eyes, but who was looking. Love was young and pretty with a sweet smile and soft grey eyes and a springing, graceful step. She wore clothes which she made herself, and which were suitable for a minister's wife in that they were understated and sensible, tailored, but they were smooth and sensuous and fitted her figure like (almost like) a glove.

Something about Love and Gwendolin that really impressed Petra was the fact that they each had a summer dressing-gown and a winter dressing-gown, floral for summer, pastel wool with satin piping for winter. Petra had never had a dressing-gown: Nancy and Greta had old, old kimonos; Cobbler had a decrepit tartan thing which he wore in the winter as he sat by the kitchen stove suffering from bronchitis.

And while we are on clothes, Gwendolin had the prettiest dresses and coats and hats around, and she wore the shoes you might have expected Petra to wear, Petra being the daughter of the shoemaker. But the saying about the cobbler's children going barefoot has some truth in it. Petra wore the cheap black boots which were usually worn by boys. And in the contrary way children have, Gwendolin envied Petra's boots. To tell you the truth, Petra had a rather sexy look in those boots. Somerset Jones always wore a discreet grey suit with a black stock and a thin white clerical collar. Cobbler Penfold, of course, was forever decked out in a leather apron.

---

shoemaker

> Her feet beneath her petticoat
> Like little mice stole in an out
> As if they feared the light
>
> JOHN SUCKLING. 'Ballad Upon a Wedding'

When Love took Gwendolin to the pantomine or the ballet, Petra was also invited. The National Theatre with its red velvet seats, red velvet curtain, gilt boxes, domed ceiling, chandeliers brought a rush of excitement to Petra's heart. They saw *The Nutcracker, Sleeping Beauty*, and *Swan Lake* performed by the local ballet school and the two girls were completely transported by the ethereal loveliness of the dancing and the music. Gwendolin collected books about ballet and she and Petra devoured them—the stories of Anna Pavlova and Moira Shearer and Marie Taglioni and Margot Fonteyn sent them wafting into rhapsodies.

Gwendolin went to ballet classes; Petra did not, but Gwendolin taught Petra some of the steps, and Petra was a very apt pupil. Gwendolin presented Petra with a framed photograph of Lydia Lopokova as the Sleeping Princess. When Gwendolin danced the Sugarplum Fairy in the ballet school's annual concert, Petra picked a basket of fruit from the back garden and presented it to Gwendolin.

A great deal of Petra's charm was genuine; in fact, sometimes I was amazed at her simplicity and generosity. But then I would be brought up smartly when she did something completely cold and calculating and imaginatively

---

Anna Pavlova; Moira Shearer; Marie Taglioni

cruel. People are so complex—that's what I have found. I imagine Adolf Hitler had his moments, that the wicked queen in 'Snow White' was probably deeply fond of her cat, perhaps even of her lady-in-waiting.

> When she recognised the young queen as Snow
> White she stood still with superstitious fear and
> rage, and was unable to stir. Then iron slippers
> were heated on the great fire, and they were
> brought in with tongs and set before her. She
> was forced to put on the red-hot shoes, and
> dance until she dropped down dead.
>
> 'Snow White' (folktale)

Some girls are so drenched in this kind of thing, this fairytale, ballet-dancer kind of thing. And they go for it. They aspire to the frail-looking body that appears to float on the tips of the satin-shod toes like thistledown, like breath, like air itself. The years and years of training and dedication, the bleeding toes, the crippled feet, the pain. The willing sacrifices made for the art of floating through the air, flying like a bird, flitting like a butterfly in a fantastic spectacle that raises the spirits of the audience, those people in the red velvet seats in the gilt boxes beneath the darkened chandeliers.

Petra didn't even have a chance to start this training, and in fact she had a native feeling that her chosen way to dance was to dance from the heart, with the feet bare. A bit like Isadora Duncan, if you like. An old, religious sense of dancing, not so much for the entertainment of others as for the expression of the soul of the dancer.

When Love took the girls to see the movie *The Red Shoes* at the cinema, Petra felt the pull of the romance, felt the pleasure of the twist of pain in her heart as the plot moved inexorably to its terrible conclusion. Petra identified with Moira Shearer herself, and also with the character of the dancer in her red satin slippers who leaps over the balcony and falls to her death under the train. And the incredible beauty and pathos of the scene where the ballet goes on without the dancer, but with a space, a ghostly gap where she would be if she were still alive.

If anything might be calculated to put girls off learning ballet dancing, you might think it would be this. As it happened, the opposite was the case. The film went straight to the heart of the matter with girls, encouraging them in their thousands to aspire to the sacrificial act of putting on the toe shoes, of seeing those shoes turn red with their own blood.

> The film *The Red Shoes* has been credited with starting more impressionable young girls on ballet careers than any other.
>
> (from the 1996 program notes of *The Red Shoes*, performed by the Australian Ballet School)

You could draw a rough parallel between the Western toe shoe and the Chinese slipper for bound feet.

The Red Shoes

But the toe shoe, while deforming the foot, allows the dancer to achieve a degree of grace and flight, allows her to transform into a sprite, a spirit, a moth, a bird, a wonderful creature of the air with a strange sensuality in her aerial beauty, a luminous sexuality that is found nowhere else. It is not her crippled foot that is fetishised, but her whole lepidopteral manifestation. She is doomed as a butterfly is doomed; so much beauty exists to be crushed and to die. In China the foot itself is the object of the fetish, and the girl is crippled for six years while her feet are prepared to be used as sexual organs.

Petra and Gwendolin were allowed to pour the milk at the monthly tea meetings where everyone gathered in the church hall on a Friday night for lantern slides and hymns and supper. Other children were simply part of the crowd, but the handmaidens, as the two girls were jokingly called, had flowery aprons and serious responsibility.

Love organised the annual concerts. Petra was eleven when they had the Blossom Ballet as the star turn of the night. The girls wore tutus made by the Ladies' Guild from old net curtains dyed in pastel shades. There were enough black ballet slippers to go around as most of the girls went to ballet classes. It was typical of Petra that even without formal lessons she could imitate the ballet exercises, the steps, the gestures of the other girls, and could then, without a teacher to guide and correct her, become the best dancer in her group. She practised in the back garden, using the low bough of an apple tree for a barre. She was one of those girls who was able naturally to dance on point. She was given the lead in the Blossom Ballet, and, because she was the acknowledged little queen of the girls, the children and even their mothers accepted this without murmur. Petra danced the role of the White Rose. A choir of younger children sang to accompany the dance:

With a toss and a twirl
And a sweep and a swirl
Down with a curtsy
Sinks each little girl

I might spare you the rest.

The Flower and Fruit Sermon

It was the day after the concert, and Love had taken Gwendolin to the dentist. Petra arrived at the door of the manse to be greeted by Mr Jones, who beamed at her and invited her in for a glass of raspberry cordial. They sat in the study, in leather armchairs beside the desk, a green reading lamp throwing light on the pages of Mr Jones's next sermon. He was smoking his pipe, making little sucking noises and letting his eyes follow the smoke as it curled up into the beam of light.

Somerset: I thought you made a very charming white rose, Pet.

Petra: Thank you, Mr Jones.

Somerset: Yes. The dance has inspired my Sunday sermon. I'm writing about the beauty of the earth, the flowers and fruits.

Petra felt a little rush of pleasure and pride that Mr Jones would speak to her about the sermon he was preparing. She was, after all, still a child.

Somerset: Shall I read you some?

Petra: Yes please.

He put down his pipe, tapping it on the side of the ashtray. He picked up the papers from under the lamp, then, as if he had forgotten something, he stood up and

---

sermon

crossed the room and latched the door. When he sat down again he held the papers up with one hand, and with the other he tapped Petra lightly on the shoulder and asked her to sit on his knee while he read.

Petra put down her glass which was still half full of cordial and hopped onto the minister's lap.

Somerset: This way, turn round this way.

And Petra straddled him as he sat in the leather armchair. He pushed the papers aside and took her face in his hands, kissing her lightly on the cheek.

(You might wonder where I was in all this. I was watching. I couldn't see that she was going to come to any real harm. Morality, you see, is not really my thing. Physical danger, I keep her out of physical danger. For instance, if Love had come home and threatened her with a breadknife, I would have had to whip the knife away.)

Somerset could feel the expectant tension in the child's body, could sense, as he had long sensed, her willingness and compliance. She gazed out the window at the roses, which were luminous in the lemon light of early afternoon, while he gently ran his hands under her dress. With a little shock he realised she was not wearing underclothes.

Somerset: Don't you wear pants?

Petra: Not always.

He pushed his finger into her soft cleft which widened to admit him, and he asked her if it hurt.

Petra: Hurt?

Somerset: Does it hurt, does it hurt unduly? I don't want to hurt you. You must tell me if it hurts.

Petra: No, it doesn't hurt at all.

Slowly he popped the buttons on his fly and then it was simple to ease his cock into her. The only thing that alarmed her was the sound he made in his throat as he came. She was startled and thrilled by the cry of an unknown animal as Somerset spurted hot and holy liquid into her. Her own pleasure was brief, delicious and silent. She rested her head on his shoulder and he threw his head back, gasping, closing his eyes from which trickled a tear or two.

After a few moments, Somerset shifted in the chair and composed himself, buttoning up and lifting Petra so that she sat again on his lap, facing away from him.

Somerset: This will be our sacred secret, Petra.

Petra (a certain knowing irony in her tone): Yes, Mr Jones, it will be our secret.

She heard him sigh. Relief? Pleasure?

She returned to her chair and he read her the flower and fruit sermon, which was pure twaddle and she knew it. He, presumably, did not. He took from the desk drawer a packet of pipe-cleaners, lengths of wire covered in white fluff, and offered her some. He said she could make giraffes and little men with them. Petra took the pipe-cleaners politely and stood up to go. She left a damp stain streaked with blood on the leather seat, which Somerset methodically wiped with his handkerchief.

Gwendolin and Love returned from the dentist, Gwendolin with a filling in a molar and a bottle of scent from Coles. Petra stayed to tea.

Somerset: Petra listened to my sermon.

Love: That was good of her. It was probably very uninteresting.

Petra: I thought it was very interesting.

Somerset: There, you see. And I gave her some pipe-cleaners. Would you like some pipe-cleaners, Gwendolin?

Gwendolin: Yes, please, as long as I don't have to listen to the sermon.

The scene in the minister's study was repeated, with variations, many times over the years. It seemed remarkable to me that he took no precautions against getting the girl pregnant. He didn't know what I know, that her fallopian tubes were malformed and incapable of conveying eggs into her uterus. She didn't know this either, at the time. I believe that Somerset used to pray he wouldn't get her pregnant, and believed that his prayers were answered. In a way, they were. Imagine his delight when he discovered she would suck him off and swallow his semen with scarcely a second thought. And she would flip up her dress and bend over and he could fuck her up the arse if he wished.

Somerset took the girls to the circus. He loved the trapeze, the girl on the flying trapeze. Petra and Gwendolin had never seen anything like it, and they watched in breathless amazement and terror and suspense. The smell of the animals, the folded old skin of the elephant, the little red jacket of a monkey. The spangles and the tinsel and the blaring music. Somerset had his arms around both girls, and they all three felt warm and elated and sexy.

Gwendolin and Petra went to the high school, and when Petra was fifteen her father said she had to leave school and go to work in the woollen mill. If it was good enough for her sisters, it was good enough for her. Lydia wept and entreated, Nancy had hysterics, but the cobbler laid down the law. Then Petra's rage, which had had little enough exercise during her early life, was something to see, and who could blame her. It had no effect on Cobbler Penfold. Good enough for the others, the mill was good enough for Little Miss. But Somerset (bless him) intervened on Petra's behalf, and instead of going to work in the mill Petra became an assistant in the Bible Shop.

The Bible Shop

So there she is, demure in a pale blue uniform, dusting and sorting and arranging and selling bibles and hymn books and improving literature and pictures of flowers and puppies and kittens and Jesus. Gwendolin went on to higher studies, went to nursing school, married a doctor and had three children: David, Jane and Natalie. I don't mean to trivialise her life by shrinking her up like that, but there's actually very little else to it. Unless you want to know that she lives to be a very old lady indeed, well into the twenty-first century, outlasting the doctor and all the children and dying quietly in her sleep when she is living in an apartment on the Queensland Gold Coast. Not exactly a novel, is it? But of course meeting her was absolutely critical to Petra's life and the way things turned out. You could write a narrative, say for something like *Who's Who*, giving the outline of Petra's life, and you could say she grew up in Tasmania, worked in the Bible Shops in Launceston and Melbourne, trained as a yoga instructor, studied kindergarten teaching, ran a type of orphanage for girls, and was well known as a spiritual leader, being a key member of a religious group based in the hills outside Melbourne. These are facts, and although the prose is bland and smoothly conceals the details, there is enough there to suggest that Petra's life would yield more interest to a reader of novels than would the life of Gwendolin Jones.

Says Gilding Littledale from the Melbourne branch: That girl in the Bible Shop, now Somerset, she's just what we need, you know, on the mainland. Just what we need. She hasn't got any sisters, then, has she, Somerset?

Somerset: Sisters, yes, but none like her.

Gilding: What future is there for a girl like that, here in this backwater, really?

Somerset: Well, I expect she'll marry and settle down and raise a family.

Even as the words were out of his mouth, Somerset felt them turn to ashes that dried his tongue and choked his throat. The imagined portrait of Petra as the respectable bride, wife, mother, as a woman who did the flowers and poured the tea at the tea meeting was sharp, ugly and fantastic. Suddenly there opened before him a swift solution to the not-too-distant problem of what was to become of the sacred secret when Petra really grew up. He realised he could pack her off to the mainland. For her own good, for her future. For his own good. He had been lucky, he had gotten away with the Petra thing for years without a hitch. He had the sense to realise it could not go on forever. There was something cold and terrible about old Somerset, but then there was something particularly cold about Petra.

Somerset (slowly and thoughtfully): I suppose, if you really wanted me to, I could speak to the girl, speak to her father, see if they would be open to the idea of her going away.

Gilding: They go away soon enough. She's what, seventeen, eighteen?

Somerset: Sixteen.

Gilding: Uh, looks older. Any romantic attachment?

Somerset: None that I know of, but what would I know?

Gilding: Quite. Can she sing? We like them to sing in their local church choir.

Somerset: Sing? Oh yes, Petra sings like an angel.

Petra had never been out of Tasmania, but her years of reading the books in the back room had filled her mind with the lure of the big wide world. She was ready to go, ready to leave behind her family, the Joneses, the familiar simple routines of small-town life for the dangers and excitement and possibilities of the big city. Lydia was the only one who raised an objection. Petra, she said, was too young for this, too inexperienced in the ways of the world. Lydia felt her heart breaking at the thought of Petra's going, and she argued and wept, but she lost. Ah, went the argument, but Petra would live with Gilding Littledale and his wife Laetitia and her sister Dodo in the manse in Murrumbeena, and what could be safer and more desirable than that? So Petra was packed up and farewelled and sent off on the boat to Melbourne. A new beginning, a new life. Before she left, Love and Gwendolin gave her a pale pink woollen dressing-gown with fine satin edges. The year was 1957, so long ago, and yet (I have to say) it seems like only yesterday.

And life was safe at the manse in Murrumbeena, safe and dull and boring in a house with many small dark rooms, of peace and quiet and bible readings and cleanliness and good manners. There was dust, and books and vases filled with dried flowers and feathers; and the sisters sat by gloomy lamps in the evenings reading detective stories, the lounge room being a musty treasure trove of

Agatha Christie and Dorothy L. Sayers. Once a week they went on an expedition to the public library to change their library books—they borrowed books by Georgette Heyer and Barbara Cartland, Conan Doyle and Noah Hill, not realising Noah Hill was really Irving Clay, of whom more later. At meals Gilding would read to them from such things as *In the Steps of the Master* by H.V. Morton, or Kipling's *Jungle Book*.

I noticed an interesting thing about Laetitia and Dodo—although Laetitia was dominant and ruled the roost and made the rules, Dodo, who appeared to be pretty colourless, was nicer. And this meant that, although Laetitia tried to undermine Dodo at every turn, Dodo always came up smiling, driving her sister mad, and Dodo also had friends. Laetitia had no friends. I find that rather astonishing. She actually had no friends. There were the people she lorded it over at the church, and the neighbours who nodded to her, but as far as I could tell Laetitia was a friendless woman who derived comfort from ruling her sparse roost and baking her mean roast and coldly and openly manipulating everyone who crossed her path. Meanwhile Dodo, after she had done her duties and chores about the house and garden and church, would be off to have afternoon tea with the Robertsons or with Nelly Whitehead, or Holly Whitaker, or the Smiths. Dodo often came home a little high on tea and cake.

In Petra, Laetitia met a particular case. Petra simply obeyed Laetitia to the letter, with no warmth, no response, no revolt, no actual engagement. This bewildered and infuriated Laetitia, but there was nothing she could put her finger on, nothing over which she could call Petra to order. Petra was expected to be a kind of servant, a role that had never appealed to her, unless it had the little quiver of excitement of the tea meetings at the Windmill Hill Methodist Church. She performed her duties as scullery maid and waitress and laundry maid with silent perfection.

Gilding and Laetitia had no children of their own, but they had fostered several babies in India, and showed photographs and lantern slides describing the progress of their lives. In one picture there was a little Indian boy sitting cross-legged on a lily pad. Petra found this one troubling and moving, as it awakened a nostalgia for the picture of the girl on the leaf in the magazine at home. (There were also pictures of children in New Guinea, known as fuzzy-wuzzy angels.) Petra wrote letters home, and letters to Gwendolin, but she never said how lonely and unhappy she was. She could see faint ripples in the water round the boy's leaf. Perhaps the leaves were strong enough to just sit there after all. She enquired of Gilding, and he said yes, oh yes, the leaves were able to support the weight of a small child.

Once, and only once, Somerset paid a visit. He took Petra out for a drive in the hills in Gilding's dark green Humber. They sat at a table in a tea room, looking like father and daughter, he pouring her tea from a fat brown pot, she dropping sugar lumps into his cup with a splash.

Somerset: I had a dream about this.

Petra: Funny dream. Not very interesting, really. Why would you bother to dream this? We are in a tea shop having tea. Why not dream you're riding an elephant in India or something. Do all your dreams come true?

Somerset: Not all.

Petra: All mine are going to come true. By that I mean all my hopes and desires, not the things I imagine in my sleep.

Somerset: What do you dream about? In your sleep I mean.

Petra: I actually think I dreamt last night about the elephant ride. But—snakes. Sometimes I dream about snakes. You never know, I might come home and work at the Snakepit. I would wear leather gloves, and milk the snakes for venom and wear snakes all up my arms like bracelets.

Somerset: Would you . . . would you come home, if you got a job? Not at the Snakepit, of course—I know you're just teasing me. Well? I miss you, you know.

Somerset's tone was wistful and pathetic. I even felt an odd twinge of sympathy for him. Petra sensibly glanced across the tea room and smiled at a hearty golfer sitting alone with a plate of scones by the window.

Actually I had a word with Somerset's guardian, a weedy individual called Niff. He said that Somerset was probably out of his depth with Petra, and although I didn't say so, I could have told him that. He did tell me that life with Love was pretty dull in the sex department, and that Somerset strayed a bit from time to time, Petra being the longest-running episode. Niff seemed to be rather fond of Petra himself—he kind of envied me the excitement, perhaps.

Petra: I'm just joking. I will never come back.

On the way home to Murrumbeena Somerset bought Petra a bunch of violets, a few of which she pressed in her hymn book and kept forever. Even the coldest people are prone sometimes to sentiment. They had a dull and awkward evening meal with the Littledales, Dodo, who rarely spoke in the normal course of events, chattering like a sparrow to Somerset and remarking that Petra appeared to be sunburnt. The conversation was dominated by Gilding and Somerset who spoke of meetings and symposiums and international movements for Christian brotherhood.

Gilding: Well then, Somerset, have you persuaded Petra to go back to the island yet?

Somerset (laughing): I don't think so. You seem to have made her very comfortable here.

Gilding: I'm glad to hear that. She's a quiet girl. Shy. Are you shy, Petra?

Petra: Oh, a bit, sometimes.

Gilding: You were right about her singing, though, Somerset. Sings like an angel all right.

That was the last Petra ever saw of Somerset; and after a while she left the Bible Shop, and left the Littledales, having met Meena, an Indian woman who taught yoga.

---

violets

Silent Knight

If you were looking for middle Australia, a bit of a time capsule, a suburb to study for your PhD, you could do worse than look at Murrumbeena. Sturdy, respectable brick bungalows from the twenties on. Trees. Nature strips. A colony of artists to lend a little spice. Places of worship. You would miss Meena's house as a place of worship; you'd count it as a house. (Unless you were passing when Meena was working in the garden wearing a green and gold sari. Then you would realise that something unusual was stirring in middle Australia.) But if you were doing a survey you'd open the low iron gate, go up the concrete path edged with lobelia, enter the dark brick porch and lift the brass knocker. The door has a panel of diamond-pane glass above the handle. (Only a matter of time, here in the nineties, I always think, before somebody smashes the glass and opens the door and gets away with Meena's TV and video and a cache of silver bangles. For Meena is still there, a wise, established yoga teacher and seer, revered as Meena of Murrumbeena and with a large and dedicated following.)

Petra used to walk past Meena's house on her way to the train. I never worked out why Meena was nearly always standing at the gate at 8.30 in the morning, but there she was, this mysterious dark figure in a sari, standing in strange silence and concentration. And there was Petra, wearing a blue uniform under a navy overcoat, and glowing like a moonbeam on a clear night, as usual. She'd go by, kind of tripping and floating the way she did, her gorgeous flares of long fiery hair pinned back behind her ears with bobby pins.

And so, after a while, Petra and Meena began to smile at each other, and nod. Then they said hello and then they discussed the weather and then they got onto the flowers and the trees and before you could say Thomas Aquinas! they were the best of friends, discussing chakras and the stars and the planets. They both loved flowers and dancing—I mean free, expressive, barefoot dancing using long coloured scarves. The Littledales saw the beginning of this friendship as the beginning of the end of Petra's soul. And it was at this time too that there were laid in Petra, in layman's terms, the seeds of a breakdown. I of course understood that Meena, far from being the evil cause of this eventual breakdown, acted instead as part of the cure.

Petra was ready to break down in order to emerge like a butterfly from a chrysalis, as the Petra Penfold-Knight the world now remembers. (I say 'the world', but in fact not very many people remember Petra now.) Petra, who is, as I think I have said or at least implied, quite a storyteller (by which I mean liar), suddenly out of the blue told Meena she had been engaged to be married but that her fiancé was drowned when he was out fishing for cray-fish on the east coast of Tasmania. She said she would never marry now but had decided to take the late fiancé's

---

Thomas Aquinas

surname in honour of his memory. Her late *fiancé*? This was all news to me, and I listened with bated breath.

Petra: Yes, I will in future be known as Petra Penfold-Knight.

Meena didn't bat an eyelid.

I thought about this choice of name, and I finally traced it back to the Joneses' Silent Knight refrigerator that had so impressed Petra when she was a child. I think I'm right about that.

---

refrigerator

The Magnetic Polarity of the Sun

Petra was in her twelfth year when she first sat on the knee of Somerset Jones; she was twenty-two when the next revolution in her life took place. There's an underlying cycle of twenty-two years in the rhythmic patterns of the electromagnetic activity of the particles of the sun. Each eleven years the sun's magnetic polarity is reversed, meaning that its north and south magnetic poles change place. This reversal is linked to harmonic cycles of vibration which result in whirling patterns of electromagnetic activity. It does not surprise me that Petra's life followed the cycle of the sun.

Call me fanciful if you like, but in any case the facts of Petra's ups and downs are as I have described them, and her life does match the sun cycles.

When Petra turned twenty-one, and already living with Meena, the Littledales arranged a party for her. I think that Gilding and Laetitia saw this as the right thing to do, and I think that Dodo saw it as something good and true and kind. I had a word with Toot who is Dodo's guardian and an amiable type, and Toot said it had been Dodo's idea, although the others would of course take all the credit.

It was a funny sort of party, a kind of afternoon tea, held in the church hall, very childish. Some concept from Dodo's own childhood. No grog. A long table with a white cloth and jugs of red and green drinks of some sweet and sickly kind. Butterfly cakes and asparagus rolls and tiny sandwiches. Balloons and streamers decked the hall. The guests were people from the parish, some of them young but most of them of little interest to Petra, who as the guest of honour received gifts and was toasted in the red and green drinks. One or two of the guests would have liked to have had something stronger to drink—I overheard one young man say to another that he would *kill* for a decent lime daiquiri.

Petra, looking gorgeously provocative and out of place in a white linen suit and scarlet sandals, thanked people graciously. She showed nothing that could be described as emotion. I believe the term is 'affectless'. She was affectless. A young man at the party said do you want to go to the pictures and Petra said no she didn't and that was that.

Gilding and Laetitia couldn't make her out. Was she saving herself for missionary work? they asked each other sometimes.

There would be psychologists who would, I imagine, say that Petra's early experiences with Somerset Jones had screwed up her emotional development. There could be something in that, but in my opinion there was an element in Petra's very nature, in her soul if you like, that sent her on the path she took. Actually (call me far-fetched), I think the gap between her uterus and her ovaries was a bodily metaphor for some gap in her nature. There, I've said it! She also had the strongest will of anybody I have ever known.

Back to the party. Meena was there in a fancy blue and gold sari, adding a kind of respectable exoticism to the church hall. She gave Petra a silver bracelet. Dodo's gift was a fake gold brooch shaped like a basket and filled with flowers made from imitation opals. If anything touched Petra it was this, a token of a kind of innocent love. She kept that brooch among her things for years, only losing it many years down the track when she left a suitcase in a cab. Dodo imagined Petra had teamed up with Meena and was going to spend the rest of her life in the house down the street, drifting about in Indian clothing, doing yoga and taking some kind of exotic drug. This was wide of the mark, but there was an element of truth in it.

Inside Meena's neat brick house there was a sunken marble bath where Meena poured oils and floated the petals of flowers, different colours for different moods, and where she and Petra took long lovely baths together. When Petra went to live in Meena's house, she had, for the first time in her life, a room she could truly call her own. She painted it blue, blue, blue, with a great golden lotus flower on one wall. Meena trained her to teach yoga and Petra was a quick and willing pupil. And by Petra's powers of persuasion (remember the Halo Effect?) they were able to rent Gilding's church hall and open a suburban school of yoga and dance.

Gilding and Laetitia gave Petra a handsome bible with gilt edges. Curiously enough it was the bible that set off the nervous breakdown thing. She was ready to crack and the bible was the last straw. (I keep saying nervous breakdown, but it was more like some state of weird

---

lotus

paralysis that she went into, and that she came out of with a new and adamantine purpose.) Petra had been reading the bible for many years, had been working in the shop where she was daily surrounded by bibles of all kinds. But she had never actually had a bible of her very own—and this was such a lovely one, the pages thin as thin, the words on the pages placed and spaced and inked with such beauty, authority and love. When she riffled through the pages of this magical volume those pages whispered to her like silk, like water, like kisses in the dark.

I said the birthday bible set her off. It happened thus.

Reality, as far as Petra was concerned, was grim and grey and unpromising, and in her heart she was ready to revolt against it. She had been waiting, perhaps without knowing it, for some sort of sign, some indication of her direction. The innocent Gilding and Laetitia handed her the handsome holy book and Petra, who had read many stories in her life, sat down in her blue bedroom at Meena's and discovered for the first time the Book of Revelation. Plenty of people read the Book of Revelation without going off the deep end, but Petra was ready, there and then, to lap up the message and make it her own.

> Blessed is he that readeth, and they that hear the
> words of this prophecy, and keep those things
> which are written therein: for the time is at
> hand.

The bible, I have always found, is a very dangerous document.

> I was in the Spirit on the Lord's day, and heard behind me a great voice, as of a trumpet.

Petra began to hear great voices in her head, but with her will still at full strength she listened and told nobody. Hers was not the mission of a Joan of Arc; hers was her very own cause, to be held in secret until the time was right. Manic depressive? Schizophrenic? Deluded? Depressed? I'm not a doctor. She was never diagnosed. There was nothing, really, *wrong* with her, in the ordinary way. As far as she was concerned she was not hallucinating; she was seeing visions of the true state of affairs.

> And I turned to see the voice that spake with me. And being turned I saw seven golden candlesticks;
>
> And in the midst of the seven candlesticks one like unto the Son of man, clothed in a garment down to the foot, and girt about the paps with a golden girdle.
>
> His head and his hairs were white like wool, as white as snow; and his eyes were as a flame of fire;
>
> And his feet like unto fine brass, as if they burned in a furnace; and his voice as the sound of many waters.
>
> And he had in his right hand seven stars: and out of his mouth went a sharp two-edged sword: and his countenance was as the sun shineth in his strength.

Petra did not just *read* the Book of Revelation; she *saw* the Book of Revelation. She was *in* the thing, herself part of the vision of Saint John the Divine. She spoke to the seven angels and wrote letters to them, willing the message out to them by the power of her mind, telling them where they had gone wrong. One of these angels, at the church in Sardis, sent me a ribbon, by which I mean a sort of ectoplasmic telegram we have, and it said, in effect: 'What's with the crazy little ice-maiden?'

You realise I couldn't stop her; she was doing no harm and could come to no harm. The really good outcome was that she upped and left the Bible Shop where she had, in any case, become worse than useless. She didn't eat; she hallucinated; she spoke to the voices who were speaking to her. None of this was seen at the shop as being particularly unusual, but it was inconvenient in a young woman who was supposed to be dusting the bibles and selling them and putting them in packets and posting them to the missions.

Chapter twelve of the Book of Revelation was actually the clincher.

> And there appeared a great wonder in heaven; a
> woman clothed with the sun, and the moon
> under her feet, and upon her head a crown of
> twelve stars.

Guess who?

Petra took all that as a literal description of herself and—oh, how can I tell you of the strength of her conviction? She didn't just think she was the woman (who later on gets the wings of a great eagle and the serpent tries to drown her, but the earth swallows the water for her and she is okay), she *understood* that she was the woman, and interpreted this to mean she had been chosen to be the mother of a great new race of people who would save the world in the new millennium, after the coming holocaust. The usual kind of thing. And Petra knew this to be true. The period of paralysis and breakdown was over. She was poised to spring her truth upon the world.

There have been times when I have read the Book of Revelation quite a bit myself, and I have enjoyed it very much as a glorious and hallucinatory kind of poetry and music. I have bathed in the Book of Revelation, and in the end I have found it to be ultimately mysterious, and I have come to suspect that the mystery, or the mysteriousness, is the essence of the thing. There are words in Revelation that suggest to me that they have me on the brink of the explanation of everything, but those words will not unlock their meaning, not to me, not, perhaps, to anyone. They are the words of the mystery, and the mystery is the point. If people or angels such as myself could in fact unlock the mystery, perhaps the whole tension that keeps things spinning would drop away, and a booming, blasting lethargy like nothing ever before seen or imagined would burgeon its blooming, bleeding vastness across all time and space.

Petra got the idea that she was supposed to eat the pages of the Book of Revelation, and for a while she took three meals a day, the meals consisting of sliced white bread, butter and a page from the Book of Revelation. (Not, need I say, from the bible presented to her on her birthday.) Sometimes in the full flight of her leadership of the Hill House Brethren, during speeches to her people, she would recite from chapter ten the bit that goes:

'And the voice which I heard from heaven spake unto me again and said, Go and take the little book which is open in the hand of the angel which standeth upon the sea and upon the earth. And I went up unto the angel, and said unto him, Give me the little book. And he said unto me, Take it and eat it up, and it shall make thy belly bitter, but it shall be in thy mouth sweet as honey. And I took the little book out of the angel's hand, and ate it up, and it was in my mouth sweet as honey: and as soon as I had eaten it, my belly was bitter. And he said unto me, Thou must prophesy again before many peoples, and nations, and tongues, and kings.'

The tone of her voice always took on a particular note of hysteria when she broke into these verses. People seemed to find this hysteria very engaging and persuasive.

The odd thing about Petra was that while had been cracking up, sliding into a state of emotional and mental paralysis, externally she was getting on with things quite normally. A kind of terrible chaos had enveloped her mind and she moved in a cloud of darkness, bewilderment and despair. This was a strange, a foreign state of affairs for Petra, but she seemed to accept it and to run with it, and in the end she came out stronger than before; it was an important turning point.

Actually, it was the life at Meena's and the yoga that kept her going. It's odd, that. People often break down and give up and give in and fall apart when their souls are in turmoil, but Petra, with her will of steel, kept the surface clean and smooth and let the inside freeze up, disintegrate, split, as it were, from the rest of her.

It wasn't until she made up her mind to die, much later on, when she had done what she set out to do and could see she had nowhere to go, that she brought the inside and the outside together and let each destroy the other. In one way her suicide was the result of her loss of faith in herself, and in another it was a statement of her absolute belief in herself, in her rightness.

You Can Smell the Mushrooms

When the petals fall from the magnolia tree and begin to rot you can smell the mushrooms.

ERNEST BEAUX, *creator of Chanel No. 5*

In the early sixties, Petra completed her training as a kindergarten teacher. In the late sixties she met Dr Ambrose Goddard from the Mandala Psychiatric Clinic; she met Dr Irving V. Clay, Master of King's College; and she discovered the beauties of LSD and psilocybin and redcaps.

She had been on quite a journey already, and it was just about to really take off.

Petra's story intersects in strange and dreadful ways with the stories of many other people. One of those people is Sylvie. I sometimes imagine that from one life many ripples move out, and these meet the ripples sent out by other lives and other lives, across time and across space. And in this way patterns and meaning are formed and the ripples go on, meeting other ripples—makes you dizzy, doesn't it?

(Just a little quote from Dr Irving Clay in his book *The Mysterious Universe of the Mind*: 'The mind is a lake

---

LSD; psilocybin; redcaps

where on the restless surface ripples of thought move constantly.')

A mind can be very free with time and space; in dreams and imaginings it can go anywhere at any time, now 1988, now 1888, now a French port, now a forest in Australia, here, there, everywhere, now and then.

How Sylvie Fisher Lost Her Mind

Sylvie Fisher walks along the gravel paths between the flowerbeds. She places her feet, heel to toe, heel to toe, so that she moves slowly round the garden in front of the house. She is a tall woman with hair that has faded from its dark blonde. She has white, white skin, long fingers, pale eyes faded from blue to a sort of colourless cloud. I keep saying 'faded' when I describe Sylvie. It's spot on. She gives me the impression she is fading out, moving backwards out of life into some ghostly form, some filmy impression of a woman, not quite here, and definitely not all there as far as the intellect goes.

Sylvie reminds me, in her fading way, of Cyane the nymph who wasted with weeping and dissolved into the water of the pool.

A broken blood vessel threads its way across the white of Sylvie's left eye, as if to remind an observer that Sylvie is not bloodless, in spite of her papery skin. She is nearly thirty-six years old, but she looks much, much younger than that. There is a childishness in her movements, in the concentration she brings to her walk, heel to toe, heel to toe, in the importance she places on the footprints she is making, faintly, on the golden gravel surface. She passes beneath the shade of a magnolia tree, pausing

---

Cyane

to look up into the branches, which are fat, twisted, velvet with age. Dark. Even ominous, threatening, evil. She follows the fragrance of the open blooms, pushes aside with the toe of her shoe the few huge creamy yellow petals that have fallen, soft dead fish, onto the path.

Images and the language of death surround Sylvie, yet Sylvie is not dead. The good mother often dies at the beginning of the story. That is how the story often starts—think of Cinderella or Snow White.

Sylvie's father was William, and he is long since dead; through the window of the parlour, Sylvie's mother, Dolfi, is watching.

Sylvie's unconscious mind, located behind her papery forehead, swims, blowing silver bubbles as it goes, here, there, everywhere, now, then, forever, bearing gifts from foreign lands, presenting presents in the present, passing parcels in the past. Present, so-called, 1988; past, ever-present, past. And before long, Dolfi will die. What then? What will become of the girl–woman in her pale blue dress and flat black shoes, the girl who sniffs the air, inhales the scent of the magnolia, of the gardenia, the alyssum, the roses, who proceeds heel to toe, heel to toe, towards an island of gravel between the knuckled roots of the magnolia tree, and kneels?

From the pocket of her soft-fold dress Sylvie (known when she was a child as the Silverfish; how she hated that) takes with her long thin fingers a small pair of scarlet shoes. Start-Rite shoes (style name, Colette) with anti-slip soles, shoes for a three-year-old, shoes that the Silverfish wore when she was three, when she ran around the magnolia chasing butterflies—some white, some black and orange. Cabbage whites and admirals. Admire the admirals, Sylvie. Sylvie is bright and clever; she admires quick pretty things, follows ants and seagulls, longs again for the praying mantis that lived translucent green for two weeks of blissful watchfulness in the heart of the bloom of a dusty pink rose until the petals fell and the insect found another home.

There's a man, there's a little man living in my rose!

Sylvie had such a vivid imagination.

As a child Sylvie *was* bright and clever. But she is described these days by the neighbours as Mrs Fisher's retarded daughter, a house where the lights are on but nobody is home, one sandwich short of a picnic. I like to pick up nifty little expressions from all sorts of people around the place—one sandwich short of a picnic always strikes me as poignant.

Dolfi long ago ceased to weep at the sight of her daughter. She has two sons who are older than Sylvie, and who are married and have children, and Dolfi rejoices in these happy facts. Sylvie is a terrible fact, something to get over, to get through, to put up with, to manage, to humour, to endure. There are times when Dolfi imagines killing Sylvie, but you can't just take a life, can you, and what would be the use? Better to live with the daily fact of a breathing tragedy than suffer the anguish that must come to the mother who murders her child. She watches from the window now as Sylvie crouches on the gravel, places her fingers inside the scarlet shoes, and gently walks them round the little island between the magnolia roots. Talking to them. Talking to a child.

Colette, she says, look at the butterflies.

Colette raises her non-existent head and stretches out her arms to the beauty of the air, to the non-existent butterflies, to the wings that are not there, to the shimmering summer sunshine that hovers over the garden beds, just out of reach, and she laughs her lovely strange metallic tinkling laugh and shows her darling, perfect teeth, like the teeth of kittens. She tosses her flaxen curls. The toes of her shoes are worn, scraped with pleasure; her stockings are black, her dress navy blue with scarlet and white smocking and a round white collar. When she goes out she wears a smart red overcoat and the smallest, smoothest navy blue leather gloves. She puts her hand in Sylvie's and they trot together to the park.

Every step felt as though she were walking on sharp knives

HANS CHRISTIAN ANDERSEN, 'The Little Mermaid'

The house with the magnolia, known as the French house, was on the edge of a forest on the outskirts of Melbourne. That's how the Fishers thought of it—always the edge, always the outskirts, not quite the rural countryside, not the suburbs, not the city. Even when time had changed all that, the Fishers still felt in their hearts that they lived on the edge of a forest. Somewhere else, some special place where the Fishers lived. It was an elaborate, out-of-place house, a house overblown on the overblouse of the far reaches of a city at the outer reaches of the British Empire.

Behind the house, and connected to it by a stone walkway, was an earlier house which August Fisher had built himself in 1865 from timber he cut from the surrounding trees. He used a hollow rock, already there, as a fireplace. The first house was built when August and his wife Ida May came to Australia from Dorset, and their six children were all born in the large room at the back of the house. Five of the children lived, and by the time the French house was imported in pieces from Burgundy in 1890, there was a desire for a place that reflected the family's prosperity. August Fisher stamped succeeding generations with his love of French things. Even Sylvie, distant from August in time, reflected in her name the romantic strain in the family. Men who worked in August's orchards, flower fields, pottery and timber mill helped him assemble the French house with its long windows, slatted shutters, veranda pillars, slender chimneys, slate roofs, attics, dormers and red floor tiles. The walls were apricot, the shutters green. Some people referred to it affectionately as Fisher's Folly, but with its quaintly gracious air it soon settled in to become the French house.

Ida May supervised the growing of herbs along the walkway, vegetables behind the cold-room, and in front of the French house she had an elegant little garden where gravel paths wound between beds of roses and alyssum, her favourites. Also several bushes of gardenias. Daffodils in great clots of butter and cream carpeted the paddocks near the house in spring, and in a corner of the front garden Ida May planted the magnolia tree that was to spread its mournful shade for over a century, and from which the flowers, as big as the moon, shed their cloying scent with its hum of dark desire, its note of slow corruption.

August and Ida May were stalwarts of the little timber Methodist church that stood by the side of the road, not far from the Fishers' cherry orchard, and first Ida May and then the eldest daughter Fidelia played the organ for the hymns. Concerts were given in the parlour of the French house, with all members of the family, and many of the people who worked for August, playing instruments or singing. The sons inherited the business when August died, and for five generations there were Fishers living in the French house. The land on which the orchards, the pottery, the mill and the flower fields had stood was gradually sold off, so that by the time Colette, great-great-great-granddaughter of August and Ida May, was born in 1968, the house was a little piece of history, an island in a sea of suburban blocks, the forest only a remnant, the road a big highway soon to be bordered with used-car yards and fast-food outlets.

Colette Fisher was born in a hospital near a home for unmarried mothers run by Sister Denise Winter in another part of Melbourne, and Colette never saw the French house because she was adopted and grew up as Celeste Penfold-Knight. But Sylvie, who was sixteen when Colette was born, never of course forgot Colette. Sylvie continued to live in the French house with her parents, never having recovered from the shame of Colette's birth.

The little timber Methodist church had long since disappeared but some of the respectability of August and Ida May had trickled down to Sylvie's parents, and

Sylvie's fate was sealed the night she confessed to her mother that she was pregnant. Pregnant and with no immediate prospect of marriage. Abortion was out of the question. Sylvie was sent to Sister Winter's for the last five months before Colette was born. Sylvie was given to understand that she was very lucky her family didn't disown her altogether, was prepared to pay for her to stay at Sister Winter's, where she did housework and washed and ironed shirts for city businessmen, barristers, judges and doctors. Sister Winter's husband was in fact one of these doctors, a psychiatrist, Daniel Winter.

Introducing Irving Clay

On the day Colette was born in 1968, the Winters were out to lunch at the house of another psychiatrist, Ambrose Goddard, and his wife Abigail. The purpose of the lunch was to welcome into a special group of doctors, academics and barristers a strange and wonderful woman, Petra Penfold-Knight. Denise Winter had already arranged with Petra that Sylvie Fisher's child, if it was a healthy girl, would go to her, but no reference at all was made to this at lunch. It was as if Denise and Petra had never met before.

Petra arrived with Dr Irving and Mrs Eugenia Clay. Irving was the Master of King's College at the university and he had talked about little else but Petra for weeks. He had been introduced to her by Sir Simon Honeychurch QC, who, with his wife Vera, was also present at lunch. The Honeychurches were parishioners at the Methodist church in Murrumbeena, and Vera, bless her, a woman of sixty who had never done much more than play a little tennis and walk the King Charles spaniels, had taken up yoga. There she would be in her new black leotard twisting and turning into oriental shapes along with the other women of the parish who drifted and then flocked to Petra's classes. And Vera would go home and rhapsodise about it all to Simon.

Vera: The lion, we do a position called the lion,

Simon, and even though I think to myself, I'll never be able to do this one, never, Petra is so incredibly inspiring that I just seem to be able to *do* it. It's quite magical. I feel so well!

Much to the alarm of Simon, Vera got down on the dining-room carpet and assumed the lion position, emitting bellows and great huffings and puffings, which were an important part of the exercise.

Then before you could say lotus position Petra was invited to afternoon tea at the Honeychurch mansion where she met (and need I say captivated) Sir Simon. This was the final step, the last link before she was to make the truly vital connection with Dr Clay. Although Dr Clay and the Rev. Littledale were clergy of the same church, the chances of Petra's meeting Dr Clay through Gilding Littledale were very slim indeed, since Dr Clay was high up in the church hierarchy and Rev. Littledale was very low down. In fact, when Gilding heard from Vera Honeychurch that Petra had gone to King's College to meet Irving, he was filled with dismay and foreboding; the silly young woman was mixing in dangerous and unorthodox circles, there was no telling where it would end. Gilding held the private view that Irving Clay was mad. (I personally am of the opinion that old Gilding was onto something here, for once.)

Irving Clay had his own theories, actually, about chance and connection and probability and fate and so forth. He had written several books on these subjects, and I sometimes wonder how he got away with it in his church. A Methodist minister who preaches on such topics as karma and reincarnation and Jung and astral travel and spirit writing and fortune telling and ghostly presences and Hinduism? Such a cocktail, for one thing. And this was the sixties, not the nineties, remember. A man before his time. He was as if drunk on the idea of some deeper and higher levels of the self, which notions allowed him to whizz about in all the most curious margins of religious thought—but you see he did it in a particular kind of pompous language that people appeared to accept, to love. He, like Petra, had the Halo Effect, and he cultivated a way of speaking and of writing that was very persuasive in its lugubrious and dreary way.

For instance: We manifest in a web of relationships so that our karma is interlinked with that of others whom we have influenced and who have influenced us.

I think myself more of the ripple effect, of waves moving out from Irving and waves moving out from Petra, and of his waves meeting her waves and setting up turbulence—but I speak only in metaphors and images, whereas Irving seemed to be very material about it all, seemed to mean that there really *was* a web in which he could manifest.

Heaven forbid!

Although Dr Irving V. Clay was officially the Master of King's, he liked to be known as the Captain, and he put around the idea that he saw King's College at the university as the Noah's Ark of intellectual life in a sea of ignorance and philistinism. (The arrogance of this was never called into question.) His white hair was what is commonly described as a shock, and it stood up from a parting in the centre of his skull revealing a healthy thick pink worm of scalp. His eyebrows were big tufts of white springy hairs above dark purply eyes (like blackberries) that remained fixed on any person he was talking to, fixed in an alarming way, and that were magnified by spectacles with rims made in Germany from (surely not, but rumour had it) the shells of real tortoises. In his buttonhole he always wore a flower, a russet chrysanthemum when they were in season. He generally spoke slowly, quietly, deliberately, with a sometimes terrible authority. He had very long fingers which he moved like the legs of a graceful but menacing spider in a rhythm to accompany his speech, as if he were conducting a company of musicians. When he spoke of how we manifest in a web of relationships, I imagined a seething mass of spiders, manifesting in their web. Not far off the mark, actually.

If people had been able to see his feet, they would have realised that his toes also moved in this curious ballet. His shoes were made a good half-size too big by Church of London, in whose remarkable archives were kept a cast of each of Irving's feet, and a dossier of detail on his skeleton, muscles, tendons, and his proneness to a stubborn form of tinea and, in times of humidity, to eczema, from which he had suffered, along with mild asthma, since early childhood. (I imagine Church of London having a section marked 'Feet of Clay'.) Aligned with the minor health problems was an allergy to eggs and fish, and a susceptibility to throat infections—but I digress. The worm on his scalp, as I said, was healthy. His mind was in a state of drastic delusion, but nobody cared. He was the Captain in dark grey suit and dog collar. His

---

chrysanthemum

teeth were false and they rattled—I could never understand why he didn't get them fixed, and I was also amazed that the clicking and clacking and spitting of his teeth didn't put off the faithful. Charisma is a truly wonderful thing.

He was able to impress such followers as Sir Simon Honeychurch, and around King's there collected a circle of powerful men from not only the church, but from medicine and the law, who were determined in their search for their higher and lower selves, keen to follow the Higher Way of which Irving Clay spoke. (Their lower selves, I would have thought, were easy enough to discover, but they nattered on about higher and lower.) They were commonly known as the Old Boy Network, these judges and surgeons and so on, and certainly there seemed to me to have been an element of play about the business for many of them (not for Dr Clay; he was serious, dead serious).

All this was fairly harmless fiddle-faddle until they began to experiment with hallucinogens on a large scale, and to replace such things as automatic writing and table rapping with the techniques and medicines of modern psychiatric practice, and until Irving Clay began to develop his community in the hills where the ideas could be put into practice and where the lives of a few dozen fairly ordinary human beings were altered forever.

In conjunction with Ambrose Goddard at Mandala, and with the financial help of Old Boys powerful in the city, Irving developed a group following known as the Hill House Brethren. Under the supervision of Ambrose, Irving began to experiment with the use of LSD. He took a preparation of carbon dioxide mixed with seventy percent oxygen and then he took fifty micrograms of LSD. He burst into a kind of demonic and hysterical laughter and saw within his head sprays of unbelievably clean and vivid colours, like lights in geometric shapes. He felt himself separating out from his own body and began to float in a space that was also within his own head, and filled with the vivid colours. He was in two forms of space at once. He soared up through a broad tunnel towards a brilliant white light, supported by a cloud of sparkling amber. He was endowed with a boundless joy, a tingling rapture, and he felt running through his mind and his body and the entire universe a current of electricity which he knew to be true and godly love. He was enveloped in love, and he was love.

It was a wonderfully pure and sexual experience. On this trip Irving had no negative feelings whatsoever, although during some later trips he saw the devil and a lot of terrible, monstrous, cancerous imps. He wrote all this up for Ambrose later, and Ambrose filed it with all the other accounts of similar experiences. The experiences were, in fact, all so similar that they made boring reading after a while. The interesting thing was that they *were* so similar. Ambrose was a collector of research material, but after he had collected it he more or less forgot about it. He simply never did anything with it, but just got on with other work—if you could call it work. He didn't even put in reports to the Swiss drug company that so generously supplied the drug.

The Weather is Bad in the World of Sexuality

People are in general not candid over sexual matters. They do not show their sexuality freely, but to conceal it they wear a heavy overcoat woven of a tissue of lies, as though the weather were bad in the world of sexuality.

SIGMUND FREUD, *Clark Lectures 1909*

Irving Victor Clay was born in Wales in 1930, and he went to Cambridge where he read classics before going to Harvard to study astronomy, physics, languages and comparative religion. He emigrated to Australia, teaching at the University of Melbourne where he took a degree in theology. He married Eugenia Phyllis Tart (unfortunate name which she was in a hurry to change—pity she didn't work up a hyphenated thing such as Clay-Tart). They had two sons and a daughter, all of whom wisely removed as soon as they could to distant countries, out of reach of their father's lunatic ideas. In 1962, having recently written the best-selling *Sensual Spirituality and the Finger of God*, Irving was appointed Master of King's. The Old Boy Network found Irving very unusual and refreshing; they were unused to a clergyman who could even bring himself to use the word 'sensual', let alone put it in the title of a book. And of course he had the good old Halo

Effect, and so soon he had the doctors and lawyers eating out of his soft white hand. Anyone could see he was mad, but nobody bothered to look. A sex-driven prophet.

The old story.

David and Solomon
led very wicked lives,
they spent the afternoons
with other people's wives.
Then in the evenings
when their conscience gave them qualms
Solomon wrote the Proverbs
and David wrote the Psalms.

On the fabulous proceeds of his books (by which I do not mean his well-known *God is a Dolphin* and *Deepest Recall: God and Memory in Trees* and *Understanding the Secret Doctrine*, but his series of immensely popular detective novels featuring Inspector [Square] Root, and written under the pen name of Noah Hill) he bought a property in the foothills of the mountains behind the city. This was Ararat, a few acres of sloping land enclosed by a rough stone wall and containing the houses of New Haven, Bethany and Hill House, as well as small cottages and workshops. New Haven was situated at a low, distant corner of the property, surrounded by a high brick wall with a heavy wooden gate. The top of the wall was studded with shards of green broken glass and through this was twisted sharp wire known as tiger tape. Outside the wall were planted cypress trees so that the house was screened by a dark hedge. It was just the place for bringing up the children, a neat little prison within a paradise.

Ararat had been built as an artists' colony, and was exactly what Irving had always dreamed of. Here was the place where he could found his religious community, where he and his followers could pursue higher thought, where they could be free from the constraints and from the clamour of the day-to-day world. The architecture was a wild romantic mixture, with leanings towards gothic, and a certain emphasis on fairytale and European monastery. You could grow vegetables and fruits and keep chickens and cows and goats. Make bread. Be carpenters and stonemasons. Worship with the whole person. The air was clean and pure; the stars shone brightly in the night sky.

It astonishes me when people like Irving find a place like this, a place that whispers 'Paradise on earth' and beckons with slim princess fingers from leaded casements, and they don't see the devil grinning from behind the tree. But Irving fell for it. He bought Ararat—where he could, of course, be forgiven for seeing himself as Noah.

He continued to live at King's, visiting Ararat at least twice a week. People began to remove themselves from city life and take up residence on the property. This was necessary, of course, for the running of the place. And gradually the group, the cult of the Hill House Brethren, evolved. Sometimes Irving felt the strong inclination to resign as Master of King's and go to the hills to be Master of Ararat. But for a very long time he resisted the urge. Ararat came to be known, in a quiet and underground sort of way, as a theological college of some extraordinary and rarified kind. The members of the Brethren were sworn to secrecy as to the details of their faith, and more and more of them abandoned their other lives and gave all to the cult.

Their beliefs were many-faceted and flexible, but there were rules, the principal one being absolute loyalty to Irving Clay—the Captain, the Master.

Sex was not, at first anyhow, really talked about, even though it was the underlying principle.

Solomon and Sheba

Things took a bright and dangerous turn when chance–fate–kismet–destiny–Honeychurch brought Petra into the picture. Honeychurch was the hoopoe that would bring Sheba to Solomon. And indeed, Irving would sometimes refer to himself and Petra as Solomon and Sheba—how did he interpret the *Song of Songs*, I wonder. Did he see it as a metaphor for Christ and his church, or did he take it at face value as a piece of oriental erotica? I suspect that old Irving was pretty split on this kind of thing. With his so-called conscious and rational mind he would take the Song as a church metaphor, but with his not-so-unconscious self he would respond to it as a juicy piece of lovely filth. I suppose it was ever thus. Is it called self-delusion? Or perhaps hypocrisy? Did he know it was poetry? Anyway, that's the way I imagine it worked for Irving.

Honeychurch: Petra is ... luminous, strange, wise—so spiritual.

Clay: If what you say is so, then it is imperative that I meet her.

So one summer evening, when the shadows of the trees and towers were lengthening across the lawns of King's, and the perfume of the ginger lilies filled the still

---

hoopoe; Sheba; Solomon

and balmy air in which sprinklers twittered, Simon drove into the college with, beside him in the passenger seat, gorgeous in a simple azure silk dress and silver sandals, our girl Petra. In the study lined with glass-fronted bookcases Irving received the two visitors. Simon stayed for a weak sherry. It was horrible, it tasted like the juice of a daffodil—in this place of temperance such was the gesture towards the grape. Then he left Irving alone with Petra.

Perhaps I should elaborate on the reason for the flavour of the sherry. The Master's wife was so earnest in her campaign against the consumption of alcohol that she used to tamper with the contents of the bottles, substituting for a small quantity of the sherry a few spoonfuls of her own urine, in an attempt to put people off. An odd thing was that some people positively liked the taste. Irving in particular, and one of the High Court judges. This fact gave rise to a nice ambivalence in the Master's wife, for whereas she had originally peed in the sherry to stop people from drinking, she developed an interest in who liked the mixture and who did not, and looked forward eagerly to the opinions of visitors. Simon Honeychurch hated the stuff but suffered it; Petra didn't even bother to sip.

Don't worry about how I come to know all that about the sherry; if I was forever going into the detail of my sources we'd be here all night. In fact the widdle in the sherry story came out some years later when a maid who had worked in the college wrote her memoirs (I do wish they wouldn't do that) and spilled not only those beans but a number of others, such as the bizarre sexual practices of Honeychurch and friends, and the requests she had to fulfil for the Captain, who liked the maids to bend over his imposing desk just before prayers in the chapel while he had his way quickly. He said it improved his voice. And the way he liked them to remove their shoes and watch while he took his pleasure with the footwear. He would then insist that they wear the shoes, just as they were, into the dining-room.

Well, Petra looked, as you can imagine, like an angelic visitor to the Master, the Captain, whose blackberry eyes were wide with wonder and delight behind his tortoise-shells. They spoke on this first occasion principally of rebirth, reincarnation and the evidence of ghostly presences. Petra agreed with everything Irving said, adding in a thrilling murmur her own poetic and imaginative phrases here and there so that he thought they were his own, and he felt lifted up with his own brilliance. It was interesting to see two workers of the Halo Effect coming together in a room, coming together with a clear and unstated intention of mutual benefit of a weird and spiritual kind. They began by both sitting in deep leather armchairs. The light was fading behind the quaint diamond panes of the windows. (Inside and out, the buildings of this college for university men resembled the castles and towers of a European fairytale. Seriously dreary masculine lives needed to be softened and balanced by golden spires and suggestions in stone of strange romantic possibilities.) Irving stood up in his excitement, he paced the room, his fingers going like those of a demented lace-maker, and then quite suddenly he knelt at Petra's feet.

There were a few flurried words about walking in golden realms of the spirit, and then, bowing deeply, he embraced her toes in their silver sandals and with the utmost reverence he brushed them with his lips. In an electric silence Petra waited until he had completed this ritual, and then she said, in her low and lovely voice, The Spirit of God is All Around Us in Gentleness.

Irving took this fairly unoriginal pronouncement as some kind of Big Idea, and when he had composed himself he took his leave of Petra and rushed into the kitchen where Eugenia in a navy blue dress and floral apron was making the gravy for the roast. He grabbed her impulsively by the wrist so that she dropped the spoon and the pan of gravy slipped from the stove, crashing and splattering on the tiles.

Come and meet this woman! he said. You have to meet this woman! She is a messenger, an incarnation. A holy one has been sent to us!

Two theology students, Paul and James, who were helping Eugenia with the meal, stared after the Captain as he dragged his wife from the kitchen into the study. Paul tapped his forehead knowingly and James made crude gestures with his fingers. Apart from the fact that they were studying theology, they were two sane and sensible young men, their actions speaking louder than any words could. They set about making fresh gravy.

I would like to be able to report that Irving did not instruct Eugenia to kneel and kiss Petra's foot, but I am impelled to say that is exactly what he did, and, futhermore, Eugenia obeyed. This regular matron in sensible shoes and, for all I know, support stockings, went down on the red Turkey carpet like a Muslim facing Mecca and smooched the pearly manicured tootsies. Petra, believing in her own charismatic powers and importance, allowed all this to happen.

Then Petra and Irving sat in a pleasant trancelike silence of meditation and a certain absence of thought at the dining-table while Eugenia and Paul and James put the dinner together and served it, a traditional English sort of dinner of roast beef and vegetables and queen pudding. I felt a certain hysteria rising in me at the sight of these people, so lately purporting to be in touch with the secrets of the cosmos, tucking into sensible jolly fare. The conversation was on an altogether wordly plane, with discussions of college history and the college gardens and the price of food. Even the weather.

It interests me that here we have these people with only one thing (sex) on their minds, and they have first of all displaced it or dressed it up in cosmic and mystical terms, and now all they can do is deny it with history, gardening, economics and the weather. I was particularly bored and spent my time resting in the study, up in the ceiling which was made from polished wood, sternly divided into small squares. Quite a few cobwebs, but I got a good view of the Turkey carpet, which I thought was a very fine example of its kind—thick, dark and of an intricate and seductive geometry. A lovely mandala. I am a bit of a connoisseur.

I can spend happy hours gazing into the patterns on carpets, finding in them a satisfying description of the basic shape of everything. If you think I am just rambling on, I assure you I am not; I mean it. It is no accident, nor even

---

mandala

any coincidence, that the patterns on ancient carpets and in prehistoric paintings mirror the shapes dreamt up by the computer of Benoit Mandelbrot; that Jung's patients seemed automatically to draw mandalas. The Mandelbrot set, the fractal, these are the essential shapes of all matter, and these shapes come readily to the human imagination, which expresses itself in visual forms. I see nothing unusual in this.

After dinner the diners at King's all came into the study and drank weak black coffee from tiny black Wedgwood cups. They had each an apostle spoon and an after-dinner mint. I tell you, it was excruciating. And they obscured the patterns I was so enjoying on the rug. Irving put on a recording of the London Philharmonic playing Handel, and when they got to 'The Arrival Of The Queen Of Sheba' he announced that this was Petra's perfect theme song. Little did he realise the trouble he was starting at that moment; Petra decided he was right, and she adopted the music as her own forthwith. She took to making entrances accompanied by a recording of some great orchestra or other playing her tune. And there was a time when she adopted Handel's *Largo* for super-solemn moments.

(I should probably come clean here and tell you that I was Handel's guardian angel. That was a great job. And of course not only did it fulfil my interest in the use of the hand in the making of music, but the man's name was a comfort to me as well. So it was nice when Petra took up with the music of my beloved George, and brought back many happy memories to me.)

These are the principal players, then. Naturally I see Petra as the central figure. Then after her I would put Irving Clay. And next I would probably put Celeste, although I can imagine that some people would say Dr Goddard would be pretty big. And then there's poor Sylvie, Celeste's mother. All these people bring more people with them, ripples going out from one and flowing into the ripples from another and another; it's very interesting to observe the patterns these things make. I could take you on ripple journeys that would sear your eyeballs and frizzle your brain with the dizzy, spinning, clashing excitement of it all.

If you start with Celeste and see that she is the best little ballet dancer of Petra's whole troupe (of which more later), you can get a ripple to her strict obedience to Petra's regime of how her girls will sleep, and that ripple takes you to Fanny Cerito who invented the sleeping method in London last century. (The idea of the method was that the girls preserve the line of their knees by sleeping on their backs with one foot tied to each bedpost.) And from Fanny you can ripple out to Queen Victoria, who commanded her performance with three other famous dancers of the time, and from there you get to Pepita, celebrated Spanish dancer who also danced for Queen Victoria. And Pepita takes you straight to Vita Sackville-West who was Pepita's granddaughter, and that brings you right back to Petra and to Dr Goddard and the Mandala clinic where some patients constructed a facsimile of Vita's famous White Garden. There, you didn't

---

Fanny Cerito

expect that, did you? Perhaps not such a ripple as a whirligig.

With all this talk of mothers and daughters and the disappearance of baby Colette, the sorrowing of her poor mother, you will have found a strand or a string (or whatever you have in your unconscious there) being plucked or tweaked or twanged, or in some way activated and giving off effects. You will have thought, or almost thought, of Persephone and Demeter. This story has the underworld as one of its locations, so it's pretty interesting. People have sometimes asked me how that girl got the pomegranate seeds down there in Hades, and, you know, I have never had an answer. I'm not sure myself what they serve there, and where they get the stuff from. Funny thing to choose, pomegranate seeds. I read that a decoction of the flowers and bark of the tree stop bleeding and purging of all kinds, and that a strong infusion of the pulp cures mouth ulcers and fastens the teeth.

I'm puzzled by that 'fastens the teeth'—from Culpeper, you will have recognised the old fellow's style. There's a great old pomegranate tree in the garden of the French house, but the Fishers were less interested in (if they were in fact conscious of) the classical reference than in the beauty of the ruddy fruit and glowing bright orange flowers and in the Christian symbolism, the fruit signifying the Church because of the unity of the innumerable seeds contained in one whole. Also the Christian hope of resurrection and immortality—and this probably derives from the old Persephone thing anyhow. Then of course there's fertility—all those seeds tucked into their glowing scarlet, juicy-jelly globules. Dripping with sex.

Personally, I can look at a split pomegranate for hours at a stretch. So in a way I probably do understand why Persephone chose the pomegranate; she liked the taste and it linked up, in her imagination, with gorgeous shining red round fruit cracking open and displaying the bloody gleam of the internal pattern of seeds in envelopes, nestling up against each other in darling little rows, full of promise, waiting to burst out of their skins and sprout new roots and leaves. Yes, I get it now. Sorry to ramble on, but I did warn you.

And I feel also that I should point out the fact that there was never any such person as Persephone. She's a character in a story. It's a story, right? One of the early stories people made up and retold and wrote down. Don't let this get out, but personally I find these made-up characters in stories more interesting, convincing and what I might call 'useful' than many famous people who really lived. They are myths, and as myths they have incredible fascination and power. And if you think of real people and their myths, you'll see that the myths surrounding, say, Michael Jackson or Elvis are where the power of those people really develops and gets off the ground. It's not the person that matters, it's the myth. Pretty hard on the person, when you think about it. The awesome, invisible power of charisma is made up in several ways, the Halo Effect being one bit, myth being another.

My own Petra caught on very early to the importance of weaving a veil of myths around herself, and then she began to believe in the myths, and her belief was so strong that its truth started to glow from her face and to register in her gestures and movements. Petra's got charisma, and you actually get a lot of your charisma by the strength of your belief in your own myth. It sounds simple, and there is a kind of simplicity to it. But it is a trick a person has to discover. A bit like when you look at those 3-D Magic Eye pictures. I love those. Once you learn the trick of how to keep a steady gaze while letting your eyes stay out of focus, the thing is simple magic. Well, Petra and her ilk learnt the trick of firm belief in their own lies about themselves. She's a super-duper confidence trickster with absolute conviction shining out of her hypnotic blue eyes, and no mistake. It's quite a thing. I marvel. If Petra had ever woken up one morning and told herself she was a fraud, the game would have been up. Not to worry; she'd never have done that. Take my word for it. Petra believed her own story from beginning to end.

There's no doubt about it, when you hear a story like the story of the life of Sylvie Fisher and her long-lost daughter Colette, named after a little red shoe, you can't help recalling, deep down inside yourself, the story of Persephone. I go to Homer for the Greek, Ovid for the Latin, and then silly old Sir James George Frazer, F.R.S., F.B.A. for the English. I've put parts of all their versions of the story of Persephone in The Footnote, of course. Persephone out picking flowers in the lush meadow always stirs in my mind the memory of Red Riding Hood as she strayed from the path and picked the flowers. Girls who dally in meadow and wood get snatched up and carried off and raped and murdered. That's one of the simpler messages of those stories, and many, many other stories all over the world, all down the ages. It's as if girls are deaf or stupid, isn't it? They read the stories, see the pretty flowers, and the moral goes *woosh!* over their dear little heads, and before you know what, they have gone out into the lush meadow and there they are picking scarlet poppies and heaven knows what, and along comes a fellow in a Toyota station wagon and bye-bye girlie.

> The badly decomposed body of a young woman was discovered yesterday in a shallow grave in dense scrub within five kilometres of the highway that runs through the Balanglo State Forest. Police estimate that the woman, whose hands and feet were tied with electrical cord, has been dead for approximately three months. She had been shot in the back of the head at close range.

A news item such as that leaves no room for levity.

I always wonder, though, who in heaven's name was supposed to be looking after such a girl. The careless guardians have much to answer for. It's a strange thing, to go back to what I was just saying about how all these girls have been told the stories over and over again, not just the stories of Red Riding Hood and so forth, but the stories in the paper every second day—girls snatched from railway stations at midnight, girls picked up outside their own houses in broad daylight. I have sometimes tested this myself, being as it were, freelance. (I should point out here that I manifest and appear to be a normal, good-looking bloke—no sign of wing or whiff of brimstone. Well, as if there ever would be.) I see a lovely creature at a tram stop at twilight and I stand at a respectable distance from her and after a while she turns to me and she says when do the trams run and I say where are you going and she says she has to find her way to Chapel Street and is it far and I say is she from round here and she says she's just moved to the city from Shepparton and she has to meet up with some people in a bar in Chapel Street and I say I'm getting a cab and I'll drop her off at Chapel Street and a cab comes and I whistle and it pulls up and we get in. Next stop the Balanglo State Forest, you might say.

It's okay—I drop them at Chapel Street. But where are their guardians? And where are their brains? It almost seems as if there is victimhood written into the blood of some of these girls. Lambs to the slaughter, sacrificial virgins. Wolf on prowl snatches chicken by roadside—beginning and end of story.

The Path of Light Leads to the River of No Return

So there they were at lunch: the Goddards, the Clays, the Winters and the Honeychurches—and Petra Penfold-Knight. There was a table set out among the trees at the end of the garden, where the river ran past.

I often see things from above, like a cameraman with an aerial long shot. If you open a newspaper or news magazine you will nearly always find an aerial long shot of a mansion or a farmhouse where something terrible has happened, such as a multiple death of some kind. You see the drive with the tops of the parked cars, some of these being police cars, and the layout of the gardens, the pathways, the pool, and the shape of the roof of the house. It has a flattening, eerie atmosphere, at once unfamiliar and familiar—familiar because the shot is so common. You get the house of tragedy down on the earth, and up above are journalists hanging from hovering helicopters, getting their pictures. The angle of vision is of course one which is entirely normal to me. No big deal.

The long shot at lunch was of two graceful weeping willows, beneath which there were white cane armchairs and small tables, and in front of the trees was a long table with a white cloth, set for lunch, sparkling with silver and crystal, and surrounded by cedar dining-chairs. People on the chairs under the trees. Two Irish wolfhounds reclining on the lawn. 'The Arrival Of The Queen Of Sheba' coming almost unobtrusively from speakers in the trees—these people were sometimes touching (and dangerous) in their childishness. And Petra in white silk with a broad buttercup sash and golden sandals making her progress across the grass towards the willow trees, her red hair rippling across her shoulders, her blue eyes blazing with high excitement and expectation. Even to me there appeared to be a path of light opening up before her as she moved—and I am very sceptical. The people in the chairs under the willows stood up as Petra approached and they moved out onto the lawn to greet her—Abigail and Ambrose Goddard both embraced her with a kind of formal warmth at which they were very practised. Abigail and Ambrose were a bit younger than the others; Abigail was beautiful and Ambrose looked okay until you saw the crazed light in his eye. He too had the Halo Effect, which had taken him far in the land of psychiatry.

At lunch there was French wine and light, delicious dishes delivered from the kitchen of the best hotel in town, served by a group of out-of-work actresses (this was the sixties, and it was okay to call them actresses then) dressed as waitresses (ditto). Take my word for it, the food was splendid; I feel no urge to go into detail about it. Abigail Goddard wasn't particularly interested in cooking, but she loved to arrange catered dinners and lunches, such as this one, theatrical events in the garden, or in the house, where the dining-room was papered in red and lit by a large and intricate Indian chandelier.

The wine was impeccably selected and even Irving sipped some of this. Eugenia, that arch adulterer of the grape, diluted hers with ice and water, much to the silent disgust of Ambrose. Sometimes, from the music room in the house, came the notes of a cello played badly by Sebastian, the son of Ambrose and Abigail. Sophie, the daughter, had gone out riding for the day. I tell you these little things simply to give you an idea of the kind of people the Goddards were, or at least the kind of people they gave the impression of being.

The lunch was successful in that Petra was found suitable by all present to be installed as the matron–mother–queen of the new experiment in raising children for the future continuity of the Hill House Brethren. It was a foregone conclusion anyway, since Irving had already decided.

Petra had told Sister Denise Winter she would adopt the baby that was due to be born to Sylvie Fisher, provided that baby was a girl. The idea was that this baby would be the first of several who would be brought up by the group, with Petra in charge, as part of the plan to develop and mould members of the cult from birth, to raise children who would know only what the cult told them, who would have as little contact as possible with society and the world outside Ararat. It was understood that the community would continue to attract members from outside, with the children becoming the core of a fully initiated, fully enlightened elite. The children would have the strength to take the group into the twenty-first century, after the holocaust. So the story ran.

(There's no story like an old story. Well, come to that, I daresay there's no story *but* an old story.)

Irving Clay was the authority and the mastermind behind the whole thing, it being an idea he had been working on for years. He had visited various experimental segregated communities in the United States, and had been struck by the fact that failure often seemed to come about through sexual jealousies arising from idealised free love, and through the communal rearing of the children of the group. He was particularly interested in the Oneida community in New York State, an experiment which began in 1850 and ended peacefully in 1880, and which was noted for its development of a particular kind of sexual arrangement called complex marriage, similar in some ways to the wife swapping of the sixties, and for its experimental breeding of children to found a better race. The race never eventuated, and the principal remnant of Oneida is the highly successful Oneida factory that produces table silver. The knives and forks on the tables at Hill House and Bethany all came from Oneida. An attempt had been made by the leader of Oneida, John Noyes, to reconcile the book of Genesis and the work of Charles Darwin, the result being the theory that mankind was descended from snakes.

Ambrose Goddard was interested to learn of the sex lives of the people at Oneida, and of the way the leader of the community could command the women, particularly the teenage girls, a key interest for Ambrose, and, for that matter, for Irving and several of the other Brethren and Old Boys. And because Ambrose was fascinated by the role of laundry in the control of women in general (and madwomen in particular, madwomen being his other speciality), he was delighted to read in a book Irving lent

---

him (*Without Sin* by Spencer Klaw) that John Noyes had also seen the virtues of the wash-house and had invented a primitive washing-machine, even including men in the ritual of washing. Taking his cue from an account of washing days at Oneida, Ambrose tried to encourage singing in the laundries at the Mandala clinic.

'Ah! our old washing days,' John Noyes had written in his diary,' the whole scene comes up before me as I write. An odor of soap suds, emanating from two large caldrons of boiling clothes, fills the atmosphere. One by one the washers come in, some looking rather sleepy. Finally the wash-boxes are surrounded, the partners standing vis-a-vis. In a few minutes all are busily washing—a pleasant hum of voices can be heard, despite the thumping of the one washing-machine in the corner.

'Anon, the whole group are formed into a grand musical chorus; now singing snatches of an old anthem, and now divided into sections, the air is soon resonant with such rounds as "Scotland's Burning", "Merrily, Merrily Greet The Morn", "Glide Along My Bobby Boat", etc. Tired of all this, all is quiet until Mr T. is prevailed upon to sing "Dearest Mae" which he alone can render to suit this audience. He is loudly applauded, and before another song can be produced the breakfast bell sounds, announcing to the astonished company that they have washed an hour and a half.'

The Mandala singing experiment was not successful.

Irving reasoned (if you could call it that) that an untried way forward would be to form a kind of convent composed of new-born baby girls placed in the care of one woman who had a group of servant women. These girls would be enclosed and trained to be the mothers of the first generation of superior beings, the fathers being the men who made up the male population at Hill House. Eventually the boy children born in the community would become the fathers of the next generation.

You might imagine that the notion of collecting new-born baby girls in Melbourne in the 1960s would present a stumbling-block to this project, but as it happened this was not so. With his Old Boy network of legal and medical men, Irving was easily able to arrange for babies to be found, acquired and brought, complete with forged papers, to the fortified house called New Haven in the hills, where Petra came to preside. The problem was not in finding the babies and securing their adoption, but in finding the woman who could control the operation. Once Irving Clay had found Petra, from then on it was more or less plain sailing, a piece of cake, or, as Irving used to say, a French kiss (nobody knew what he meant).

The Sexual Privilege

The little community of babies and nurses at New Haven was only one part of Irving's Hill House Brethren; Hill House and Bethany were situated within walking distance of the walled enclave of New Haven, and were houses where some of the followers lived and which other followers, still engaged in important matters medical and legal in the city, visited. Some of the babies who ended up at New Haven had their origins at Bethany, where the women of the group lived. Baby boys born at Bethany were sent away to one of Nurse Winter's homes for a few years so as to separate them from their mothers, and then were brought back, but no boys were brought in from outside.

The men of the community lived at Hill House, which was a large, grand fantasy–gothic house commanding a view of the distant city as well as the rolling hills, forests, flower farms and lake. There were no formal marriages, the women leading a more or less conventual life of work and prayer, and the men working on the small farm and going out to lecture on their faith from time to time. They were able to apply to Irving for permission to mate with one or other of the women. Oral contraceptives, a new invention, were supplied to the women by the doctors in the group, and when Irving decided a woman should bear a child, these were discontinued. Women who then failed to conceive were severely punished, no blame being attributed to the men. Punishments were forerunners of things Jim Jones did to his erring faithful in Jonestown and took the form of pushing red hot peppers into the woman's vagina, and administering electric shocks to her brain without an anaesthetic by the use of a machine called Bigfoot, supplied from Mandala by Ambrose. All the women had to pass several tests conducted by Irving before they were allowed to join the community; one of these tests was officially known as the Sexual Privilege—it was a great honour to be fucked by Irving—and the procedure was commonly known as the Captain's Road Test.

Petra had the sense to see that if there were anything sexual between herself and Irving, the game would be up as far as she was concerned. He was powerfully attracted to her, but she held herself aloof, in a kind of holy virginity. She differed from mad Wanda in that way. Since the old days on the knee of Somerset Jones, Petra had actually lost interest in ordinary sex, being disappointed in the men she ran into, seeing them, as, for one thing, fools. Petra was more interested in the use of her sexuality to obtain power. She used her sexual charisma to hold men to her in hope, but she distributed no favours. This strategy placed her above Irving in the power structure, with him referring to her as the Queen. She was ideal as the head of the little babies' convent at New Haven where other women did all the hard work.

In the years since she had arrived in Melbourne, worked at the Bible Shop, got into yoga, acquired a certificate to teach kindergarten, she had formed no real bonds with men or women, unless you count Meena, who was a kind of professional contact. These were years of cold hard work and very little play. Petra had no romantic leanings, no attachments; her contempt for most of the human race rendered her a special kind of celibate. In this she differed utterly from so many charismatic and lascivious men who choose to lead the faithful out of the wilderness into the light, men such as Irving. Irving saw sex with the women in the group as both his duty and his right, a gift from the gods to the god. I know it sounds peculiar, but I really think he believed all that stuff, in his own weird way. And Petra believed in all her stuff, and so there they were.

At first I wondered how people were recruited into the Brethren, but it soon became clear that many of them were ex-patients from the Mandala clinic, and therein lies a tale.

Sheba Walks on Solomon's Face

Irving had prayed for someone as special as Petra to come into his circle, for he saw that in order to make a success of the New Haven experiment in child-raising he needed a powerful female spirit. He found it a nice coincidence that the Oneida community had at one time lived in New Haven in Connecticut, and little things like this served to inspire and encourage him. And he was not to know that Petra would soon outrank him in the cult. Sheba walks on Solomon's face. The anima rises up to destroy or at least unnerve the man who needs her. Petra was a key attraction to new members; she could out-charisma old Irving any day, and Irving had at least the wit to go along with her. Once she was accepted and established in the Brethren, there was no stopping her. Ambrose Goddard fancied that he himself would one day have sex with Petra. If he only knew how low he appeared to her to be. She admired his set-up at the clinic and the way he could get the LSD free with government approval, and could manipulate the patients, get just about anybody to do his will, but Petra's eye was fixed in the narcissist's mirror; she was her own god and she was going to be everybody else's god as well. An ambitious girl. As I said, cold.

Brethren were found in two basic ways—they were the friends or colleagues of people already in the fold, or they were 'discovered' at Mandala. Usually the members of the first group lived in their own homes in the city, coming to the meeting hall at Hill House once or twice a week. The meeting hall, the former ballroom of Hill House, was known as Mount Meru, the name of the Tantric mountain that stands at the centre of the universe and also at the centre point of the human body. Sometimes people would stay for a weekend of retreat, and occasionally they would stay for a longer period to be instructed in some higher aspect of the faith.

The Brethren who lived in the city formed a central core of Believers in the World, successful professionals who were profoundly empty and unhappy in their personal lives, desolate in their souls, and therefore prepared to be beguiled by the doctrines of leaders such as Irving and by the mysterious and dazzling Queen Petra. People were drawn to Petra as moths are drawn to a flame. They were also attracted to Irving like filings to a magnet. The magic, which can be analysed but never truly described, was in Petra and Irving. And there was also secrecy and a specific reserve about them. You could come just so close and no closer; there was a point at which the sanctuary of Petra, the holiness of Irving was set aside, was beyond the reach of ordinary mortals.

They spoke, also, with absolute authority. Petra and Irving could (and did) utter the most garbled twaddle and you would see their followers just lapping it up.

'You stand within the portals, on the threshold of a gleaming new and shining clean and beautiful life, wandering from a world of ignorance, darkness, grief, despair and folly. You come to this spiritual place, this temenos, this holy ground of the heart and soul where the Captain and the Mother will guide you in your journey through the jasper sea of profanity and pollution towards the glory of transparent enlightenment in the new time, the new eternity, where the veil will be drawn back and you will be as a child at the breast, as a sponge in the sea, as a flower in the field of eternal light.'

You see what I mean?

There was no written doctrine, no catechism, for the rules would change from week to week. There were texts for study, such as the Book of Revelation and the Bhagavadgita, and so forth, but the general idea was that Petra and Irving were going to steer the ship of the faithful into the next century, beyond the coming holocaust, and into a brand new reality which only Petra and Irving could possibly imagine. Take your drugs, obey the Mother and the Captain, have sex how and when they say, shun the outside world, even when you are in the outside world.

'We guarantee you power, the power of the vision of spiritual truth, innocence and light. The power to transcend the darkness of sin. The power of the visioned heart. The power of the beatified mind. The power of the body perfected in the fires of truth. The power of holiness. The plagues and earthquakes and poisons will come. The air and the waters of the earth will destroy the peoples of the earth. Yet the Brethren, obedient to the visions of the transcendent heart, will prevail, and their children will prevail, and their children's children will inherit the new world beyond the century, beyond the flow of time, beyond the rafters of the rays of eternity.'

When you heard Petra or Irving deliver one of these

speeches, you were gone, lapped in the warm waves of faith. And the Brethren who worked out in the world, in hospitals and courts and universities, were promised a special entry to the world beyond the century, when the time came, in recognition of their selflessness in remaining outside the walls of Ararat. The Brethren who lived at Ararat followed daily rules of segregation by gender, except when called upon to produce children, or to receive Irving's Sexual Privilege. They worked in the community of Ararat, living simple, rigid and busy lives.

I used to look at the Brethren in their black clothes and red slippers and they seemed to me to resemble toys. They were, I think, the playthings of Petra and Irving. Like children tired of their games, one day Petra and Irving would walk away from the Hill House Brethren, just as John Noyes walked away from his Oneida community.

The Brethren who lived outside were as vital as those inside. They were people who had a certainty of power in the professional world, and they gained a strange satisfaction in being close to the seat of other-worldly powers. They were the lawyers who created the false identities of the babies by writing the deed polls needed to forge birth certificates, and sometimes even passports. They were the psychiatrists and other medical men who wrote the prescriptions for the drugs needed to keep the faithful in thrall. They were the nurses who brought Irving and Petra to comfort lonely, wealthy people who would subsequently leave large estates to the Brethren when they died. It was not even necessary to wait for the people to die, better to hasten the end. They were also social workers who brought to the Brethren babies for adoption or sale. Social life went on as usual for these professionals, their non-Brethren colleagues having no inkling of the complexities of the faith of the Brethren on the Hill. They constantly and subtly recruited new members.

The helpless psychiatric patients chosen to be Brethren by a committee consisting of Ambrose Goddard, Irving Clay and Petra were first of all separated from their family ties, making them utterly dependent on the Brethren. Men were instructed to leave their wives, wives to leave their husbands. For these old ties were dangerous to the group, and were presented to the prospective Brethren as being dangerous to their own souls, to their spiritual enlightenment, as being a deadly insult to God.

Porcelain Man

Roger Nichols was the husband of Anna, a woman who died at Mandala during a session of Deep Sleep Therapy. Roger was a school teacher and it was thought that he would be a useful tutor for the young people at Hill House and Bethany, and as an education supervisor for the children at New Haven. If the story of Roger that I am about to tell appears to be a curiously elaborate way of going about getting a tutor for the community, remember that this was no simple religious group. This was a group that not only delighted in intrigue and torture, but required secrecy and extreme loyalty for its very existence.

After the death of his wife, Roger, who was beside himself with grief, was for a time admitted to the clinic to undergo a course of treatment with LSD. As I've said before, the LSD at Mandala was brought in free, with government approval, from the Swiss manufacturer, on the understanding that it was being used therapeutically and to a certain extent experimentally. The clinic charged the patients for the drug—the theory being that if they were not charged they would not believe in the usefulness of the drug. Roger was given doses of LSD every day for a week. He lay naked in bed in a darkened room.

The first time:

Enter Petra in blue silk and a nurse in pink polyester.

Petra wears a strange blue crystal on a cord at her throat. The nurse, according to the rules at Mandala, wears a Mickey Mouse badge. (A thing I have noticed about the world, no matter where you go—a women's military convent in Libya, a remote hill tribe in Wherever—you will see on a sleeve, a cap, a backpack an image of Mickey Mouse. Forget Jesus, forget Elvis, forget Diana. The Mouse rules.)

The nurse gives Roger a needle of sedative and then a needle of LSD while Petra speaks soothingly to him: You will see a pattern through the pain. So much beauty and truthfulness and a light, a beautiful light. Bow you heart and accept the journey, for this is given to you as a child of light and good. Open your hands and grasp the staff for the journey. I will go with you. I will help you, lead you as the sunlight touches the flower, as the lotus opens above the surface of the waters of night. We will go through together.

On she went with her amazing, garbled talk. But her voice was pitched to a note that somehow entered the man in a place that was not his intellect. She would sometimes touch him gently, softly, intimately, like a loving being from another world. It was horrible to watch, but the nurse in pink seemed to take it all in her stride. All in a day's work at Mandala.

The first time, it was important that Roger should start out trusting and relaxed, and so Petra stayed with him for an hour, murmuring, humming, uttering strange and colourful nonsense. Petra left, abandoning him to his own madness, leaving the nurse in pink to take some notes about his gestures, and leaving a tape-recorder running.

For everything Roger said and did was going to be studied and used in the attempt to bind him to the Brethren. Even the nurse got bored eventually and left. It was one of Petra's methods that she would collect information about the patients when they were not conscious of having given it, and then she would repeat this to them when they least expected it. This gave the impression that Petra had psychic powers and special knowledge and understanding. It amazes me that Roger could have been persuaded to go anywhere near Mandala, except perhaps to torch the place, after what had happened to his wife. But such was the smooth tongue of Dr Goddard, and the complexity of guilt and depth of helplessness and need within Roger himself, that there he was, seeking sanctuary in hell.

And such was the power of Petra.

Roger was kept in an almost continuous state of hallucination for seven days and seven nights. At the end of this period he was stark, raving mad. Trapped within the prison of his own head, he had been on an electric and fluorescent journey to the end of space, had been inside the skins of serpents, behind the eyes of giant ants, been trapped in the writhing roots of fig trees, sucked into the indigo mouth of a great jellied anemone, had seen and heard and felt the heartbeat within an icy cube of sickly yellow glass. And he was spinning, forever spinning, forever caught in violent metal spirals. He could hear, from within his own head, the roar of a waterfall mingled with the constant crash of breaking glass. And the lights. And the stench. And from time to time he was almost conscious of the nurse in pink who came to change the tape or to give him another injection, sometimes before he had come down from the last. Was that his own laughter? Was that his own scream? His own shit. His own tears. He was drenched in tears and urine and sweat.

And he babbled through the night: Of, of, of, of, na, na, na, na, ann, na, anna. Work and of, and bub, bubububub, da. Mi, mmm, kakish, rolly rolly rolly victory scrub of of of of of poor, poor me and you and ann and me, poor poor ann, poor man, porcelain man, poor slain man and ann and poorpoor slain paw paw man paw and claw and wolf in wolf-clothing goes woof woof woof.

Of, of, of, of—he babbled softly hour after hour, saliva dribbling from the corners of his mouth. Then he would reverse the sound and begin to say fo, fo, fo and fee-fi-fo-fum and ffffffuck. Then he would fall silent for a long time, before starting up again.

On and on, but the only listener was the tape-recorder. The boundaries of his own body dissolved, and his mind spread like bubbles of grey and yellow soapsuds. Occasionally the nurse would take his blood pressure, and she would sometimes seem to Roger to be a glowing, all-powerful priest in jewelled robes, sometimes a giant spider nipping him with pointed, poisoned fangs. A dark webbed veil hung before his eyes, and viscous liquids dripped and seeped across his brow.

He later wrote up his impressions of the experience in a journal which he called 'Rip Van Winkle: To Hell and Back, and Back to Hell'. He never heard the tapes. The journal was so bizarre and horrible he burnt it.

And when this man, after sessions of LSD over a period of six weeks, was reduced to jelly, Petra came back to him and he fell physically and emotionally at her feet, begging her to save him. Save him from torture. The victim turns to the torturer with love, hope and obedience.

He ended up selling his house, handing the proceeds over to the Brethren and going to live at Hill House, where first of all he was treated gently until he appeared to have recovered from his ordeal, and then he was put to work on the strawberry farm. He set up the shoemaker's shop, and he also taught in the classroom of the children living in the community—a few boys at Hill House and some girls at Bethany, and later the convent girls at New Haven. He appeared to be well and happy; I think he was.

I have no idea what his ex-family made of all this. Sometimes the families of Brethren caused trouble and tried to involve the police and the courts. They didn't have a hope, of course, because Irving and Petra had the ears and the hearts and the minds and the balls of such lawyers as mattered.

Roger is just one example of how things worked between Mandala and the Brethren—there were variations, and people who joined were told they were free to leave at any time. However, anyone who tried to leave was punished, persecuted, threatened and pursued. Their professional and personal lives were over. Sometimes, in fact, they were murdered.

Going Out

A few people who attempted to escape simply disappeared from the face of the earth. They were given a lethal injection at Mandala, put down like sick animals at a veterinary hospital. Whereas the treatment with LSD was known as Threshold, this terminal treatment was called Going Out, or else the Light Treatment—as in going out like a ~. The word would come from Petra and Irving, and Ambrose would put the operation into effect at the clinic. No paperwork needed.

You occasionally hear of a woman who leaves home without her purse, leaving a half-eaten tuna sandwich on the kitchen table and the TV running, talk shows and soaps twittering out into the empty lounge-room, cat not fed. Well, one or two of those in my experience have answered a ring at the doorbell, received a swift hypodermic in the upper arm, been folded up in a van and carted off to the back door of Mandala, where they are popped into solitary, given the big one, folded up again while still soft, and stashed down the old well behind the laundry building.

Since those days, the gardens of Mandala have been gloriously improved and are now a visitors' paradise; the well has been filled with concrete and covered over with a herbal knot-garden. Rosemary for remembrance. Thyme, bergamot, the works. And you see the families of the missing people—on TV—forever wondering and yearning and begging to know where their loved ones have gone. Ding-dong-bell, you might say.

Redcap and Magic Meru Soma

When redcap mushrooms were in season up in the hills, parties of Brethren would go out and joyfully collect them and bring them back to Hill House, where they would dry them for use during special meetings at Mount Meru.

A great fire was lit in the courtyard in front of Mount Meru, the mushrooms were boiled in a cauldron, and the intoxicating liquor was then drunk. On other occasions the Brethren swallowed the dried mushrooms in large chunks, without chewing, and washed them down with cups of cold water. An hour after eating the mushrooms the Brethren began to have fantastic hallucinations and visions, great kaleidoscopic mandalas accompanied by heavenly music and a magnificent feeling of wellbeing and power, the whole experience having a deep undertone of terror, with sensations of one's body becoming by turns enormous and minute, too big to fit into this world, small enough to pass through the eye of a needle.

If you think of *Alice's Adventures in Wonderland* in connection with the effects of various hallucinogens, you might conclude that Lewis Carroll was describing the sensations of a trip. The caterpillar smokes a hookah, and Alice eats the mushroom, and things look very different from the way they looked before.

There were two-day festivals at midsummer and mid-winter when Petra was the only person permitted to eat the redcaps. She would then supply three chosen disciples with her urine, and they would pass theirs on to nine more, and so on until everyone had drunk what they called Magic Meru soma. The effect of the mushrooms was progressively magnified in the urine until the fourth round of drinks, and then it began to fade. Petra claimed never to have had a bad trip from any of the hallucinogens she took, always to be transported to a pure and brilliant vision of the fusion beween her own inner life and the spirit of the whole of creation, of the life before birth and after death, of the meaning of light, the meaning of life, death and the stars. Petra lied about this. She had many a bad trip.

Around the grounds of Hill House, beneath the trees, there were stone replicas of redcaps, giving the place an atmosphere of fairytale, a picturesque reminder that the work of the imagination is frequently stimulated by hallucinations. In the damp weather, the real redcaps came up to put the imitations to shame with the brilliance, the gleaming succulence of their scarlet and white heads.

White Shadow

As I tell this story, I have begun to see that Petra was a kind of white shadow in the lives of the people she touched. As if the halo reached out, radiated, and cast a cloak of strange and evil negativity across all in her path, a clear jellyfish entrapment, a cloud of poisonous ectoplasm. It is horrible to realise this, but the more I think about it, the more I believe I am right.

I have reflected often on the confluence of Petra and Irving, on how they were somehow fashioned for each other, made for each other. If Irving had not found Petra, would his great scheme to establish a new world, beginning with girl babies at New Haven, ever have gotten off the ground? If Petra had not met Irving, what would have become of her warped maternal instinct? And of course I always end up back at mad Wanda and her knitting needle. What if Wanda had succeeded in puncturing Petra's envelope way back then? And what if Wanda hadn't died young?

This is a foolish line of thinking, but in this case it is very tempting. I have been able to describe Petra's movement towards Irving as a more or less straight line, from the Bible Shop to the yoga class and on to the meeting at King's, but if you think about it you'll see that there could have been many a slip that would have kept the fatal pair apart; if the ripples of the lives of Petra and Irving had never met, then the lives of many other people would have been quite different. The lives, in particular, of the babies, and of the true mothers of those babies.

Shalimar

The old brass nameplate on the gate of Sister Denise Winter's Home for Unwed Mothers said 'Shalimar'. It was the name—oriental garden of love—given to the house by the first owner, a man with a wife and five daughters. A family named Chetwynd. The house was grand, with a tower that looked out over the city in one direction and out to the hills in the other. On the lawn at the front of the house stood two graceful palm trees. The reception rooms had long windows to the floor, and deep marble fireplaces with vast looking-glasses above. The ceilings were very elaborate, having moulded urns and shells and swags of flowers round the cornices, and deep, voluptuous centre roses from which hung brass chandeliers. There was the yellow drawing-room with its portrait of Mrs Chetwynd and three of the five daughters, each figure in a different shade of yellow, from gold to cream, a little golden dog in the foreground and a river winding away in the amber distance. The rose room, all pink and magenta brocade, opened onto a lawn that led down to the sunken garden.

It was a ritual that each morning the girls would arrange fresh flowers in the entrance hall and the main rooms before they went about their own business, going to school, practising the piano, keeping diaries and reading books. The place was furnished with pieces from

England, although the dining-room was rich with red Chinese lacquer cabinets and inlaid teak table and chairs. The daughters each had a spacious bedroom, and there were several bathrooms and guest rooms besides.

The grounds, which had once held a tennis court, an orchard, kitchen garden and a rose arbour, had shrunk over the years as subsequent owners had sold off bits of the property. Four of the Chetwynd girls married, and one became the headmistress of a school, and gradually the family that had made the walls of Shalimar sing like the walls of a garden of love disappeared. Sometimes children of the fourth generation would have the house pointed out to them—that's where the Chetwynds lived, that's Shalimar. Because all the children had been daughters, in the end there were no Chetwynds.

When Sister Winter bought Shalimar, it had for many years been a boarding house, with the large rooms rented out as bed-sitting rooms. So the place was inhabited by the spirits of strange, lonely people as well as by the happy ghosts of the Chetwynd girls. The *pit-pat* of the tennis balls on the non-existent court; the plaintive drift of a cello; the flutter of ribbons on a hat; the shush and whisper of silk; the bubble of laughter. It was a bit of a sad irony that into this down-at-heel garden of love straggled the saddest people of all—young, bewildered, frightened, humiliated women who should have been celebrating the child they were carrying, but who were forced into ambivalence and dread and hatred of themselves, even of the child. Their bodies and their hearts told them that this was a joyful, mysterious and holy time, but their minds and their families and their society and their churches told them they must be ashamed, must hide behind the walls and hedges of Shalimar and weep, and hate themselves. They would never even see the babies to whom they gave birth, and they would return to their former lives forever changed, forever wondering how things could have been different.

If you think back to Wanda Penfold, you can see that she was lucky, in a way, for she at least had a family that would nurture the child. Although they could not quite acknowledge that Wanda was Petra's mother (and how might things have turned out differently, for everyone, if they had), at least they did not abandon Petra to strangers at birth.

Girls were admitted to Sister Winter's Shalimar only on the understanding that the child was going to be put up for adoption. This was a business from which Sister Winter reaped a tidy profit. On a grey and inauspicious day, up the path, carrying a small brown suitcase, there slowly walked Sylvie Fisher, sixteen years old, alone, four months pregnant. Sylvie noticed very little as she headed for the front door; she didn't even see, that day, the huge old palm trees with their heavy scaled trunks, plated like the backs of prehistoric animals. She didn't see the delphiniums blue as peacocks by the gate. Later on she saw them; later on she came to take in every last detail of Shalimar.

Sylvie told her mother about the baby one night after tea. They were standing at the sink and Dolfi was washing the dishes and Sylvie was drying, and she knew she was pregnant even though she hadn't been to the doctor, and she knew she had to tell her mother. Tonight. A sad girl in a green dress, her eyes clouded with trouble, holding a green and white dinner plate loosely wrapped in a tea-towel in both hands. Mum, she said, her voice strangely hollow and unworldly, I think I am expecting. Then she dropped the plate, which split into three pieces on the floor, and she fell to the floor after it, hunching over the pieces, almost fainting, unable to sob, finding a dry, hot place within her throat where all feeling lodged and numbed.

Her mother asked Sylvie when and who and how and why. She got no answers from the girl who by now was beginning to sob into the tea-towel, was folded up small on the floor, as if protecting the broken plate. What Dolfi did not do—she did not offer any comfort, any warmth, any hope. She knew it was the end of the world, Sylvie might as well get used to that.

Her mother told her father.

Her father washed his hands of both Sylvie and her mother, blaming both of them for what had happened. Who is the boy? (he called him a boy, and he was right) he asked, but Sylvie wouldn't tell, and her father ranted and raved and went through every standard, sad cliché. He took his shotgun from the wall and threatened to shoot Sylvie if she didn't tell him, saying he was going to go and shoot the boy when he found out who he was. He said words neither Sylvie nor her mother had ever heard him use before. He called the boy a Jesus-fucking shithouse murdering thief. He called Sylvie a whore and a slut, and he hit her in the face with the back of his hand. Then he left the house and went out and got drunk, even though he was teetotal. He got into a fight at the pub, accused everyone in the bar of being the father of the child, thus broadcasting in his drunken delirium the secret he was trying to keep.

> She confessed her sins and the executioner cut off her feet, and the red shoes danced away with them into the dark forest. The executioner carved a pair of wooden feet for her. She kissed the hand that had guided the axe and went on her way. The red shoes danced in front of her.
>
> 'The Red Shoes' (folktale)

William and Dolfi wished for Sylvie to be out of the house as soon as possible; the question of termination never even came up, not in their emotional discussion, nor in Sylvie's thoughts—she was no Wanda, she had a reverence for the child, however frightening the reality of that child was.

The idea, if the truth were known, did cross Dolfi's mind often in the dead of night. She would lie awake imagining, even praying, that the baby would abort spontaneously. There was no image of the knitting needle, the gin, the hot bath, the concoction of herbs, the back-yard abortionist with the dirty kitchen table and the syringe. Dolfi had known a girl, long ago, who died after an abortion; the story was the saddest and most terrifying story Dolfi knew. It haunted her. One day the girl was working in the bakery; the next day she had disappeared, and the day after that she was dead. Girls had to be kept away from boys, somehow, until they were old enough to get married.

Start-Rite Anti-Slip

Mother: Sylvie, I want you to light the incinerator, please.

From the top of her wardrobe Dolfi has taken a shoe box containing small treasures and mementoes of Sylvie's childhood. This childhood is over now, corrupted, destroyed, and the memories will be consigned to the flames. In the box, preserved in tissue and dusted with naphthalene flakes against moths, is a small cream silk dress embroidered with pink and blue and lilac grub roses and sprays of minute daisies. There is a yellowing knitted bonnet the size of an orange. An envelope containing photographs of Sylvie as baby and as child. A paperback copy of *Sylvie*, the strange French novelette Dolfi was reading before Sylvie was born. (The note on the author said he was a schizophrenic who finally hanged himself in the rue de la Lanterne using an apron string that he believed was the garter of the Queen of Sheba.) A pearly celluloid rattle in the shape of a doll; a pair of silk bootees; a pink smocked frock; a blue knitted jacket; a handmade felt mouse, faded green with a long leather tail bearing the marks of tiny teeth. There are also the teeth, wrapped in a twist of silk, and some dark curls of hair. And the red buckle shoes that Sylvie wore when she was three. Start-Rite, Anti-Slip. The toes are scuffed, the straps worn thin where the buckles have cut into them.

The mother will destroy the evidence of the existence of the wicked daughter.

The old iron incinerator with its big black chimney is roaring, sparks twirling up into the air, flying up into the branches of an overhanging almond tree.

Mother: Watch out for the tree! Don't put in so much paper.

Pale smoke twines through the branches of the almond tree. Sylvie stands by the incinerator waiting for her mother to bring out the things she wants to burn. Innocent Sylvie. She has really no idea of what is about to happen.

Mother (not wishing the girl to witness the full meaning of what is happening): Well, you can go now. Go on, go inside.

But Sylvie has seen the shoe box and she knows what it contains. She has seen the name of the shoes stamped on the end of the box: Colette, cherry red. A small black hand clutches at her heart and she is as if hypnotised. She can not move from her place beside the incinerator.

Mother: Well, don't then. You might as well see anyway. And what would you care? What do you care about anything? Look at you.

Something bright and vicious had gotten into Dolfi's blood and was glittering in her eyes. Her hair, dark with some streaks of grey, fell in strands across her face which was red with embarrassment and rage. Dolfi threw the lid of the box into the mouth of the incinerator, and then began to toss the contents of the box one by one into the

---

cherry

flames. The silk dress caught and curled quickly, spurting with a pale yellow splash and breaking up into little flying rags which sailed off up into the leaves of the almond tree—charred wings of silky butterflies that came too close to danger.

As Dolfi stood there feeding the flames, she too became hypnotised by what she was doing, and she felt the heat of the fire on her body, and was drawn into the warmth and the light, and her task took on the nature of a ritual, her gesture was the gesture of dance. And while Dolfi performed her bitter function, Sylvie suddenly sprang into life. She pushed Dolfi aside, grabbed a pile of photographs, tossed them into the fire, and then she gripped the red shoes with both hands and, like a wild cat, she leapt away, up the path and into the house and through the front door and past the magnolia and out into the street before Dolfi knew what had happened.

Sylvie stopped and came back inside the gate to where the tap was connected to the hose, and she turned the tap on full so that the hose spurted into life, a great red snake writhing and leaping and spraying all over the path, the garden, the front of the house. And Sylvie, the red shoes tightly enclosed in her hands, ran and ran and ran down the street until she came to the edge of the river, where she paused, panting and weeping, and lay down under a tree and hugged the shoes to her body, between her body and the dry earth among the roots of the tree. The place where she lay was not far from the place, close to the iron bridge, where the baby had been conceived. And she stayed there for a very long time, until her tears were spent, and she sat up and wondered what would become of her, not in the years to come but in the next few hours.

She went slowly home, where nobody took any notice of her. The hose was once again rolled up behind the gate. It had been disconnected from its tap. Sylvie went into her bedroom and swore to herself that she would never, ever be parted from the little shoes. She put them under her pillow; she called them Colette. How could she be sure they would not be taken from her? Perhaps she would have to part with them in order to keep them safe. Like hiding a beloved child from some great threat of danger. In time of war. In time of the massacre of innocent children. They seek out and slaughter all the babies so that none can grow up to be the Messiah who will come to overthrow the king. You hide the baby. Where do you hide the baby? As Sylvie asked herself, she picked and fiddled with a little cylinder of metal on the buckle of one of the shoes, a little cylinder that spun round and round and round and round. It rattled.

The ashes of all the burned and blackened treasures in the incinerator were cold.

The Archangel Gabriel, you know, is made from fire.

The Almond Tree

Sylvie suddenly knew that nowhere was ever safe for anything. Her thoughts went spinning from digging a hole in the cellar to bury the shoes, to being very rich and having a bank vault where she could deposit them. But then there would be an earthquake, and the cellar and the bank vault would amount to the same thing, and the shoes would come rushing to the surface like dying fish in a storm at sea. Nowhere was safe. One day she would lose the shoes. Maybe she should just go back down the yard and put them in the incinerator after all.

But then she thought of the almond tree, and a recollection of something in the story of Cinderella drifted gently into her mind like a balm, and she knew in her heart that the almond tree would guard the shoes. So she kissed each shoe, and then she wrapped each shoe in a scrap of old plastic and tied ribbon around them. Then she went out in the dark and explored the tree with her fingers until she found what she had sensed would be there. Into a crack in the tree she pushed the shoes, push, push, until they disappeared into the tree. Even if she could never get them out again, she had saved them, had consecrated the precious memory of her own early time on earth. If the tempest came, if the lightning struck, and if

---

almond

the tree gave up the precious shoes, so be it. Nowhere was really safe.

> What if I die or if I kill myself? Who will ever find the shoes? Will it matter? It won't matter. If the baby is a girl I will call her Colette.

Sylvie never went to school again. She was taken to the doctor for a proper diagnosis—four months—to the minister for a moral talk. You have done wrong. You have committed a sin. You have disgraced your mother and your father and your church. You have angered God, you have made Jesus sorry and sad. What have you got to say for yourself?

Nothing.

She wasn't even sure now what she and the boy had done, exactly, to bring all this about. Half an hour of intense pleasure in the grass by the river and her life was changed forever. She never saw the boy again, never had any contact with him at all. She hated him now. The story went around that she was ill, was going to a sanatorium—this suggested she was tubercular. The child would be born, would be adopted, and that would be the end of things, and Sylvie would come home and get on with her life as best she could, get a job, get some training, perhaps even marry in the long run.

Those minutes of joy when her head spun and the soles of her feet burned with a rapturous flame and she took the first step towards her own madness, have put in motion the life of a child who will be whisked off into the nightmare fairytale of New Haven.

Once when Sylvie was very young she was walking with her little dog on a hillside behind the French house. It was late afternoon and the sun was breathing a peach haze over the golden blooms of the gorse bushes. The bees were gone, perhaps the trill of a cricket embellished the hilly silence. The dog ran, Sylvie ran, the air was clean and lovely and silken on her face and rushed like crystal into her lungs. And she had a sudden understanding that the hillside was alive, was breathing, was luminous with its own spirit which was akin to her own.

It was a brief moment, a vivid window into knowledge that opened up and closed almost as soon as it had opened. She had never forgotten the moment, but somehow, when her father hit her in the face with the back of his hand, she began to forget, everything began to fade, and a greyness, and then a darkness, a fog of deep, deep, slow and watery sadness, began to engulf her.

The minister put the family in touch with Sister Winter, who recommended Sylvie consult a doctor at the private hospital near Shalimar. Sylvie was not aware that the big old house she passed on her way to her first appointment with the doctor was the place where she was going to spend the next five months.

At Shalimar, Dr Sparks, touching a switch that set a recording tape running: This is strictly confidential, Sylvie, just between you and me, some things I need to know so that we can give you and the baby the best possible care. You don't have to tell me the name of the father, but I need to know various things about him, such as his health record as far as you know it—was he, for instance, asthmatic, hem?

Sylvie: No.

Sparks: Now, was he interested in sport, hem?

Sylvie: Football, tennis.

Sparks: How, hem, tall?

Sylvie: Tall.

Is the doctor trying to get out of me who the boy is so they can go after him?

Sparks: And his eyes, what colour were his eyes, hem?

Sylvie: Blue.

Sparks: Good. Um, hem, his hair, then?

Sylvie: Blondish.

Sparks: And did he get good results in his, hem, exams?

Sylvie: Yes.

Sparks: I hope you are being completely honest with me, Sylvie, because a lot depends on this. You are being, hem, honest?

Sylvie, feeling herself going into a light trance as the man's irritating speech defect hem-hemmed at her across the desk: Yes.

Sparks: And what were the hobbies of this, hem, chap, apart from getting girls to take off their pants, hem?

Sylvie stared at him for a moment and then she fainted.

She woke up in a cubicle in the hospital, in a cot with bars. Her wrists were chained to the bars. Her clothes were gone and she was in a pale green hospital nightdress.

A little nurse who resembled a frail white butterfly flitted in and out with a worried frown on her insect brow.

Dr Sparks arrived, and because Sylvie was now lying down and he was standing up, Sylvie could see that he was very large and very round, with an enormous abdomen. He looked like a great big bee in a fancy waistcoat with gold chains. And Sylvie's mind flicked back to the room where he had interviewed her, and her memory of her impressions of the room were more vivid than her observations had been at the time. It was as if when she was in his office she was mindlessly collecting material which she had now assembled, and which she could now call up as a background to this big fat man with big fat hands. The room where Dr Sparks saw his patients was decorated with the doctor's collection of medical curiosities and memorabilia—ancient surgical and obstetric instruments—the room was known to his friends and colleagues as Sparkie's torture chamber. Through the window behind the doctor's head the sun was shining, the light filtered by the leaves of a peppermint gum.

Dr Sparks in the hospital: We can't have you fainting like that, Sylvie. That will never hem do. When you have quite hem recovered we will send you home in a cab, and in a few days you will move to Sister hem Winter's home where you will get the very best of care, and where I will visit you to see how things are hem coming along.

Sylvie never wanted to see this man ever again, and here he was promising, threatening, to visit her on a regular basis.

I think I just want to die. I can't go on with all
this. I will have to kill myself. Razor blade in
the bath.

And you know, hem, Sylvie, you must take very good care of yourself. No more fainting, no getting up to hem tricks like slashing your lovely little hem wrists in the bath.

He knows. Oh my God, he can read my
thoughts. Or maybe I said it aloud. Or maybe I
said it when I fainted.

She will remain here under hem observation until tomorrow, nurse, and then the car will take her to her home. I will contact the hem parents.

The afternoon drifted into twilight and Sylvie was given a small but delicious tea of chicken and vegetables and bread and butter pudding.

Must keep your strength up, whispered the butterfly in her tissue-paper voice.

The night caved in on Sylvie. The darkness wrapped her waking mind in the smooth embrace of half-death. She stared out from her black pit towards the window where a sprinkle of stars spoke of far-off worlds and of music and poetry.

The branches of a tree were visible in the black, and a wind came up and stirred them and moaned through the leaves. Sylvie filled her spinning mind with the words of old poems and hymns as she forced herself to forget the boy in the grass by the river, to forget the baby, the past, the present and the future. Sylvie lay in the cot in the bare dark room and willed herself into oblivion.

The Wind that Walks on Air

And did those feet in ancient time
Walk upon England's mountains green?

    Oppressed with sin and woe
    A burdened heart I bear
    Opposed by many a mighty foe
    But I will not despair

All things bright and beautiful
All creatures great and small

    Believe not those who say
    The upward path is smooth
    Lest thou shouldst stumble in the way
    And faint before the truth

Bring me my bow of burning gold
Bring me my arrows of desire

    The buttercup glistens
    He's cheerful and kind
    The cuckoo-flower listens
    To the song of the wind

She woke in the early hours of the morning with a sense of dread, a feeling that she was a stone on a beach being lapped by the waves and slowly and steadily dragged, dragged out into the ocean where she would sink. Drown.

She tried to think of nicer things, tried to tell herself stories, tried to remember 'The Little Mermaid', but her memory was dull and all she could think of was the idea of walking on red-hot knives. She put her hands flat on her belly and had a momentary sensation and belief that it was empty, that she was hollow and that there was nothing inside her at all but dark air.

Dark, dark air. But her breasts were very tender, and there was in fact a constant feeling low down in her abdomen of tiny, unusual activity, a kind of faint little electric shock.

The cuckoo-flower listens to the song of the
wind.

Cuckoo-flower, lady's smock, ragged robin, cuckoo, cuckoo. Listen to the sound of the wind, the sound of the wind. There is a wind in the tree outside the window, a wind in my mind, it has blown my memory away, cuckoo, cuckoo. I am a ragged robin in a lady's smock blowing away in the wind on the water and the water is dragging me—am I a flower; am I a stone—the water is rushing up towards me, great navy blue breakers rolling up, up and over me and breaking into white and creamy lace foam,

---

mermaid

froth, star bubbles, snowflakes in the wind, listen to the sound of the wind, the song of the wind, the wise old, cuckoo old gold and silver white-frost wind.

I am the wind, the wind that walks on air. The Wind that Walks on Air. I try to say those words aloud, but no words will come; I am the weightless, wayward breath of the wind, white-frost winter wind, cuckoo west wind, like smoke, like spirit, like thought. I look down from the air where I am walking and I see my body lying so sadly on the bed beside the window, and I see again the gorse blooming golden with the bees on the hillside, and the hillside is alive, and I am alive, live wind, cold, fresh, living wind. I run on the air, I am the air. I hear the dog barking in the golden gorse, and like a drop of water that falls and blends with the waters of a deep dark pool I fall and I blend with the body on the bed, and I am awake in the mind but in the body I sleep. The wakeful mind exists for a timeless moment in the gap between the teeth of eternity, where the light is split into its rainbow parts, where the sound is the sound of soundlessness.

I have paid a great deal of attention to what went on not only in Sylvie's life, but in her mind and heart. When a subject interests me as she interests me, I can lay my hands on most of the material available. The universe is, for us, an eternal library. The World Wide Web is a pale shadow of the infinite resources that we can use for research.

In matters such as this it is necessary for me to clear my research with the subject's guardian. Sylvie's guardian is a sincere but somewhat ineffectual individual called

Yip, but I am grateful to him because he gave me entrée into Sylvie's life and heart and thoughts. He felt it might help her if I did this, but of course by the time I realised I needed to go in, it was too late and her mind was shot to pieces. The sophistication of her thoughts and mental and spiritual language need not alarm or surprise you; all people of whatever age or intellectual ability have this at their command, it's in the human stamp, goes with arms that bend forward and legs that bend back, but only a few people know they have got it, so it can sound weird and prodigious. What Sylvie did after a while, of course, was to dip right into the place of this knowledge and language, and shut herself in there; she imprisoned herself in an occult space. It took about a year after the birth of Colette for her to shut herself up finally in this prison of the mind. She was, naturally enough, diagnosed as insane, borderline schizophrenic, and put on a strange cocktail of medication for the term of her natural life.

A car came for Sylvie and she was driven back home—where her mother stood in the doorway of the bedroom as Sylvie packed her case to go to Shalimar. A small case, a few necessities; a simple, penitential collection of soap and towel and hairbrush and socks and shoes and nightdresses and underclothes and some smocks hastily manufactured by Dolfi from old curtains and tablecloths. Cardigans, a raincoat. A hymn book. A bible. Once, long ago, there had been talk of sending Sylvie off to boarding school. Sylvie had been a little afraid, but excited by the idea and had sometimes imagined the special uniforms and books and equipment she would take with her. This packing, this leaving, this humiliation, this disgrace, it was a pale and mocking shadow of the glorious and thrilling day when she might have left to go to boarding school. Now she slipped into the case a book of poems and a photograph of herself with her puppy Billy—he was older now, and was sleeping in his kennel in the back yard. When her mother left her grim post in the doorway, Sylvie swiftly went down to the kennel and she buried her face in Billy's neck, and wept and said goodbye. He stared at her with sad and knowing eyes, and licked her cheeks. She kissed him and ran inside the house, never looking back. Billy died a few weeks before Sylvie's baby was born. Nobody told her.

She caught a bus. Arrangements had been made for a small allowance to be paid to her each week. She was on her way to Sister Winter's, on her way to produce the girl-child who would satisfy the criteria laid down by Petra and Irving, who would become the first baby member of the little convent at New Haven. Colette. Celeste. Within weeks, three other girls would have babies who also went to New Haven. These were to be Celeste's first three sisters, Selina, Zora and Stella. More would follow.

Sylvie shared a dormitory with the mothers of these babies. Between the girls there developed a strong loyalty, a silent union of strength against the authority of Sister Winter and her staff. But the girls were given false names from the bible and forbidden to make any significant contact with each other. So Sylvie became, for five months, Sarah, and she shared the room with girls she called Rachel, Rebecca and Hannah, and she never knew their real names. In spite of the attempt to keep the girls apart, they did form deep, sad bonds with each other, but so afraid were they of every little thing, they never confessed to each other who they were. They told each other instead stories of romance, stories of their hopes, of the things they were going to do when all this was over. Perhaps the lives of the other three took on some of the glamour they wished for. They told each other the fairytales they remembered from their childhoods. They comforted each other as best they could.

A girl known as Ruth from another dormitory disappeared in the middle of the night; the story was that she had gone mad and was taken to Mandala for Deep Sleep. She never came back. Madness was greatly feared among the girls; everything was fearful, they could not really trust each other. They walked carefully, at Shalimar, on a sea of broken glass. They had no visitors except for the wife of the local Church of England minister and some of her Guild ladies.

These women came on Fridays, wearing hats and being cheerful and forgiving and nice. If the truth were told (and of course it never is), two or three of them had been in much the same situation as the girls, in their time. There was a softness and kindness to them of which Sister Winter and her staff disapproved and despaired, but which they had to tolerate since the parish made generous donations to the work of the home. They brought cakes and books and sweet-smelling soaps, shampoo and posies of flowers. The books were paperback romances, and the girls had to hide them under their mattresses and read them at night by torchlight.

The Guild met the girls in a group in the dining-room and offered themselves for advice, but the girls could think of nothing to ask. Tea and biscuits were served, and there was a kind of charm and sweet formality that came as a comfort after the harsh week gone by. There was one prayer and no bible reading, but an attempt at chatter and a lot of knitting and sewing. Some of the girls had their first lessons in these arts at the Guild afternoons. The ladies supplied wool and fabric and patterns, and the happy little hum that came from the dining-room as Fridays wore on was so very soothing to the girls. The making of baby clothes in any form was forbidden, and so the girls made aprons and kettle holders. The more advanced ones made kimonos and embroidered them with flowers and birds. By forbidding all reference to babies, Sister Winter, a cold, strange, frightening ogre of a woman, was denying any outlet for the one thought that really obsessed the girls, and this caused them to be even more sad and despairing.

One of the ladies, a tiny, thin, elegant woman called Mrs Tamara Eagle, regularly brought the girls acid drops and chocolate mice. This Friday afternoon meeting was an incredible oasis in the desert of life at Shalimar.

The name of the minister's wife was Mrs Allura de Wolfe, and we must not forget her. It is so easy, in this world of woe, to forget that bright, good people such as Allura are walking about in a true spirit of selfless kindness. She might be seen as the good fairy who was not present at the christening, but who came round sixteen or so years later to try to make amends, to make good the harm that had been done in the meantime. Her husband, Rev. Nicholas de Wolfe, was almost her equal in his tireless and wise administration of his parish. He had no ambition to rise higher, to be a bishop; he was called to serve in the little parish of Saint Anselm, and if he and Allura were a bit High Church for people at times, that was their only visible fault. By saying that I do not mean to imply that beneath the veil of goodness they were seething with corruption; on the contrary, I am really only suggesting that they might have had some imperfections that I didn't know about. I am sometimes accused of telling the stories only of the bad (or at least the mad) people, and of thus ignoring all the good and noble folk whose lives I could well be describing. There might be something in that, but if you think about it, I wouldn't even be talking about Allura and Rev if they hadn't come into contact with the baddies at Shalimar. Where would the story of Jesus be without the sins of the other characters? Not much of a story. Snow White without the wicked queen, Cinderella without her highly unpleasant stepsisters? Goodness makes no sense, you see, unless there's evil. A pity, but that's the way it is. Light is not light without darkness. And often the thing that people like about the light is the way it shows up what's going on in the dark.

Well, that's how it looks from where I'm standing, but I'm no expert.

Look on the bright side.

The girls were not allowed out to go to church, and so on Sunday afternoons Rev would come round and conduct a little holy communion service in the dining-room. All the girls attended, without exception, Rev operating on some ruling of his own making that no matter what their beliefs they could all, under the circumstances, partake of the consecrated Body and Blood. And he was so funny and so sweet and so handsome and so fatherly. The girls were kind of in love with him. He let them sing 'Jerusalem' every week.

And did those feet . . .

They loved the music and the thrill of the words—'bring me my chariot of fire'—although they had little understanding of what they might mean. Sylvie played the piano, an old black upright splashed with drips of green paint, out of tune, tinny, but adored. The Infant Jesus was kept to a very low profile because he was a baby, although it was impossible to follow the Winter rule and bleach him out of things altogether. Rev and Allura were the light of the girls' dark and frightening lives.

Its Name is Baby

Day in and day out the girls worked in the laundry, washing and ironing. They dug the vegetable garden, cleaned the floors and windows, and cooked the meals. One day when she was digging the garden, Sylvie unearthed a small white china doll the size of her finger. It was very old, with a broken foot and with traces of paint on its cheeks. There were fragments of rotting green velvet and scraps of a rose-pink silk ribbon, as if the china baby had been wrapped in cloth by childish hands and tied up with a bow. In fact, the youngest Chetwynd girl had bitten off the doll's foot in a moment of strange, intense love, and fearing punishment had pronounced the baby dead and wrapped her in a little shroud and tied her up, and had conducted a solitary funeral during which the china doll was ceremonially buried in the ground, the grave marked by a wooden cross.

> There shall be a resurrection of the dead, both
> of the just and unjust.
>
> Acts 24:15

It was the rising of the china baby, planted in the earth so long ago by one child, found now by Sylvie and cradled in her childish heart as a sign, a talisman of something good and kind. A treasure. A small prophetic gesture of generosity from the heart of the earth. A love token. An emblem of hope, a message from the underworld. Persephone rising. Oh, do not eat the pomegranate seed, little Sylvie. Yet whatever it was that Sylvie ate while in her purgatory at Sister Winter's Shalimar, it was very like, in its effect, Persephone's pomegranate. For a kind of death came over her, a death of the mind and of the spirit. The baby left her body and went off to have a life of its own, but Sylvie was left behind in her own underworld. She tenderly washes the small white china doll under the garden tap, wipes it on her apron, and slips it down into the space between her ankle and her sock. A secret blessing from the dark earth. She keeps this little baby all her life, always concealing it somewhere, either in her bedroom or else about her person. Its name is Baby.

Nobody would ever take Baby away from Sylvie.

When Sylvie went into labour she wrapped Baby in her face cloth and folded this up in her sponge bag. She was whisked away to the hospital. Stripped. Shaved. Enema.

Hours went by. Sylvie was determined she would not cry out with the pain. Butterfly nurse was very frightened about this fact; she kept looking in on Sylvie because she thought the girl might be dead. But Sylvie clamped her jaws shut, and although every nerve in her body begged her to scream, she would not.

I will not scream, I will not scream, I will not
give them that satisfaction.

Persephone

They gave her no medication for pain. Nothing. They let her writhe and vomit, gave her only cubes of ice to suck. It was as if the staff in that hospital, dealing with wicked wayward girls, had had their own inclinations to compassion surgically removed. Yet the girls were their livelihood; from these naughty little machines would come the babies who could be sold for a handsome profit, no questions asked. But if they treated the girls too badly the babies might die. It might not matter so much if the girls themselves gave up the ghost, but first you had to get the babies.

There was the case of Ruth. We might assume Ruth never made it. Perhaps they saved the baby; perhaps not. Her parents would not be interested in knowing what happened to the baby, and if they got Ruth back as a corpse, they would trust that Dr Sparks and Sister Winter and Dr Goddard had done everything possible. They would even be grateful; they would also pay handsomely.

Sylvie lay with her feet in stirrups in a weird haze of silent pain. Dr Sparks and the nurses touched her and held her and suddenly somebody pushed a pillow over her face. She turned her head to the wall, able to see there a shadow dance of heads and arms, and suddenly a strange numbness came upon her, as if she had hit a pain barrier and could no longer feel. She saw on the wall a shadow of a baby held upside down by its feet, a shadowy string leading down from its middle. Then the image was gone and she heard, through the muffling of the pillow, a baby's cry.

That was all.

Sylvie never saw the baby. They told her it was a girl and presented her with papers to sign; the sooner they were signed, they said, the better for the baby. And for Sylvie. Tidy it all up. Go home. Get on with life. Sylvie called the baby Colette and when she signed the form she held the pen very, very tightly, and wrote in the tiniest, saddest writing she could. It was a message from her sad heart to the little shadow she had seen up on the wall.

Colette.

They gave her an injection to dry up the milk, but her breasts remained swollen and painful and dripping for over a week. Weeping great tears of milk.

That was all.

To the other girls in the dormitory she said nothing. They didn't ask. She packed her things, including the china Baby from the vegetable garden, and was sent back home to the French house. Sylvie cried, alone, in silence, without eating, for days.

Then she emerged from her room, dressed, and went and sat silently beneath the almond tree, not far from the incinerator where her life had gone up in charred butterflies of rag. Her dog, her Billy, was dead. She seemed to be too numb to mourn; of course Billy was dead. Everything was dead. Everything was over. She held in her hand the china Baby; she imagined the red shoes safe in the belly of the tree.

Sylvie has gone off her rocker. We should send her to the loony bin, but maybe we can just keep her here for a while, see how she goes. The while stretched out into weeks, months, years, and Sylvie grew older and the family settled into a new pattern around her. Sylvie the quiet, mad one. She never went out, not even to church. She would sit in the front room for hours and play melancholy pieces on the piano. When visitors came she would drift into her bedroom and close the door. Generally, people did not ask questions. Sylvie's relatives and their children gradually accepted mad Sylvie, who remained in her room when they came to visit. Even on Christmas Day Sylvie was in her room with the door shut, eating a lonely meal of roast chicken and plum pudding. Lonely. She shared it in whispers with Baby and with Colette.

For one day, about six months after Colette's birth, Sylvie had gone down to the almond tree and fished out the shoes with a pair of pliers. A grotesque parody of the doctor with forceps, she reached into the split in the bark and gripped the plastic parcels with the pliers and pulled and dragged until the shoes were born. Her face was white and wet with tears as she kissed the dusty plastic, unravelled the ribbons, and then laid her cheek against the little red shoes. She took the shoes and placed them in the highest cupboard in her wardrobe, pushed behind a neat little pile of woollen pullovers. Safe. As safe as possible in this slippery, shadowy world.

And Sylvie began to knit. She made baby clothes with fine white wool, her stitches even and exquisite. Loop after loop, twist after twist, stitch by stitch. She sat in an old floral armchair in her bedroom beside the window and she made bonnets and bootees and dresses and coats and singlets and capes and shawls and jackets. Dolfi would take the finished articles and donate them to the Red Cross shop. This went on for years and years; Sylvie never knitted in anything except white. Mrs Fisher's poor daughter became a legend at the Red Cross, people coming back again and again to buy her baby clothes. By a sad little irony, some of the babies over the years at New Haven got to wear things knitted by Sylvie.

Sylvie's father scarcely ever spoke to her again, and six years after Colette was born, he died, leaving Dolfi and Sylvie together in the French house.

The Arrival of Celeste

The baby girl was sent in her basket, accompanied by Nurse Butterfly, out to New Haven, where three women from Bethany had already moved in. These women, Faith, Hope and Charity, would be the nurses and nannies for the collection of baby girls; Petra would be the chief, the Mother, and the children would call her Mother or Mama.

There was a nursery with six standard wooden cots into which the babies went from birth until they were almost three. There was a spareness to the decoration, no concession to sentiment. The walls were lemon, the cots white, the blankets blue—all flat colours with no decoration or relief. The window was without a curtain and was barred, as were all the windows in the house, keeping the children in, keeping the world out. There was a white venetian blind. The floor was covered with dark blue industrial carpet. One white cupboard and a bench. No toys. It was clearly the scene for an experiment, which was what was going on. The babies were to be the guinea pigs in Irving's new project.

Petra had moved into the corner rooms at New Haven, a bedroom and a bathroom which looked out over the base of the valley. From the bedroom window, which was placed above the line formed by the top of the cypresses, Petra could see gum trees and rocks and sky. This was in fact the first decent room Petra had ever had to herself in her life. The rooms at Meena's and at the Littledales' had been small and makeshift. She hung on the wall above the bed a picture of a Spartan youth in red boots, the boots they wore so that the blood they waded in would not discolour the leather. She had already decided that her children would all wear red shoes and she had an inkling that she would soon have the power to place red footwear on the feet of the adult Brethren. It would happen more or less by stealth, until it became the norm, and then the rule.

The Atrophy of Angels

Faith, Hope and Charity were women in their thirties. They had all started out, at different times, as members of Irving's tutorial on the history of religion at the university, and had all been separately captivated by the Captain. They were absolutely ready to act as the nurses for the babies at New Haven, following strict rules of discipline, reward and punishment. The nurses slept in a room off the nursery, their beds lined up, spartan, as in a dormitory for schoolgirls—this was the way in all the houses at Ararat. Petra had rooms at Hill House as well as New Haven. Irving had an office, bedroom, sitting-room, dining nook and bathroom when he was in residence at Hill House, but everybody else slept dormitory style.

A large room at New Haven would become a schoolroom, a yoga, dance and music room, as well as dining-room. It would be furnished with tables and chairs, a piano, a barre and a wall of mirrors. The tables could be stacked in the corners of the room and the chairs hung from pegs high up on the walls.

And what I saw happen in this place, New Haven, was something I had heard of but had never actually witnessed before. This was the withering and atrophy of the children's guardian angels. They had to hang about all day and night with these babies, and they lost their energy, their light dimmed, they became lethargic, imprisoned and depressed; they wilted and faded. They reminded me of the nymph Cyane as their outlines slowly melted away and they grew more and more ghostly, less and less able to protect the children in their care. The human keepers, on the other hand, gathered strength as they tested their power and their sadism on the bodies and minds and spirits of the babies.

There was a big ceremony of welcome to Petra and her baby at Mount Meru, where Irving presided. Celeste was the first of the members of what he called the cradle of the future, and Petra was the supreme mother. She stood in front of the community with the baby in her arms, radiating love and joy and hope and certainty. I think it was the certainty that really got them in. They played a tape of Handel's *Largo* and everybody came forward and brushed Petra's foot with their lips and kissed the top of the baby's golden head. Celeste slept throughout the ceremony. Each member of the community brought a gift which was handmade. Petra was particularly interested in the man who gave the baby a pair of white felt slippers—here was her cobbler. It was Roger, one of the people recruited from Mandala when under LSD.

Irving made a speech about how Celeste was the first of a community of babies who would grow up firm in the faith of the Brethren, who would carry the truth with them when they and their descendants survived the holocaust at the end of the century. Unsullied by the sins of the world beyond the walls of Ararat, these children would shine with a purity and strength never before seen in the world. Petra, as their mother, would provide them with the example and the discipline needed to train them in the Higher Path. Theirs was the gift of the New Truth.

And as Irving spoke, all eyes were on the blue and white vision of Petra and Celeste, around whom shone a light that was not of this earth. This moment was the real turning point at which Petra's star rose in the community, and at which Irving's star began to fade. He stood in a pool of artificial light, but Petra and the child glowed with a radiance that seemed to come from within. And in a curious way Irving accepted this state of affairs; even though his belief in his own power and wisdom was fabulously grand, he was also convinced that Petra was the incarnate spirit of truth, an embodiment of the Christ, of the Buddha—you name it. I'm not sure how he figured this but it went over well with the Brethren, who were people longing to believe that the walls of Ararat enclosed the ultimate miracle and that they themselves were chosen to touch the Highest Truth.

Irving told them:

'You have been chosen to participate in the great spiritual journey of adventure. The Brethren who live within the walls of our community, and those who live outside working for truth in the world, giving the appearance of ordinary citizens—the lawyers and nurses and doctors who are indistinguishable, on the surface, from their neighbours—all these Brethren have been specially selected by the highest spirit in the universe to be in this place at this time and to co-operate in the nurture of this child and all the other children who are coming to us. Only a great spirit, as much at home in the other dimension as in this one, could be entrusted with the supervision and raising of these children, entrusted to carry the project through to its great conclusion. The Mother has been sent to us, and now the children are beginning to come. The Mother knows when and where and to which parents the children are coming, and she knows too what qualities and potential these children are bringing from their past lives. A future age will see these children as custodians and bearers of the truth, of the work the Brethren have set in motion. After the holocaust these children will rise up and come forward to bring about the glory of a new and shining age.'

(If you read in the Manual the section quoted from the great Maurice Maeterlinck, you will find a poetic description of the Azure Palace where the children who are yet to be born are held in waiting, in thirty thousand luminous halls, enough children to last until the end of time. Everything shimmers with intense and radiant blue, and the children, robed in azure garments, move at their tasks, cultivating the growth of fruits and flowers, playing ancient musical instruments, constructing temples. These children are of a supernatural purity and goodness, the strange blue of their eyes glowing with the light of truth.)

'And these, my Brethren, are our children. These are the children who are coming to us in their sovereign and solemn beauty, coming into our care, into our sacred trust. We will not disappoint them.'

The Brethren fingered their Manuals, thick volumes of collected wisdom and poetry. Some turned to the Maeterlinck quotation, but most gazed ahead in rapture

---

manual

at the sight of Petra and the child, the sacred trust. The Mother of the Brethren stood in her own aureole of radiance in Mount Meru; she gleamed white and blue, smooth as marble, and in her arms she held the child Celeste.

Something I will tell you about Petra, she had an incredible constitution. She could keep going for forty-eight hours without a break, drinking water and not eating, whenever she wished. She lived in perfect health, with the exception of a few mild colds when she was a child, all her life. As a consequence of this, she had no patience with illness and believed all infirmity, not to mention accidents of any kind, were the responsibility of the victim. Part of her training for the children in her care was based on this belief, nurtured by her own apparent mental ability to control her health and wellbeing. Siddha yoga, she would tell the Brethren, was the key to this. Perhaps it was, but things are never really as simple as that. You have to take myself into account here, to consider my role in Petra's charmed life—but, wisely, Petra never mentioned me.

Yet Petra was also fascinated by certain kinds of illness, in particular mental illness. Her mother had been mentally unstable, no doubt about that, but Petra knew very little about Wanda. The mentally ill are so utterly in the power of their keepers, as are the very old and young.

A few of the Brethren came down with fevers after the ceremony to welcome Celeste and the Mother. Everybody must have known or at least suspected that the fever was the result of drinking the water in which two girls in white had ceremonially washed the Mother's feet, but of course nobody said a word. The sufferers, all women (perhaps the men didn't actually swallow the water?), were placed in a dormitory together in Bethany and prayed over in an atmosphere of incense and flowers until the fever passed. Hail to the jewel in the lotus, they chanted. The fever was taken to be a sign of the women's closeness to the Mother and of their being singled out as specially blessed. Lucky they weren't dead.

I can tell one happy story of a baby who very nearly fell into Petra's clutches, but who was saved in the nick of time by her guardian. The story of the child's mother is just the old story of a nice girl who goes to the drive-in with a nice boy and who ends up pregnant after something that happened somewhere between the middle and the end of *Rear Window*. Then later on this girl winds up in Shalimar and her guardian, as it happens, is more alert than many. He sussed out that the guardian of the unborn child was going to be Argol, and got in touch. I've known Argol myself for centuries, and he has a really professional attitude to his work. He consulted me and explained that he wished to keep his human out of range of my human, and asked me what would be the best strategy. I said that if the baby was a boy there would be no danger, since Petra was only interested in girls. However, to safeguard a girl who might be born, he had better attend to the colour of her skin. Although the parents were blonde, there was almost bound to be a gene or two for colour hanging around somewhere. I told him that if he could see to it the baby was born darker than had been expected, she would escape. He found a Tasmanian Aboriginal ancestor on a remote twig of the family tree and decided to intervene before the birth, a thing not often done.

The ending is even happier than you might expect, since Sister Winter and the doctors were so startled and afraid when they saw the little piccaninny that they quickly banished the mother and her baby from Shalimar. Mother and baby went home to the grandparents and were welcomed with open arms and tears of joy. When the baby was two the mother married an Italian count and they all lived happily ever after in Milan, a place that has always particularly appealed to Argol, who is very fond of opera.

We must, however, return to the sad story of Celeste, who fifteen years after her welcoming ceremony was sent, in the company of Charity, by air, by night, to the remotest north-western tip of the island of Tasmania, where she was instructed to type out the story of her life so far, as she had led it in the Brethren.

She called it 'My Life', but I think it would more aptly be titled 'Celeste Spills the Beans'. A truly frank and unguarded document. Her guardian is some kind of fool, although to give him his due, he has had his work cut out just keeping the child alive at Ararat, and he has faded to a shadow of his former self. As I have said before, the angels seemed to atrophy after a time at New Haven. And the atrophy of angels is not a pretty thing.

My Life

by Celeste Penfold-Knight, 1983

I am afraid. I have always been afraid. Fear is a normal part of my everyday existence. Since I was very young I have developed a way, a kind of trick, of dealing with my fear—this is to go right up to it and look right into it and glide over, through and past it. I always enjoyed listening to the story of 'The Youth Who Went Forth to Learn What Fear Was'; I think the accounts of tests he underwent probably helped me. And yet my fear is deeper than anything found in a story—it's as if part of me really were fear. Perhaps instead of writing that I am afraid, I should write that I am fear. But I am many things. I am also joy and laughter and love. I love my mama and my sisters. I have no papa. Our lives are Chosen and we are Different.

My mama is the Mother of the Hill House Brethren, and my sisters and I live in a house where we are cared for by nurses and teachers. I am the eldest, and I share with three of the others the fact that Mama gave birth to us. All the others are adopted. My name is Celeste, and the others are Stella, Selina, Zora, Solange, Zephyr, Vivia, Kiku, Uma, Iris, Lydia, Aurora, Giselle, Bathsheba and Golden Jade. We once had a baby sister called Swanilda but she died when she was nearly three. Golden Jade's name sounds Chinese but she isn't. She was born with deformed feet and Mama considered this to be a portent. When Golden Jade was six Mama had her feet bound according to ancient Chinese rules, and Golden Jade is the only one of us girls who has a little bedroom all to herself. She cries with pain much of the time. When she is twelve her Threshold will take place in the Mother's bedroom at Hill House, and she will live at Hill House from then on. The rest of us expect to live at Bethany with the other women Brethren. We derive great pleasure from sewing and embroidering little slippers for Golden Jade; these are made from crimson satin and we secretly compete with each other to do the most beautiful designs on them. Golden Jade is rather like a toy to us, although she is often very sad.

The only real toys we have are three teddy bears Dr Goddard gave us. Toys are not important. (Secretly, I always long to take one of the teddies to bed, but this is not allowed. We are also not allowed to get into bed with each other, as the desire for comfort is a sign of weakness. Although I should say here that Golden Jade is allowed a little rocking-chair because it takes her mind off the sharp and ardent pain in her feet and stills her crying.)

I have been directed by Mama to come here to this Apartment where Charity and I will live alone for six months in order to chronicle my life story and prepare myself for the next stage of my life, during which I will move from our house, New Haven, into the women's house, Bethany. On each day, as I sit down to work at the pages of this chronicle, I will draw a mandala in pastels, bringing my mind to a state of concentration and allowing my deepest thoughts and feelings of the night just passed to come to the surface in colour and pattern. I will then meditate for a few minutes on the mandala of the day, trying to move into a primary state of self-abnegation, of self-elimination. The Mother speaks in the meeting hall often of the importance of achieving this state, and she says that when she herself has completed her work on this earth she will ritually self-eliminate totally and move on to a higher level. This could come at any time; only she will know the time and the place and the manner of her leaving. Every day one of the women in the community gives her a special pedicure—she says she will walk into eternity. She has a massage that involves the use of reflexology.

The houses of New Haven and Bethany are two of the main houses on the property which is called Ararat, after the mountain in the Holy Bible where the ark was saved. (And the ark rested in the seventh month, on the seventeenth day of the month, upon the mountains of Ararat.) The 17th of July is a big day of celebration at home. The other important house is Hill House, which is a very large mansion like a palace in a fairytale and this is where Mama mostly lives, and where the Master, Dr Irving Clay (we are permitted to call him Papa Irving), lives some of the time. The Mount Meru meeting hall in Hill House is the centre of our lives; it is where we worship and attend lectures and practise some of our yoga, and also where we give choral and ballet performances and where we have our most important ceremonies in which we use special chemistry to bring about visions of the Higher Truth.

---

reflexology

The other buildings on the property are the bakery and the shoemaker's and the carpenter's and the pottery. Roger is the shoemaker and is also responsible for our general education, for seeing that we have the chance to learn all the things we will need to know. The women at Bethany make gloves from soft, fine leather, and these are sold to shops in the city. They are the most beautiful things, the gloves. We have a lovely vegetable garden and many fruit trees, as well as a whole strawberry farm and a flower farm where we grow chrysanthemums. The strawberries and chrysanthemums are taken out on the cart, which is pulled by Nijinsky the draught-horse, and sold to people in the streets around our home. I am filled with a terrible dread of the world outside. I have not often been out. The journey from New Haven to the Apartment was the longest and strangest I have ever known.

I was prepared for it for months by Charity, who is one of the nurses who has been with us ever since I was born. It was night when we set off in a car with Papa Irving driving and Mama sitting next to him, with me and Charity in the back. We drove for a long way, and I was medicated to keep me calm in the face of my great adventure. Then Mama and Papa Irving said goodbye to us and we got in an aircraft chartered from Reg Hughes Air.

I hadn't been in a plane before—it was a very strange experience. It was a very small plane, just me and Charity and Reg Hughes the pilot and another man called Tek. But I was not particularly afraid because a great feeling of serenity and wellbeing had come over me and I was floating in the clouds.

Tek said something to Charity—I remember

exactly—he said, You have a very pretty daughter. And what Charity said was, Empty flattery is very bad for her, and she is not my daughter, actually.

I was really embarrassed. And hurt, somehow I was hurt. Because Charity made it sound as if she wouldn't care to have me for a daughter, as if she didn't like me very much.

You have a very pretty daughter.

When Charity wasn't looking, I smiled at Tek, and he winked at me. I had never heard anybody call me pretty before.

It seemed to take a very long time to get to the little airport by the sea, and then someone came to fetch us in a car and drove us through very dark forest till we arrived at the Apartment. It is a funny name. Mama called it the Apartment because it is set apart from the world. It is very cold here, and the wind howls about all night. We have a fire going in a little pot-belly stove downstairs all the time. This is a tiny little place, tall and narrow, wooden, and all alone in the scrub on the headland. There's a kitchen and bathroom downstairs, and a staircase leads up to two small rooms, one for me and one for Charity—it is nice to have a room all to myself. We each have a window that looks out to sea, just sea, as far as the world can reach; limitless, frightening. A bed, a lamp, a cupboard, a table and chair.

On the table I found the typewriter waiting for me. I am to type ten pages and then Charity will send them off to Mama, who will keep them for me until I have finished.

Before she sends them, Charity has them copied by Mrs Edmunds at her post office, which is down the road. For safety in the mail, one copy is sent to Mama and one to Dr Goddard at Mandala. Mama says this work of mine is an important document; it feels good to have such personal responsibility.

It feels strange and lonely and sad not to be with my sisters. I have never been without at least one of them before, ever, and usually we are all together. We can get on each other's nerves at times, but I am used to them. And I wonder how they are all going without me. I have often taken the role of a sort of mother with them, even though I am practically the same age as Zora and Selina and Stella. Those three were all adopted. The next one, Kiku, is one of Mama's real children (I am not meant to say that, but I don't know how else to make myself clear) and so are Uma and Zephyr. All the others are the children of Brethren who have elected to give them to the New Haven family so that they can become a part of the great breeding experiment devised by Mama and Papa Irving. It is a program that grooms and trains us to survive and take over the earth after the holocaust which is coming at the end of the century. We will be the Brethren of the New World. Sometimes other children come to stay with us and they are partly trained, but we are the core spirits. As the oldest, I have always felt very responsible and proud of my position.

My early memories are of being with Zora, Selina and Stella, and of being also with the nurses—Charity and Faith and Hope. More nurses came as more babies came. Mama has a room in New Haven, but she really lives in much more beautiful rooms over at Hill House. As

Brethren, we all wear a uniform and this sets us apart as spiritual people, and also saves time and leaves our minds free to dwell on matters more important than dress. Another important aspect of having our uniform is that it is a type of discipline, and this is a vital part of our lives. When we were tiny babies we wore white knitted things exactly like all other babies, but when we were one year old we began to wear our black smocks, big white collars, black stockings, black pinafores, red ribbons and red shoes. We have black overcoats and red capes. All the Brethren except Mama and Papa Irving wear mostly black when they are at Ararat, or out in the world on official business such as selling the flowers. They wear red shoes, and in the meeting hall they wear special red slippers. If they go barefoot on the property in the summer the women paint their feet with bright henna in pretty designs. Some Brethren, such as Mr Honeychurch, move about in the world freely and wear ordinary worldly clothes. Sometimes I have thought of that and how it would feel. Strange but exciting, I think.

We often hear ourselves described as a flock of black butterflies with red and white markings, and of course our appearance is even more uniform than it might otherwise be because of our hair. Our nurses give us protein treatments which bleach all our hair to the same degree of white, and it so happens we all have pale eyes, blue or grey or green, except for Uma and Zephyr whose eyes are darker—brown, but not very, maybe hazel.

Our lives have been so far very strict, and I am always frightened of something. I spoke to Dr Winter who is our psychiatrist about that and he gave me some drug therapy and some electric shock therapy and also suggested to Mama that I might come here to the Apartment and write my fear out of my spirit. I will try to do that, I will try to look into my heart and see what it is that frightens me so much. Dr Winter even tried to joke me out of it by saying whenever he saw me, How's the Nameless Dread? But it didn't help at all, I became tearful and embarrassed. Mama calls my terrors my *bhaya*—a Hindu word for fear.

My project is to go back over my life as an important record for the archives at Hill House, but also to help me to understand my fears, instead of just gliding past them the way I have taught myself to do. If I can't get to an understanding, Mama is sure I will not be able to grow up into full responsibility within the community. It is also part of my progress towards the Realisation of Myself.

I have been encouraged to be frank and honest, and I have been told that even if I feel afraid that some of my remarks may be critical of Brethren, even of Mama (which is a very scary idea), I am to go ahead and speak my deepest, truest thoughts. In any case, the Mother knows already every single thing I know, everything I will write. The important part is that I write it down for my own evolution.

That is a very difficult thing to do; some days I hardly know how to begin.

This small house is built from silver tiles of cedar, smooth and soft to the touch, silky in appearance, comforting, sad, like the beautiful wings of a moth. The walls inside are lined with cedar too, palings going straight up and down, with patterns of veins and whorls on the surface of many of them. Between the inside and the outside there are sheets of silver material, an insulator, and you can see glimpses of this between some of the boards, like shiny silver fish. The roof is made from corrugated iron, painted silver. So it is a tall thin silver house with windows and a door and a chimney. The door is painted blue and the colour has faded in the sea air, and clumps of silvery grasses cling to the ground, making odd tufts from one side of the door, right round the house and coming back at the other side of the door. We have a rope between two trees out the back—that's where we hang our washing, although it doesn't always dry in the sea air. Outside the door there is a pile of firewood for the stove. At night we bring in the washing and hang it on a wire above the pot-belly to dry out properly.

I fancy I am a princess in a lonely tower, that Charity is my jailer, that I am waiting for a prince. Every once in a while we see movies in the dining-room at home—*Snow White* and *Tales of Hoffmann* and *The Red Shoes*. And of course we are forever reading and studying the stories of the Brothers Grimm. Mama uses these stories partly to illustrate the dangers that we face in the world outside the Brethren; the world is a place of evil and darkness and terrible dangers, full of murderous villains and tricksters. The discipline in our lives is a shield against danger.

I listen to the wind and the sea and the cries of the sea birds. I wish for a cat, a dog. It is lovely to look out the clear glass of the windows at the sky and the sea; at home we have bars on the windows because the world is full of evil and we must be kept safe. In the Apartment, Charity keeps me safe.

At home we have many cats and dogs; we love them,

but above all Mama is devoted to them. She believes that the animals are actually more highly evolved than her children. Children are imperfect, sinful creatures, and we need to be strictly disciplined in order to bring us to a higher level. We must be beaten and starved and ridiculed. When one of the cats peed in the porridge pot we were made to eat the porridge, which was the most terrible thing you could ever have tasted. But Faith said waste not, want not, and she said she had been in telepathic communication with Mama over at Hill House and that Mama had instructed her to make us eat it. Yuk. The funny thing was that although some of us vomited (I was one), nobody got really sick. Of course we were beaten for vomiting.

Beatings are so frightening. A ritual. We take off our shoes, then our tights and then our underpants (which are always white) and bend over a hard red wooden stool. One of the nurses then hits us on the behind with a long heavy ruler, and if they get carried away, as they often do, they start hitting on the head and arms. Everybody else is lined up and forced to watch, and if you look away you have to take your turn at the stool.

Because of the strict rules about food, we seem to be always hungry. Mama knows this, so I am not at all afraid to write it down. She says our hunger is a warning that we are very, very unrealised. Very low. She has a horror of fat people, a real phobia, because they are examples of evil and low development. So it is very important for us to be as thin as possible. Every morning we are weighed and our intake for the day is adjusted accordingly.

We sleep with our feet tied to the end of the bed to keep our legs, our knees straight. This was a method invented by Fanny Cerito, a great ballerina from last century. We begin the day with a cold shower, and people who have wet the bed have to wash their sheets and hang them out and are then beaten and put under the hose out in the yard. Then there is hatha yoga for half an hour in the dining-room. Next we practise ballet for half an hour and then we put the tables and chairs back where they belong and have breakfast. This consists of porridge and fruit and fruit juice. The nurses have tea and toast and butter and jam, but this is the wrong food for us, even though we long for it. The smell! We are vegetarian and there is never any meat at all in the house except the tins of cat and dog food, which we often share with the animals. If we are ever caught eating this we are punished by being taken naked down to the old well under the house. The lid is lifted from the well and we are held by our ankles until our head goes under the surface. This well holds the contents of many years worth of chamber pots. After that you are hosed down in the yard. We also eat seed that is put out for the birds, and we eat grass and dirt and mouse and possum droppings, and we know which wild plants you can eat and which ones you can't. Nasturtium flowers are a big favourite with us. The nurses know we do this, but there is only trouble when they catch us at it.

I remember when Swanilda was caught eating the dog food from the bowls outside the back door. She was a very hungry child, nearly three years old, and Faith came out and found her sitting next to the bowls with big smudges of Chum all over her face, and her fists closed tight over handfuls of cat food. I saw Faith grab her and hold her up and shake her. Faith was yelling at her, but Swannie wouldn't open her mouth or her fists. She had gone white and rigid, and her eyes were as big as big blue plates. Faith ripped off all Swannie's clothes and banged her head against the wooden veranda post and finally Swannie screamed and then she wouldn't stop screaming and her little fists flew open and brown stars of cat food went flying in Faith's face. Faith was really foaming at the mouth like a mad dog and I could see she was going to kill Swannie. There was blood running out of the baby's nose and mouth and she suddenly went limp and Faith threw her apron over her and rushed into the bathroom and turned on the tap in the sink—we were standing in the hallway, staring, unable to lift a finger. There were no other adults there at the time. I stared at Swannie's blood on the white tiles of the bathroom, the walls and the floor. Sometimes the memory of those sad big spots and smears of blood comes back to me with a terrible rush of tears. Faith put Swannie in the sink and splashed her, and water was running everywhere. Fill the bath, fill the bath! Faith yelled at me, and I turned on the taps hard but forgot to put in the plug. Faith pushed me aside with her elbow and she nearly dropped Swannie. Then she put in the plug and lowered Swannie into the water. Swannie was no longer crying, and Faith was kind of humming in a strange way. Then Faith asked me to help her again and not to be so stupid, and I had to get Swannie's pyjamas and blanket and Faith went and put Swannie in Mama's big bed.

This frightened me very much because whenever a dog or a cat dies they are put on Mama's bed, on top of the red velvet cover, for three days and we keep vigil and chant and burn incense and candles. Was Swannie dead? She wasn't, but she was in the right place to die. Suddenly Mama was there, serene and beautiful, and we were told to go back to our lessons and not to worry. Swannie was evolving.

She did get better, but she was never the same. She stopped talking and the light had gone out of her eyes. She stayed in her cot all the time, and she got thinner and thinner and just stared up at you. She went back to having her food in a bottle and she could hardly hold on to it. Somebody always had to be there. A doctor came and gave her injections. She never cried. One day she choked on vomit and then she was gone.

When Swannie disappeared I think that was the most frightening thing, maybe, I can remember. The most frightening real thing. One day she was there and the next she was gone—we didn't have a vigil on Mama's bed—Swannie was just a space, a space where Swannie used to be. Faith wrote a notice and put it up above the bowls of pet food—it said 'Do Not Eat the Pet Food'. It only stayed there for a day or so. Then it was gone too.

We were told that the right thing to do was never ever to speak of Swannie again. Somebody, I forget who, told me Swannie had been a dream. This was very hard, and I used to cry at night thinking about her, feeling guilty that I had been powerless to help her at any stage. I blame myself for the disappearance of Swannie. How can this be? I suppose my fear is really in my own powerlessness, somehow. Mama is an incarnation of the World Mind and I am nothing. Everything I know comes from Mama. So I am frozen; deep inside me I am frozen.

Writing this makes me so very unhappy that I will turn to more everyday events.

Every morning here Charity and I do yoga toether, and I do some ballet exercises. There is no piano. This is sad. We have a tape-recorder and we listen to Mama's talks and we also listen to music. I like Tchaikovsky. I listen to *Swan Lake* a lot, just listening and staring out the kitchen window at the sky. After breakfast I do lessons and write this journal, and Charity goes for a walk to get supplies. For lunch we have lovely soup and toast—imagine, toast! Charity is very kind to me and everything is different to what it is at home—although I do miss the others and I miss the animals too. And the piano. Charity is a good cook. I didn't know that before. Of course we still fast once a week. We have to be careful that I don't get fat while we are here. Getting fat is unforgivable to Mama. Then I do some more lessons and in the middle of the afternoon we put on tracksuits and runners and go down to the beach for a run and then a swim. Every day! This is the most wonderful thing, swimming in the ocean. We were taught to swim in the pool at Hill House and that was fun, and nice, and we swam there once a week, but here we go in the waves, with the smell of the sea and the sand, and the great sky and the huge stretching water that goes to the end of the earth. I love to stand on the edge and let the waves curl over my feet and feel the water run and trickle off, and see the wet sand being sucked away. We swim and run and collect shells and seaweed, which we take back to the Apartment and put on the kitchen window-sill. When I go home I will take my shell collection. And the sound of the sea is white magic; the songs of the seabirds so forlorn, so strange. I play with the seagulls and throw them little pieces of dried bread and they come running up to us and go—snatch! Sometimes I think I would like to write music and poetry.

Charity lets me have a bath every day if I want to. At home we only use the bath on rare occasions. So at night sometimes I have a bath and then we sit by the pot-belly and listen to a tape of Mama or music and read. Quite often I get on with my French translation. This is one of the things I have to do here. Madame who comes to Ararat twice a week to teach us French has set me two books to translate—one is *Le Grand Meaulnes* by Alain-Fournier and the other one is *Les Filles du feu* by Gérard de Nerval. I enjoy them very much. Daughters of Fire is a lovely idea, like a ballet. Well, there is a ballet called *La Fille de feu* but this is nothing to do with it. Gérard de Nerval was fascinated by volcanoes—I think he was dreaming somehow about girls as daughters of the volcano, daughters of the fiery earth. The main story in the book is 'Sylvie'—very dreamy and romantic and sad. There's even a part in it about a rural festival on the feast of the Massacre of the Innocents, about which I know quite a bit because we are descended from Queen Catherine de' Medici. It is fun to find such reminders of reality in stories. The other books I have are my French dictionary and grammar, the Manual of course, and a few collections of fairy stories. Most of the stories we hear and read are the fairy stories or folktales of the world. They are the foundations of truth, and sometimes very puzzling.

Gérard de Nerval

The only time I go out is when Charity and I go to the beach. I have to stay in and get as much work done as possible. There is not very much housework—we do that quickly together in the morning before I start writing. Charity cooks and I do the dishes and wash the clothes in the sink. At home we have a picture book with pictures of the Three Bears' house—this place reminds me, sometimes, of the illustrations in that book. I always loved those pictures. The Apartment has bare boards on the floor, with rugs in mandala patterns, and I always like to let my eyes wander round and round in the mandalas. It is a form of meditation, and I think of the rugs as magic carpets. We have set up a shrine to the Mother in the kitchen by the pot-belly—just a picture of the Mother and an incense burner and a cup of grasses and wild flowers that we pick on the way back from the beach.

One day when Charity had just given me a protein treatment for my hair and I was drying it beside the pot-belly, a little white cat came to the back door, which was open. It was so sweet and I was so pleased to see it. Charity got some cat food the next time she did the shopping and now we see it often. I call it Snowflake and it lets me stroke it and comes in by the stove. A white cat is a very special animal, very magical in stories. Snowflake has blue eyes and is deaf, and appears at the door silently, like smoke. To tell the truth, I would be happy to welcome any animal, and in fact the animals at home are the things we turn to for comfort. Charity is nice with me but she does not comfort me; we have been taught not to touch people, although my sisters and I do secretly look to each other for strength and warmth.

Among the things I miss here are the nights when we go to the meeting hall for Magic Meru soma, which sometimes affords us beautiful visions of the truth beyond the veil. But I have to say I am relieved that I don't have to Threshold while I am here. I know that one of the first things that will happen when I get home will be that I will have to Threshold again.

This brings me back to fear.

I like it here, all alone in the wild, with nothing to see for miles but the grasses and the rocks and the sea. But it frightens me too. I imagine that Charity and Snowflake and I are truly alone on the earth, that we really are the last people, and I don't know where it will end. My rational mind tells me this is not so, for Charity goes off and comes back with bread and milk and vegetables and fruit. And even Snowflake must belong to somebody who is not too far away. But in my heart I feel as if I am completely singular, a speck of dust on the wind. All I have of home is what I remember, what has gone into my head somewhere, and I wonder if that can be real. I think of lessons, of Madame, and of Mischa who takes us for ballet, and the stories Mama reads to us, and the English and maths lessons with various nurses, and the music which Hope teaches. She also taught me to type.

The sound of the typewriter is comforting; it pushes back the fear.

I will have to write at some stage about Threshold because this is an important event in my life, yet each time I go to write about it I pull back.

It was the thing that changed me most.

I am knitting a red cardigan for Golden Jade.

I have here the same vitamin tablets and also energy and serenity tablets that I have at home. Vitamin C tablets are like lollies (which we are forbidden to have) and so we use the tablets to trade, like money. For instance, one vitamin C will cost two apples. Serenity is Largactil, which we have every day.

Mama is a gifted healer and she has designed a program of diet and vitamin supplements and also special medicines for us. She spent some time in Switzerland and Paris studying, and she has been in Tibet where she studied healing and spirituality for many years. All the nurses are very good at healing and have their own systems and styles. Hope collects her own urine and drinks a quantity before each meal, and she washes her face in it. We all have Valium and Mogadon every day, apart from the Largactil, and also Stelazine and Tofranil. Some of the little ones who are subject to temper tantrums are prescribed Tegretol. Initial Threshold is the name for the first use of LSD by each child and it marks a milestone in our lives; it is our initiation ceremony into full membership of the Brethren. It is a sacred rite and we look forward to it with eager anticipation and a great deal of dread. We are told that the experiences we have had with soma are pale imitations of what we will see and understand at the time of our first Threshold. In the Manual it says that it will be possible to be outside time, to be outside place, to know what it is to be, just to be, and to approach a state of true ecstasy where there is no fear, but only bliss. The Manual warns that in order to attain this state, the Threshold will

---

urine

in all probability take the subject to the far edge of fear, to the evil depths of the inferno.

I could only begin to imagine what it would be like. Afterwards I knew they had been right—I had been to hell. I was given the Book of Revelation to study in preparation for my Threshold. The Mother said that that was all that was required, a close study of this book. Prudence, who is another one of the nurses, helped me in this work. And the Mother spoke often of the possibility of Cultivating the Vision of the Rose—by this she meant concentrating on the mental image of a rose, allowing it to unfold from within, throwing out a constant succession of soft thick petals, unfolding, unfolding, brighter and brighter—until the mind becomes the rose. This is a very difficult exercise, but if it is practised and perfected, it makes the experience of Threshold somehow smoother.

The first Threshold for me came about six months after my first period, when I was thirteen. For three nights and days before the Threshold I was not allowed to go to sleep, and I was also on a medium fast.

On the day of the Threshold I got up at the same time as the others, but while they went off to do their yoga and everything I was given a hot muffin for breakfast. I had heard of muffins but I had never seen one. This was dream food. I was about to enter the dream. Then the Mother, wearing her most beautiful gown of morning-glory blue, led me to the bathroom where she told me to get into the bath. This was incredible; I had only ever had about two warm baths in my life, when I was about four and we had a nurse who thought warm baths would be good for us—she was told to stop. While I was in the bath there was a tape of *Swan Lake* playing, and the Mother had lit candles. Then I was taken to the Mother's bedroom and told to put on a little nightdress and get into the big bed with the red coverlet.

The Mother gave me a piece of paper impregnated with LSD and with a mandala printed on it. She called it my dream medicine. She told me to chew the paper and close my eyes and relax. The blinds were shut and the room was dark and absolutely quiet. After a while, keeping my eyes closed, I felt my whole self begin to move up into my brain, and I knew this was happening but I couldn't stop it. I was in the grip of a great and mysterious force. The inside of my head was alight and whirling in colours more luminous than any I had ever seen. I ceased to exist in any ordinary way and I was pulled at a great speed, inside my own head, round and round in a vortex. I could hear screaming and I knew it was my own scream but I was unable to stop it. I tried to open my eyes but they would not open, they were stuck and had a great weight like a silver ball balanced on the eyelids.

The Mother came in several times during my Threshold and she gave me more of the drug each time. I don't know what I told her, but she told me that my thoughts about sex were wrong and dirty and evil, and that sex was something pure between men and women for the production of children for the continuation of the Brethren and the coming of the New Truth. The whole Threshold lasted for three days, I think, and at one stage Dr Goddard from Mandala came in and said the Mother had ordered him to treat me for my evil thoughts. He was naked. I am quite accustomed to seeing people naked, as they swim in the pool at Hill House with nothing on, and also sometimes in the meeting hall there are Magic Meru occasions where most of the adults are naked. But Dr Goddard was very frightening when he came into the room during my first Threshold. Everything was frightening then. He spread me out on top of the red coverlet and pushed my face into the pillow and got on my back and had sex with me. He let out a great roar and I thought I was going to die from pain and suffocation, and yet the most frightening thing was hearing the Mother laughing on the other side of the room. There was no refuge. This was hell and I was in hell. I do not remember getting any sight of heaven.

Other people have told me that as well as the terror, they have seen the beauty and have known the ecstasy of moving outside time and place, but I have never had this experience in all the Thresholds I have done. If I am very tired and very hungry I sometimes have uncontrollable flashbacks to parts of Thresholds, frightening flashing lights and the sensation of being pulled against my will into a vast dark place in my own head. In dreams or nightmares I sometimes flash to the scene of Dr Goddard on my back, he is a shiny balloon full of heavy poison and it is impossible for me to escape him, impossible for me to shake him off—and I can not scream, partly because my face is pushed into the pillow. One time I saw all the tissues and blood vessels in my own brain, and then I saw the whole structure slowly dissolve and disappear—I say I saw this, but the verbs of ordinary speech are not adequate for the actions that take place in hallucination. I saw and I did not see; I knew and I did not know. I saw a woman in red with an enormous gaping laughing mouth where I could see the teeth were all black and rotten; red milk—it was not blood—was spurting from her huge breasts and the red milk was chasing me, squirting all over me, trying to hit me in the eye and kill me.

Sometimes I think of the two sides, the two very distinct sides, to my life and the lives of my sisters. We have all the very strict discipline that goes with the teachings of the Brethren, and then we have the music and the stories and the ballets which are so much a part of everything we do. It is not hard to reconcile the two parts of our lives, as I see quite clearly that without one you can not have the other, but there are times when I long for the beautiful things to take over and for the fear and pain of evolving to sink back, to fade away. Mama tells us that beauty is like a water lily, like the lotus, for without the mud and slime and darkness beneath the surface of the water, it would not be possible for the lilies to rise up and break into all their luminous grace and pure colour above the pool. And she points out that every great achievement is made as the result of vast quantities of work that has taken place in the dark, beneath the surface, behind the scenes. We studied the life of Madame Curie as a perfect example of this fact. Mama speaks of the unconscious mind, where so much activity goes on behind the scenes of our everyday lives.

When the inspectors from the Ministry for Education come, every so often, to look at us and see how we compare with other children of our age in other schools, they always find we are doing very well, and we are even more advanced in many ways than other children. Once we put on a display, in the meeting hall at Hill House, of music and yoga and free dancing and a performance of part of *Swan Lake* in front of the inspectors and the Brethren. The senior inspector made a speech at the end complimenting us and our parents and Roger and our other teachers on what they had seen. I danced the part of Odette-Odile and Mama was pleased with me, but she took me into her bedroom at Hill House afterwards and made me strip off so she could beat me with the heel of her red stiletto. This usually happens because we have to understand that pride in our own achievement is a very low emotion, and must be tamed.

Mama's bedroom at Hill House is much more beautiful than the one she has at New Haven. It is like a room in a fairytale, like a room out of the *Arabian Nights* or something. It is very oriental and glowing and mysterious and old-fashioned, and highly decorated in wonderful blue, as well as gold and scarlet. In one corner of the room is a glass case containing the prize pieces of Mama's collection of red shoes. A pair of stilettos made by Manolo Blahnik, a copy of Dorothy's ruby slippers which Mama got Roger to make, as well as the most silky and shining pair of scarlet ballet slippers, which have never been worn, and a minute pair of embroidered silk slippers for Chinese bound feet. One wall of this bedroom is a huge cupboard which contains shelves lined with red velvet and mirrors; on the shelves are Mama's shoes. Ordinary shoes and also shoes made by Robert Clergerie and Salvatore Ferragamo and more by Manolo Blahnik. Of course,

---

swan; Salvatore Ferragamo

many of the shoes are red. There is something horrifying about opening the doors and seeing all those pairs and pairs of empty shoes pointing at you.

Mama's favourite colour for herself, especially for her dresses, is blue, a gorgeous morning-glory blue. Of course, the blue reflects the colour of her eyes, which she says are exactly like mine—I hope so, her eyes are so beautiful. When she appears in the meeting hall in her flowing blue gowns, and the carpet is blue, and the lighting is also blue, she glows with a wonderful and unearthly light, and you can see people's eyes widen in adoration and love. In every single known system of faith blue is the only colour that has no negativity. (People speak of being in a blue mood when they mean a very sad mood, and blues music is sad, but it is also soul music.) Blue is the colour of truth and revelation and wisdom and chastity and peace. The colour of the heavens, the colour of the deep; the colour of the great sky deities such as Jupiter and Juno, of Venus the goddess of love, of Indra's rain-cloak, of Dharma-Datu, of the Virgin Mary, of the Great Mother. In our bedrooms at home we always have blue lights burning in glass burners.

Mama is the only member of the Brethren permitted, when at Ararat, to wear anything but black. The women at Bethany make many of the black smocks and shirts, and so on, that are worn, and Roger and some of the other men make all the red shoes in the cobbler's shop which is next to Horus the violin maker's. I enjoy it when we are allowed, on rare occasions, to visit the workshops. Also the carpenter's where it smells of sawdust and we are permitted to make things with little pieces of wood. Roger makes red sandals and red slippers and red shoes with straps and buttons, as well as red toe shoes. Mama is the only person who wears red stilettos, which she buys from a shop in the city. I have never been to a shop in the city—it sounds very exciting but also very frightening and confusing. We are safe at Ararat, safe from the terrible dangers that fill the world outside—the danger of war and hunters and the police and rapists and murderers. Once Zora saw a man with a gun stalking in the gully below New Haven, and Faith sent a message to Mama by telepathic impulse and the man disappeared instantly.

I do not have the gift of telepathy. I wish I could develop it somehow. Mama says that if we work hard enough during Thresholds we will possibly come to a stage where we can do it, perhaps when we are older. I feel so weak and imperfect and sometimes I despair of ever being able to evolve. Being here at the Apartment is helping me to advance—particularly writing this chronicle.

I have done the back and one of the fronts of Golden Jade's cardigan.

One day on the beach when Charity and I were running on the sand, we saw in the distance another runner coming towards us. Closer and closer, and he was getting larger and larger, clarifying out of the hazy distance into the sharp lines of the here and now. Our feet were pounding and his feet were pounding, pounding on the hard sand, and suddenly he stopped and waved to us. It was strange, somehow, the empty beach with the solitary runner getting bigger as we got closer. It was Tek, from the plane that brought us here. We stopped because he stopped, and I felt very awkward and a little bit afraid.

Enjoying your holiday? he said to us. And I knew I

was not supposed to say anything, so I just stared at him, and Charity said yes we were having a very good time.

Let's know when you want to go back to the mainland, then, he said.

And Charity said she would let him know.

No worries, he said, and then he said ooroo and waved and kept on running.

I felt a strange urge to run after him, to run and run and take off in his plane and fly into the heavens and never come down, never come back. Never go home, just go on and on and on into the sky forever. I stood on the sand and stared after him until he had disappeared around the headland. Charity said nothing to me. She stood there too, staring out to the horizon, out across the water, to where the water meets the sky.

Tek is the only person I have seen here.

I keep hoping we will meet him on the beach again; it was nice to see him, even though I didn't say anything or do anything. I confess I still remember how he said I was pretty. I hope I am pretty. I hope I am not vain, but I hope I am pretty. Mama does not allow us to think about our own physical appearance in this way. But I do secretly hope I am pretty, and I long for Mama to say she loves me—I yearn with all my heart for Mama to love me.

Does Mama love me? We are trained not to give way to such soft emotions as love for humans—love is reserved for our prophets and teachers and for God and the Mother and the Captain, a pure and holy and selfless love that is prepared to give all and to die for love. A different kind of love. I long to be loved for myself—I am very lowly and unevolved. I struggle with the horror of my weaknesses.

I talk to Snowflake when Charity can't hear me, and I say to Snowflake to go and find Tek and take him a message from me, to go and say yes we want to fly in his plane, we want to go somewhere. Somewhere, somewhere. Sometimes I imagine I don't really want to go back to Ararat. This is an impulse of heresy and treason and I freely confess it here; I do not always want to go back home, although I know I must. There is nowhere else to go, after all.

But I long to see my sisters and all our pets. I don't look forward to seeing the nurses very much, but I would like to see Madame and Mischa—my translation is going well, but my ballet is rather pathetic. Mischa would laugh at me and get very angry and put me down at the level of the little ones. I can dance freely on the beach, and sometimes I do. We follow two traditions of dance—one is classical, and the other is in the manner of Isadora, inspired by the wind and the wave and winged flight of bird and bee.

The only sister who doesn't study with Mischa is Golden Jade. Our feet bleed and cause us terrible pain when we wear toe shoes, but this is very little compared with the pain, the *pain* she must suffer. If we ever cry or complain, one of the nurses is sure to remind us that up in her room Golden Jade is experiencing agonies and martyrdom the like of which we could not even imagine. And in Golden Jade's case as well as in our own it is all in the cause of discipline, of putting down the flesh, of creating art, and of giving pleasure. I am permitted to go to Golden Jade's room sometimes in the very early morning to read stories to her. Her favourite is 'The Little Mermaid'. I wonder what she makes of the bits about the pain in the mermaid's feet.

As well as Mischa's ballet classes we have Mama's lessons in free movement and dance. These are so much more fun, and when we do well Mama's voice pours into our ears like silk and honey and we know we are really good and that she really loves us.

When Mama is angry with somebody, whether that somebody is one of us or a stranger, she writes the person's name on a piece of paper and freezes it in an iceblock in the fridge. After a time decreed by Mama, she takes the iceblock out and puts it in a pot of boiling water, and then she takes the paper and dries it out and then she burns it. Mama loves the extremes of fire and ice; she speaks sometimes of the Archangels Michael and Gabriel. Michael is made from pure snow, and Gabriel is made from fire. Mama says that the centre of hell is full of the coldest, hardest ice. The fridge at New Haven is locked because we get so hungry we are always trying to steal food. There is no need for a fridge at the Apartment, it is cold here most of the time and we do not store food very much, just the oats for the porridge; other things Charity goes out and gets from Mrs Edmunds' shop quite frequently.

I dream of ice, of a land of ice, of a world where everything is choking on sharp white crystals, sparkling, deadly stilettos pointing up and hanging down, like the teeth of a glass shark.

My sense of dread, my eerie haunting terror, hangs on the edges of my mind, in the deepest recesses of my heart, as if nightmares never leave me, or only for a little while, for a fleeting moment such as when I am dancing or playing the piano or the violin, or sometimes when Mama or somebody is telling a story. Specially Mama. For when we are all there around the table and Mama is in her big carved chair at her end of the table, we are all safe, and we are quiet and happy and Mama is beautiful and reading to us in her lovely voice. We know then that she loves us even if we are below the dogs in our evolution.

But when we go up to bed afterwards, the feeling of serenity doesn't last. I am not afraid of the dark, it's not that. I believe I am afraid of the great nothing. That is what I have secretly named it. The Great Nothing. I have never spoken about this before and I scarcely know what I mean. But I have somewhere in me a feeling of the Great Nothing. And I am afraid.

A strange thing happened once. It was years ago now, and I was one of the children sent out with the horse and cart to sell flowers. Children don't do any of the selling, we are there to look decorative on the side of the cart among the chrysanthemums. Suddenly we were outside the walls of Ararat, and then we were away, away, and Ararat was nowhere to be seen. We were surrounded by tall trees and sky, the wide blue yonder of the world. Horus was driving the cart and two women Hattie and Zilla were in the back among the flowers with me and Iris. I was overcome by a feeling of intense loneliness and sadness. I knew I was forbidden to cry, but I went completely silent and could not smile for the whole day. I was almost frozen with nameless terror. Strangely enough, my demeanour was very popular with the people who came to buy the flowers. I was wordless and, I suppose, other-worldly or something. Anyhow, they liked me. Other times when I went out on the cart I felt quite different and normal, and I was probably less popular with the public. Horus was Tchaikovsky in one of his earlier incarnations, and whenever he drove the cart he sang, and the songs he sang stayed with me for days, as if he had put them into my brain.

The flowers and the strawberries are at the very simplest level of the Brethren's existence, and these things, as well as the yoga and medicine, appeal to people outside, and sometimes even interest people and bring them into the community. The real work of the Brethren is the work of souls and self-evolving, self-realising, and ruling the world after the holocaust. For this vital work to continue there has to be a great deal of money, and the solid financial base of the Hill House Brethren is in international property and investment. The Mother travels overseas quite often, attending to these and other matters, and recruiting new members for the Brethren. It is said that the only sure way to welcome new people is to give them a meeting with the Mother. I know this to be true.

If I have not already written that Mama is very beautiful, I should say this now. She has long auburn hair that gives off ripples of light, and she is so graceful in all her actions. She has a wonderful smile, and of course I have already described her eyes which are really hypnotic and blue, like pale sapphires, maybe star sapphires. Her skin is very smooth and soft, and pale, like a pearl. Whenever she comes into a room it is as if the brightest star has come gliding in, and when she leaves there is a lingering loveliness. Sometimes, after she has left a room, she will suddenly return, materialise, and she will come up to somebody and touch them on the forehead with her finger. This is known as the Touch and it confers momentary illumination on the person. I have never had the Touch. I long for it.

I felt that day outside Ararat how easy it would be to just give up and go mute. One of my sisters, Solange, did this for several years. It began when she was very little and she had been beaten every day for wetting the bed. This day was no different, and the beating was just the same—one of the nurses stripped her and she had to bend over the red stool and they hit her with a stick until she fell down half conscious. This time she just lay rigid on the floor for a while, and when she crawled away she had a little set look on her face, and she simply never spoke again for about five years. Then one day she just began again. Began talking as if nothing had ever happened, as if she had never stopped. It was weird. She is a little bit backward, but very pretty and very sweet.

There have been storms here at the Apartment, and a strange thing is that when the wind is raging and the sky is dark and the rain comes down in sheets and the sea from the window is a terrible, terrible boiling grey, I feel safer than I mostly feel. I feel sheltered by this little house, embraced by a spirit of goodness, alive and safe in the eye of the storm. My pervading sense of dread leaves me, and a peace comes into my soul.

When I came here for the first time I was very nervous, and I longed to return to New Haven. I have become accustomed to being here alone with Charity and Snowflake and my thoughts and my writing, and my home has faded a little. I still long to hear my sisters' voices and to do the things we do every day; I long to go to Mount Meru and listen to the music and chant, and hear the Mother speaking to us, perhaps to receive the Touch. But I suppose I am torn now between what I know at home and what I have come to know here at the Apartment. This knowledge must be good, for the Mother has set this task before me. I will not fail her. I will complete this task—there are only a few days to go—and I will return to New Haven joyfully.

A Child Alone

That sealed it for Celeste. The detailed and revealing chronicle of the life of Celeste went into the archives at Hill House, under a file marked 'Judas'. Charity returned to New Haven and life went on as usual, except for the absence of Celeste.

Charity told the police that she had gone for a walk on the beach, as she often did, at about ten o'clock at night. As she was returning at about half past eleven she suddenly saw a column of flame shoot up into the sky behind the trees on the top of the hill. She stopped in fright and amazement as the single lily of fire bloomed up into the darkness with a volcanic thrust, and then she began to run. She ran towards the house where she and Celeste were staying, ran up the path that led from the beach to the house. And as she grew closer it dawned on her that the only source of the fire she could see was the house itself.

By the time she arrived the whole house was in flames, the windows had split and sparks were falling on the surrounding scrub. Unless Celeste had escaped beforehand, she would be trapped inside. I always lock the door when I go out, Charity said. It is the safest thing to do. A child alone.

Charity ran down the road to the shop where she used to buy the vegetables and fruit and use the phone and post the letters, post the chronicle home to Petra. Frantic, she battered on the door until Mrs Edmunds came out in her dressing-gown. Mr Edmunds was a volunteer fireman, and he called the base and then he and Charity got in his jeep while Mrs Edmunds rang the police.

By the time Charity and Mr Edmunds got back to the Apartment, the building was falling. Celeste's bed, containing Celeste's sleeping body, was visible deep in a twisted cage of glowing and burning timbers, in a scarlet and golden inferno that spat and crackled and laughed as it burned. Two men from the fire base came in a water truck to douse the fire and spray the surrounding scrub; the policeman arrived. Like a bird of prey homing in to feed on a fresh corpse, a helicopter came. It contained a police doctor (the pilot was Reg Hughes) who pronounced Celeste dead from asphyxiation. Celeste, a mound of bubbled dark flesh stuck with charred scraps of sheet and blanket and pyjamas, was taken in the back of the policeman's jeep to the small hospital not far from the airport. She had inhaled smoke while asleep, had not regained consciousness, and had then burned in the bed.

There was a local inquest. The finding was accidental death caused by the inhalation of smoke from a fire of unknown origin.

Charity stayed with Mr and Mrs Edmunds for two nights.

– So the poor child was sound asleep.

– Yes, she didn't wake up when the fire started—something, a nightdress or something, must have accidentally fallen onto the pot-belly.

– And that was it.

– Yes, that was it. If only the little white cat had been inside, she would have smelt the smoke and cried out; I think she would have run to Celeste to tell her. She acted more like a dog sometimes, very devoted and intelligent. But she wasn't there. She came and went as she pleased. She wasn't there.

– And the door was locked?

– Yes, the door was locked for safety. Celeste would have climbed out the window, I know that. But she never woke up.

– No, the poor little thing, she never woke up. You did everything you could. You mustn't blame yourself.

– Oh, but I do. I will never forgive myself. Never. A child alone. Alone like that, and she never woke up. It just shot up like a volcano. And the house was a tinderbox.

A tinderbox.

Charity Was Devoted to the Girl

Tek buys his smokes at Mrs Edmunds' shop.

– So you were in the plane they first came over on, Tek?

– I was on the plane, working for Reg. That Charity, she was devoted to the girl.

– It's a shocking tragedy.

– I used to see them running on the beach.

– They went for a swim most days.

– She was a quiet little thing. Celeste.

– A very pretty girl.

– Very pretty. Charity was devoted to her.

– These things are hard to understand.

– Hard to come to terms with, Mrs E.

– Accidental death.

– Accidental death.

Dissolve

So much for Charity *in loco parentis*; so much for Petra, Celeste's so-called mother. I wondered at first why Petra went to all that trouble to get rid of Celeste, why she didn't just drop her off at Mandala one day, book her in for a lethal injection and a place at the bottom of the well. Then I realised that I was really looking at the envy and rage the wicked queen felt towards Snow White, that Petra was threatened by Celeste in all the most profound ways. It wasn't only that Celeste was a danger because she had revealed her true knowledge and thoughts about the Brethren. It was deeper and more primitive than that; the fifteen-year-old girl was the age-old enemy of the other woman. So Celeste had to go out in the fairytale fury of fire, in a dangerous public display of flame.

And what of Sylvie? Round and round the magnolia tree she trots the little red shoes called Colette. She knows only loss and the madness of her own imagination; the true fate of her baby she would never even begin to dream. Who could? The wicked queen succeeds in destroying the beautiful young Snow White in a burning tower on the edge of a far-off cliff. What, indeed, of Celeste's guardian angel? Half asleep, head in the clouds somewhere. Inept. Atrophied. Too late.

Charity did not return to New Haven for a long time. She was kept at Mandala until she had recovered from what was officially described by Petra as her shocking experience, an experience that shattered her nerves. She needed very much to readjust to things, to life, to the memory of Celeste. She had to learn to forget Celeste, let Celeste fade out, dissolve. For in truth Charity had, during the months at the Apartment, grown very fond of Celeste.

She had done what she had been ordered to do, she had doubled Celeste's dose of Mogadon, she had sprinkled the dry clothes with lighter fluid and had let them trail down and touch the stove. She had run an apron string from the inside of the stove up to the flannelette nightdress above. She had quickly locked the door and run down to the beach. She had read what Celeste had written, and she knew that the child was signing her own death warrant. There was no going back. She had considered trying to talk to Celeste, trying to explain to her that she should write only pretty stories in her chronicle. But Charity knew at some level that to try to unprogram the child, to try to undo the bond that tied her to Petra was utterly impossible. She knew that as Celeste wrote out her own death note, she also wrote out Charity's lifelong allegience and loyalty to the Brethren. Charity was now in it up to her own neck. Just as well she believed in the teachings; just as well she was ready to die for the cause, die for Petra, do the will of the Great Idea. Evolve.

When Charity came out of Mandala and returned to New Haven she was peaceful and happy and in tune with herself and the universe. While she had been away Irving had arranged for a full cremation of Celeste's remains at a city crematorium, and a simple ceremony of memorial at the meeting hall took place. Celeste, the Brethren were told, has moved on. Yes, she has moved on, Celeste's sisters who loved her were told. Celeste has moved on. She has been called to a higher level, and we rejoice. Hail to the jewel in the lotus. (Too bad about Golden Jade's cardigan.) There was a performance of the Dying Swan where Celeste appeared in the form of a dancing light. This I considered to be over-the-top tasteless, but it was absolutely true to form, for Petra. Horus was given the task of scattering the ashes among the chrysanthemums. He was not told what the ashes were or where they had come from.

One of the rules of the community is not to ask questions; this becomes easy after a while. The memory of Celeste just faded away.

Petra reviewed the treatment of the children in the light of Celeste's chronicle. But it was not really possible to change much. If you took the incriminating things out of the chronicle there wouldn't be much left. It was a highly valuable and serviceable document from that point of view. And in Petra's twisted way of looking at things, it only confirmed her beliefs about the discipline of the girls at New Haven. Rules were tightened. For one thing, children were no longer permitted to go out on the cart with the flowers. It seemed to give them funny ideas.

The children, of course, never forgot Celeste. They talked about her to each other in secret. Gradually she became a kind of saint, a saint who had gone away to be apart and study for her movement to a higher level, and had moved so swiftly on to that level that she was never seen again. Her spirit haunted the dining-room after dark and her ghost was seen in the room of Golden Jade, where it would sometimes come in the early, pearly moments of dawn and read stories.

Celeste's chronicle, though it was written in innocence, signalled to Petra the need for serious thought and action on how to manage the girls as they grew up and developed, in spite of all their training, minds of their own. As the girls became too old to continue at New Haven, they needed to complete the transition, somehow, to Bethany.

Some of the girls were easier to manage. Zora and Stella were sent over to Bethany for a trial run when they were sixteen. This was one of the best ideas Petra had had for a while. Zora and Stella took to Bethany—ducks to water—where the other women, starved for children, welcomed them as if they were little princesses. The girls threw themselves into the housework and laundry and gardening with zest—it felt like freedom to them. They were replaced in New Haven by a two-year-old and a baby, Athena and Saffron. And this became a regular thing—one girl moved out and a baby moved in.

When babies were born to women in Bethany, those babies were sent out to a location outside the community, to one of Sister Winter's homes, for fear the mother would grow too attached. When the babies were two they could be brought back, but the mother was not supposed to know it was hers. Saffron was the child of a woman in Bethany, but this was never acknowledged and the woman seemed to show no particular interest in that child. Baby boys came back to live at Hill House when they were five, having been elsewhere all that time. Raising boys was in fact of less interest than raising girls, for the girls were a set of playthings for the men, they were a key factor in the recruiting of male Brethren. A few boys were tolerated, permitted to grow up within the community, and on the rare occasions when the education inspectors came to New Haven, the boys were placed in a small group in the dining-room as if they were part of the school.

You may be wondering about the gay element in all this. Homosexual behaviour was completely disregarded, as if it did not exist. Petra herself professed to having a horror of it in any form. You can be sure there was enough of it going on under her nose, behind her back and before her very eyes.

Petra and Irving had some idea that the Hill House Brethren would continue at Ararat until the end of the century, at which time the world would end—the rest of the world would end, for the Brethren were chosen to survive. The living Brethren and the children trained at New Haven would inherit the earth and carry on the good work, building on the foundation developed at Ararat and using the basic skills learned in the workshops and gardens. People outside the community have tried to apply logic to the ideas of Petra and Irving. This is a foolish enterprise. We are beyond logic here. We are in the realm of Higher Truth where faith and obedience and charisma and a certain amount of LSD and Magic Meru are all you have to go by.

Underneath the Concrete at the Bottom of the Well

The first really big thing to shatter the confidence of Petra and Irving was the violent suicide of Ambrose Goddard in 1987, and the subsequent closing down of the highly useful Mandala clinic. Ambrose shot his dogs and then he shot himself. It was no longer possible to recruit Brethren through the hospital, and the deaths in Ambrose's Deep Sleep program, connected as they were with the Brethren's LSD program, attracted the attention of the authorities, although nothing much happened as a result of this. In any case, Ararat cut all ties with Mandala. Many records were destroyed. The disappearance of Mandala was really the beginning of the end. Recruiting had to be done differently now.

Would anybody ever think to investigate what lay under the concrete at the bottom of the old Mandala well? Probably not. So much, so much lies buried at the bottom of the Mandala well. Not just the bodies of people who defected from the Brethren, but the hopes and fears and souls and meaning of those lives. Families are forever conducting endless searches for their loved ones—when all the time the bones are lying in the ground in a quiet, respectable suburb where the old Mandala, which was once a convent, has become a big fancy conference centre. Flocks of delegates from all the right social and business worlds and from all over the place arrive there to be wisdomed up on every subject under the sun, while walking over the bones of the unquiet dead.

Crossroad

Petra had come to a crossroad, a crisis, a turning point—one of those things. The girls were suddenly grown-up problems with minds teetering on being their own, and bodies beautiful and threatening to get out of control. Petra's naïve dream of creating a convent of little girls living under strict rules and following the codes of the Hill House Brethren, living out myths and fables and fairytales, dancing and meditating, and worshipping the Mother—all this was cracking and crumbling. The idea of bringing in more babies and repeating the process had grown—well, tedious. A hopeless treadmill had been set up at New Haven. In truth, Petra had lost interest.

Things came to a point in the nineties where Petra was simply going through the motions of her leadership. Nobody knew, nobody noticed except me. I knew. Petra, in her cold and complex heart of hearts, knew too. She still got togged up in her morning-glory blue gowns; still entered the meeting hall to 'The Arrival Of The Queen Of Sheba'; still delivered her ravings from a lectern lit by a lovely blue light; still handed out the communal cup containing urine impregnated with redcap mushroom; led meditation, administered the Touch, dispensed mysterious wisdom, beat the children with her shoe. She still went over to New Haven and read stories to the children. But a darkness, an emptiness, a chill was moving in on her.

You could say that Petra had lost touch with reality a long, long time ago; that the image of herself on the lily leaf, herself dissolving into air, was a moment of split. Hard to say. I keep going back to the memory of poor mad desperate Wanda with the knitting needle. I somehow imagine that that was the moment of—what shall I call it?—truth. Some would argue with me, would say that a foetus is not really capable of realising that its very lifeline is after it with a stiletto, but it seems to me that Petra sensed what was going on. Having negotiated the battle of the cold steel knitting needle and won, Petra was already beyond reality, and the stage was set for all her unusual ways to follow. She could imagine the moment of disappearance from the lily leaf because she had looked annihilation in the face, at point-blank range, and lived. She had grasped life then; could she live forever? Surely, surely she could live forever? Would live forever? Yes?

Yes. Petra decided that she knew she would truly live forever. She adopted wholeheartedly the delusion that she would be better off when she gave up the ghost, self-eliminated, died.

How can I persuade you that she believed this? Her body would fall asleep and her soul would slip away into the great beyond. She would reign from the great elsewhere; she would evolve. Lift. Transfigure. I can not be sure how, can not be exactly certain in what terms she saw, in her heart of hearts, her new and shining self, but I know she was convinced. I can't give you her words, for there were none; I can't even give you her thoughts—at times like this she had nothing that could be described as thoughts. Petra operated on feelings and what she might describe as instinct, or intuition, or spiritual gifts of deeper truth. You get my drift.

The Captain's Decision

During all the years that the community of the Hill House Brethren lived and worked and grew behind the high walls of Ararat, and the little population was more or less secure and happy in its way, and Petra and Irving and a few others grew more and more mysterious and powerful and rich, there was the sure hope in the hearts and minds of the faithful that the end of the century would bring glory. They were the chosen people. The new heaven and the new earth would come to pass. The children of New Haven would rule the New Order.

But time, that remorseless master of human life, caught up with Irving. Or should I say time came to the window and tapped with the head of his blackwood cane and warned Irving that one fine day things, or at least things as far as Irving was concerned, would come to an end. His wife Eugenia, that patient woman who made the gravy and pissed in the sherry, developed a brain tumour and died slowly and painfully and very sadly. Her illness happened far away from Ararat, and the Brethren scarcely knew of it, for Eugenia had never lived in the community, Irving himself living half in and half out, keeping in touch with important city forces in business and medicine and the Church and the law. But the loss of Eugenia, the loss of his wife in the world outside Ararat, this was a very great loss to Irving. He had looked upon Eugenia as a fixture, in spite of all his strange and wonderful philosophies and theories about astral travel and the evolution of the soul and the embracing of the Great Idea.

After the funeral, which was a grand affair in King's, Irving retired to Hill House where he went into a period of retreat and mourning, attended only by Petra and some of the women from Bethany. To tell you the truth, he sat in his study drinking brandy and watching television.

He prayed a lot and studied his books. He kept returning to the line in the gospels where it says Jesus gave up the ghost. By some remarkable and twisted thinking he persuaded himself that it was time for him to give up the life at Ararat, at Hill House. He would give up all he had known and believed in and move away. He read again about the Oneida community, where the leader removed himself suddenly after thirty years from the place that he had made and from the people who followed his teachings. Irving selected a young woman from Bethany, a woman called Isis, and he announced that he and Isis would move to a retreat house in Queensland, leaving Ararat in the sole care of Petra. Forget Solomon and Sheba—Irving was now a drowning man sensibly reaching for a lifeboat. Isis. There was to be no communication between Irving and the Brethren. The property of Ararat would pass to Petra upon the death of Irving; if Petra predeceased Irving, it would pass to a Hill House Trust at Irving's death. The remainder of Irving's considerable estate would go to his own children and their families. Death, the unthinkable, was in the air.

Irving's so-called retreat house was an apartment on the Gold Coast and it came as a shock to Isis, who had lived at Bethany for a long time, but she soon recovered and she and Irving lived there together quite happily, keeping themselves to themselves. Because Irving retained his old Halo Effect, the Brethren forgave him, they understood, they admired him, they envied him; they imagined, in the end, that any course of action he took was approved by God. He continued, in his retirement from academic and religious life, to write his Inspector Root novels, which were always very popular; Isis worked, as you might expect, as his secretary. His teeth continued to clack, his fingers to wave whitely in their spider dance.

As time went on, Gwendolin Jones (that was) moved into the apartment next door to Irving and Isis. Life has a way of manufacturing coincidence. But the Petra connection between Gwendolin and Irving was never revealed to them, and they remained ignorant of the amazing woman they had in common, a woman they had both, in their way, loved, even worshipped. And Gwendolin, need I say, was a great fan of Inspector Root, and was unaware that Root was her neighbour's creation.

The scene is the tropical foyer of the Gold Coast apartment building. There is a great deal of glass, marble, and greenery and subtle lighting, and soft music. The time is five years after the turn of the century. The holocaust predicted by Petra and others has not happened. Life goes on, you know, life goes on.

Gwendolin: Good morning, Mr Clay, Mrs Clay.

Irving: Mrs Thing-thing, good morning, how very good to see you.

Isis: Thing-thing.

Gwendolin: Glorious weather.

Irving: Glorious.

Gwendolin: Well, enjoy your day.

Irving: Enjoy your day.

Isis: Enjoy your day.

So the Captain was gone, Mandala was gone, Celeste was gone. Petra's world was beginning to crack, to crumble, to wither, to fade, to die.

But in Dreams Time Does Not Exist

This is 1995 and Petra is asleep, dreaming. In her dreams she returns to the dark room at the back of her childhood home, but the room is empty and cold and darker than it ever was before. The room is a hollow shell where Petra is trapped, where the logic of nightmare gives her no books, no pictures; no drifting, dreamy thoughts of other worlds and power and beauty, and magical, fantastical leaps from the lily leaf to the dissolving nothingness of the sky. She is in the grip of a dark figure, semi-human, with demonic arms and hands, claws with a steely hold. This is the past and the present collapsed in the mind of the dreamer; she is a child, an adult, an infant, a crone; her own time swings in slow, hypnotic pendulums within her head, within her heart. She is asleep and she is not asleep. Nothing is real except for the frantic beating of her dreamer's heart. The dreamer has no personality but fear, and she is abandoned in a tempest of black rain that never ends, never stops falling.

But time returns with the dawn, and Petra is lying in her golden bed in her crimson bedroom and the sunlight is playing in the leaves outside the windows, throwing little glinting lights across the shifting, shiny surfaces. Petra lies, queenlike, on the bed, covered by a white sheet and a crimson coverlet, her fiery hair spread on a pile of snow-white pillows. She admires her hands, stretches her feet beneath the covers, turns her face towards the sunlight—

and in this moment she knows what it is she has to do, what it is she is going to do.

Petra has decided to die now.

The final and only way to win, to cheat death, is to make your own arrangements. Kill yourself. This line of thought is consistent with all of Petra's ideas. Take charge. Get in first. Don't hang around waiting for the spook in the black cloak and hood to tap you on the shoulder. Kill yourself. Go out in style, your own style. It's not as simple as it sounds, but Petra is prepared to give suicide her best shot.

Her farewell speech begins to form in her mind. She will leave the Brethren in body, remaining forever with them in spirit, giving them by her physical absence greater strength to confront *mappo*, the chaos at the end of the century. She will call upon the Great Spirit to take her. One moment she will be with the Brethren and the next moment she will vanish, she will be gone, she will have travelled beyond the farthest star. She will be with them always, even unto the end of the world.

The words roll round in her head; she is in love with the words; it is very easy, lying in the bed in the sunlight, to believe them. She is basking in her own Halo Effect—a trick she perfected long ago, but I never thought she would bring it into play for the big goodbye. This was self-elimination. I was not a player.

Angel of God, my guardian dear
To whom God's love commits me here
Ever this day be at my side
To light and guard
To rule and guide.

Not a bad prayer; and I was always there for her, until this, until the idea of the coming *mappo* got a grip on her imagination and overwhelmed such reason as she might have had. My hands were tied, my wings were clipped, my voice was stopped.

She called in Daniel Winter—if Ambrose Goddard had still been alive she would have talked to him, but Daniel Winter knew his stuff, and doctors such as he are above the law. They mixed up 9g of phenobarbitone sodium, 10ml of propylene glycol, 50ml of orange syrup, 15ml of purified water, and 20ml of vodka. After taking that she was going to take 1g of the beloved LSD, of which the community still had a huge supply stockpiled. The only other people in on the act were Faith and Hope, to act in the role of reverse midwives. For someone as interested in shit as Petra had always been, it is no wonder she paid careful attention to the matter of containing her bowels after the big sleep. It was a job for Faith and Hope. And a job for the men in the carpenter's shop was to construct, with no explanation given, a transparent perspex coffin. I had never really imagined that Petra would get round to doing all this, to actually doing the deed, but I began to see that orchestrating her own end, her own exit, was consistent with the way she had lived: truly remarkable theatre.

She called Simon Honeychurch in to finalise her affairs, he knowing nothing of her secret plan to die. At her death her property was to be divided among the girls at New Haven, and her shoe collection was to go to Roger, with specific instructions about how it was to be preserved. The bedroom at Hill House would become a shrine. She sent her regards to Vera Honeychurch, who was still a devoted, and by now very advanced, follower of Meena of Murrumbeena and her yoga classes.

She had a great final dinner with the girls in New Haven, all the snowy heads around the dining-room, black smocks, good manners, vegetable soup and the story by Hans Christian Andersen, read by Petra, of 'The Red Shoes'. The girl dances forever on the bleeding stumps where her feet used to be. Petra mixed this story with the Book of Revelation. I couldn't seem to connect the two narratives myself, over dinner, but the girls listened with their usual polite and rather blank wide and beautiful eyes. They didn't know this was the last supper. Petra broke up some dried mushrooms and walked around distributing bits to the girls, saying, Take, eat. This was very special, as the girls didn't usually get to have chunks of the mushroom's flesh. They went to bed that night high on mushroom and Mother. That was how Petra wanted it to be.

Then Petra fasted for a week, living on water and infusions of herbs grown in the gardens at Ararat. She took no drugs whatsoever for that week so that her body would be ready to receive its final and glorious dose. Faith administered an enema, flushing out stuff that might stain the deathbed. I should stress that Petra was not physically ill; she had simply made her decision to leave the scene, believing that she was going to a higher level, that her spirit would prevail in all its beauty and mystery. I really think she believed this. Her mind, as anyone would realise, was by this time shot to pieces. She had Horus apply for a permit to have a bonfire on the 17th of July, the anniversary of the deliverance, of the day when the waters of the earth abated and the Ark rested at last on the mountains of Ararat.

The Bonfire of the Scarlet Slippers

A bonfire was built in the courtyard in front of the Mount Meru meeting hall, and in the evening, a crisp, cool, starry evening, all the Brethren were bidden to the hall.

The music of 'How Beautiful Are The Feet' from Handel's *Messiah* was playing in the hall, which was lit with dim blue lights. A charge of strange excitement was running through the Brethren, a reverent and still mass in black, with their red ecclesiastical slippers, all in the lotus position before the podium. They had sipped from little cups of Magic Meru soma. The music changed to 'The Entrance Of The Queen Of Sheba' and slowly Petra, in flowing pale blue, came gliding in, a lighter blue spotlight following her, resting on the back of her head. From time to time in her progress she stopped to rest her finger on, give the Touch to, one or other of the faithful. And then she took her place at the podium and she led a chant—simply 'How beautiful are the feet of them that preach the gospel of peace'.

She began to speak in a low, compelling tone: As you know, I have not slept for seven years, and I have visited the entire world every night; I have visited the planets from time to time, and I have been given a great gift—I have been granted the privilege of Lifting. I will be with you always, even until the end of the world, I will be with you in my lightened instrumentation. Forever and ever. A great peace has been shown to me, and a light. I must follow the light which is a light of beauty beyond earthly understanding. Once upon a time, in the dawn of time, we were all children and we knew the possibility of the Great Everything, we heard at that time the music of honey, the laughter of stars. In the house of the Great Mind there are many, many mansions, many, many levels of pure and shining thought. *Mappo* will come rushing upon the face of the earth, but the Brethren of Hill House will prevail against it; at the coming of the sword of fire, the Brethren will stand firm and will go through the fire and will inherit the universe. I have come tonight to tell you that I have accepted the gift of Lifting. Do not think that I am leaving you; know rather that I will be in every one of you, and at the last trump I will be there, and I will know you, and you will know me.

And she held her hands above her head in a stark gesture of blessing, and light radiated from her fingertips, and the Brethren, their eyes wide, their spines taut, felt the power of the light as it entered their souls.

Then Petra instructed the Brethren to remove their slippers; she had never asked them to do such a thing before. This was the signal for Horus to light the bonfire, and then Petra led the flock out into the courtyard, to the strains of 'Total Eclipse' from Handel's *Samson*. In the courtyard they were further instructed to consign their slippers to the flames. She led them in a slow procession around the fire, in which all the Brethren's files were already burning, and one by one they threw the slippers in, and an eerie silence prevailed in the courtyard, a silence broken by the crackle of the bonfire, a darkness illuminated by the lustful leaping of the flames. The only member of the Brethren who did not dance was Roger. Barefoot, he stood in the darkness by the wall as the shadows of the dancers leapt and writhed in monstrous shape and gesture. He stood, a porcelain man pale in the flickering firelight, very still by the wall, and he watched all his shoes burning before his eyes, and a slow stream of hot and terrible tears coursed down his face.

And slowly Petra, barefoot, began to dance on the cold flagstones of the courtyard, and the Brethren fell in behind her, Horus playing on his fiddle an old Turkish folksong. As the flames leapt up, scarlet and golden lilies, swiftly unfurling roses of desire, and as the sparks sputtered and flew into the darkness, the company circled the fire where their red shoes cracked and burned, and the smell of the leather was in their nostrils, the rhythm of the music thrilling in their hearts, and they whirled and danced, demons in the darkness, the black skirts of the women billowing like lanterns, like sails, the flailing arms and legs of the men the legs of wild, demented spiders, until Petra stood still.

From my vantage point high above the scene, all was beautiful, a turning mandala-wheel, a flaming dance of death. The dancers all stopped and looked up, the flicker of the fire on their pale, expectant faces. Petra stood on the steps of Hill House and she gestured in silent blessing, turned in a graceful, regal movement like a snow queen in the darkness, and was gone.

Before eternity, you dance without shoes.

In silence the Brethren returned to their quarters, and Petra and Faith and Hope went up to the scarlet bedroom. It was a most breathtaking sight—the great red and black mandala of the magic carpet on the floor, the doors of the shoe cupboard wide open, all the lights in there glowing, the shoes sitting on their racks like hundreds of parrots on a perch. The perspex coffin was placed on a stand at the end of the bed. Candles and spicy incense burning. Handel's *Largo* playing softly. Petra took a slow, deep bath and put on a white silk nightgown; her pampered feet were pedicured and massaged, with great attention to the rituals of reflexology, for the last time. The women moved about the chamber silently, reverently, in the presence of a saint.

I took up the position I knew she wished me to have, above the head of the bed, hovering. Human beings have to die of course, but I had never had one go like this before. Uninteresting old age has usually been my thing. Poor Handel was blind when he died. Petra was already treating herself as 'the body' and Faith and Hope followed her lead. They placed towels under her. Placed the glass of goodbye juice on the bedside table, the LSD in suspension beside it. Then they waited for the Touch, and left the room to report to Daniel Winter, who was waiting downstairs in Irving's old office, watching television, enjoying a brandy (the good fire-water) and a cigar.

Halo Effect Survives Death

I said goodbye to Petra. They always ask you, on television, if you had time to say goodbye. Yes, we said goodbye. She took her poison and I held her in my arms and she looked into my eyes. Feathers falling—feathers falling like snowflakes, she said. Goodbye, Beau. She squeezed my hand and I whispered goodbye. She closed her eyes and drifted into unconsciousness. At some point I sensed that beneath her eyelids the light went quite suddenly from her eyes, breath fluttered out of her, and she was dead.

After two hours, as agreed, Faith and Hope returned to the bedroom, and Petra was dead. Beautiful in death, as always. Even though the starry periwinkles were softly closed, I swear a light still radiated from her face. Halo Effect Survives Death! But she was as dead as a doornail, of that there was no question. Since souls are not my department, I know nothing further. I am unable to shed any light on the existence or otherwise of the soul after death. I have thought about it a little, and the stumbling block for me is that living human bodies give enough trouble for the universe—who wants more of the same in a spiritual realm?

The two women called Daniel Winter and he confirmed the death, filled in the papers. Petra had died, said the certificate, of an asthma attack, to which attacks she had been more and more frequently prone. She was sixty-six years old. (Well, fifty-five was nearer the mark, but she insisted she was older. And she liked the idea of sixty-six because she said it was twice the age of Jesus when he died—Jesus, one of the great self-eliminators.)

Faith and Hope prepared the body as they had been instructed, washing it in vanilla and alcohol, embalming according to modified Egyptian rites. They put on her feet little white kid slippers, and in her hands a crystal skull the size of a baby's head. Her face glowed pearl and alabaster; her hair flamed out over a white satin pillow. They put Petra in the glassy coffin and closed the lid. Although my job was by then, strictly speaking, over, I stayed around because it was quite interesting in its way.

Music and incense and candles and flowers—and the Brethren filed past, barefoot, without ceasing for two days, in a kind of stunned and reverent wonder. There was some stifled sobbing, and Golden Jade, who is very highly strung, had hysterics. But generally, it was as if Petra had truly gifted them with her leaving. The charisma, I swear, never left her. In fact I think it came on stronger as she lay in her glassy box in the flickering, spicy light. It seemed to be a big turn-on. Always sexy and cold and just out of reach, now Petra was the Holy One enshrined as if in amber.

There came a time (it was the dead of night) when the body was put in a teak casket and spirited away to the city crematorium, the same crematorium that had dispatched the pitiful remains of Celeste. And within a few days there was a small ceremony of ordinary public burning. People such as the Honeychurches and the Winters came to this.

And curiously, a woman who turned out to be Natalie, one of the daughters of Gwendolin Jones, following her mother's old childhood friend to the grave. It was a strange and touching moment, bringing back my memories of the days at the manse, in the garden, by the pond, dolls sailing on the lily leaves. Natalie did not resemble her mother.

I went to the cremation, of course, wishing to see the thing through to the end, and I found myself staring at Natalie. What was it about Natalie? And suddenly I knew—well, I think I knew. I can never be sure, but I saw that the beautiful pearly alabaster skin of Natalie and the high dome of her forehead resembled, duplicated, the forehead and the skin of her grandfather, Somerset Jones. It was a skin and a skull that had passed Gwendolin by, but that had come to light again in Natalie. It had also come to light in Petra Penfold. Could it be, I asked myself, could it be that Petra's mystery parent was none other than Somerset?

It could.

I thought of the day Somerset took Petra out to tea in the café in the hills, how their appearance and demeanour was for all the world like father and daughter. Holy Smoke! They *were* father and daughter. Just as well Petra never twigged. Did anybody know? Apart from Somerset?—who is now cast in an even poorer light than he was before. You seduce one underage girl, abandon her, she dies, and you seduce the (very) underage daughter of the first union. Murky business. I don't suppose anybody knew. I weep, you know, for Wanda.

Two weeks later, Petra's ashes came to Ararat. They

were placed in a golden sphere in a glass case above the podium, where a blue light shines perpetually upon them.

Ararat won't last, of course. These communities all have their use-by date. And with Irving gone to the Gold Coast and Petra reduced to a pile of ashes in a golden ball, there is nothing much to hold things together. The Brethren will scatter like a nest of ants where boiling water has been poured. Ten years, and Ararat will more or less revert to being a colony of artists, and a few religious nutters. The people who actually stay on the property will be the druggies, they like their mushrooms. And they will still grow the chrysanthemums with their flaming pom-pom heads.

One good thing I know is that Golden Jade somehow links up with Allura and Rev de Wolfe, and goes to live with them, becomes known simply as Jade, and has a lot of surgery on her feet. She teaches music.

I'd like to be able to report that something really good happened to Roger, but to tell you the truth I don't know what became of him. Porcelain man.

It was the burning of the shoes, I think, that really heralded the end of Hill House as it was in the hearts of the Brethren. When the Mother said burn the slippers, that was it, and round the bonfire the dance of life became the dance of death and the figures of the dancers wove the body of the serpent who swallows his own tail. Such a dramatic, simple order: Burn the slippers. The faithful burned the slippers, and when the dance was over and the fire was dying down and the Mother had gone, they trailed away in bewilderment, tired and strangely unstable, returning to their dormitories, as was their duty.

The files, such as the Judas file, had been burned. The remains of the scarlet slippers lay in the ashes, blind broken hearts, crisp and twisted fish.

I will miss Petra but, in a lot of ways, I'm glad she's dead. The strongest feeling I had, most of the time, was one of shame, but she was my given responsibility and I did my job. She did a hell of a lot of harm. I can find no excuse; I can not forgive her. But then, that's not in my brief. Forgiveness.

I can sign off now. But before I go, you might want to know how many angels there are on the head of a pin.

Just the one.

THE FOOTNOTE

It is on the whole probable that we
continually dream, but that consciousness
makes such a noise that we do not
hear the dream.

C.G. JUNG

All stories rest on other stories
which have gone before.

N.E. SOLOMON

The material in The Footnote is like the life that moves beneath the surface of a pond. The Narrative exists above the water, partly dependent on the matter below.

ALMA

This romantic ballet, also know as *La Fille de Feu,* was first performed in 1842 with Fanny Cerito at Her Majestey's Theatre in London. It tells the story of an animated statue, Alma, who is under a spell and who will revert to a statue if she falls in love. In Spanish, the word *alma* means soul.

see also FANNY CERITO

ALMOND

The shape of the almond resembles that of the human vaginal opening, and the sharply pointed almond design is depicted in ritual and religious art to represent the female genitalia, or yoni, and is known as either the mandorla, or the vessel of the fish. The shape often surrounds an image of the Virgin Mary, and symbolises virginity and self-reproduction. As the first flower of the year, the almond blossom is the awakener, and signifies watchfulness. This watchfulness is signalled in the Jewish candlestick of the tabernacle of the ark, which is fashioned from almond designs in accordance with the text of Exodus 24:32–34.

In Chinese myth the almond symbolises fortitude in sorrow as well as watchfulness and feminine beauty. Chinese men delighted in eating almonds placed between the toes of a woman's foot, once the bandages that bound the foot had been removed.

see also FOOT

ANDERSEN, HANS CHRISTIAN (1805–1875)

Hans Christian Andersen wrote an autobiography which turned out to be largely a fictitious account of his life, but it makes lively reading. He once described himself as a 'swamp plant' and this is a very interesting way of looking at him. He was born in Odense to a very poor family, and yet by the power of his imagination he was able to create items, stories, of such charm and beauty that he grew up to mingle with the nobility.

His grandfather was insane, yet a woodcarver of entrancing and strange toys which he sold from a basket as he went about the countryside. He sang madly as he went along, and would return from the woods decorated with beech leaves and wild garlands of flowers. Hans would tell other children that he himself was visited by angels who came to talk to him.

He slept with his parents in the one-room shop where his father was a shoemaker. His mother was a washer-woman who became addicted to alcohol, and Hans tried to forget his early life and his family as he aspired to move in much higher circles. However, he often harked back to incidents and motifs lodged in his memory, and many of his stories refer to cripples, feet, shoes, reminding the reader of the writer's childhood in the shoemaker's shop. Hans Christian Andersen wrote dozens of tales of fantasy and wonder, including 'The Little Mermaid', 'The Snow Queen' and 'The Red Shoes'. A writer who inspired him early on was E.T.A. Hoffmann, and in one of Andersen's first stories, 'Journey on Foot to Amager', the main character hears Hoffmann's book *Elixire des Teufels* telling its own story.

He visited the Brothers Grimm and also Charles Dickens. He was hopelessly in love with the Swedish Nightingale, singer Jenny Lind. A statue of Hans Christian

Andersen's Little Mermaid sits in the harbour at Copenhagen and is a constant reminder of Hans Christian Andersen.

see also E.T.A. HOFFMANN, MERMAID, SHOEMAKER, THE RED SHOES, THE SNOW QUEEN

ANGEL CAKE

INGREDIENTS

4 oz plain flour
1 teaspoon cream of tartar
10 oz castor sugar
11 egg-whites
1 teaspoon pure vanilla essence
good pinch of salt

METHOD

The dry ingredients will be sifted eleven times.

Sift the flour four times. Add cream of tartar and sift. Sift sugar four times. Combine dry ingredients and sift twice.

Beat egg-whites until stiff. Using the sifter, gently add the dry ingredients to the whites while the whites are still beating. Add vanilla and salt to the mixture.

Flour but do not grease the cake tin. Bake in moderate oven for 40 minutes.

Leave cake in the tin until it is cold, then turn it out and ice it completely with rough white vanilla frosting. The cake should not be cut with a knife, but gently pulled apart with two forks placed back to back.

see also TARTAR

AQUINAS, THOMAS (*c.* 1225–1274)
Thomas Aquinas was educated at the Benedictine monastery of Monte Cassino and the University of Naples, and became a mendicant Dominican friar, against the wishes of his family. He had the power of intense concentration, being able to dictate four different texts at once to his scribes.

His most important writing is the *Summa Theologica* (begun in 1265 and unfinished), a large work containing his thoughts on all the Christian mysteries and which continues to be an authoritative statement of Christian doctrine. On 6 December 1272 in Naples, Thomas experienced a revelation of God, after which he stopped writing, saying that all he had written was straw in comparison with what he had now seen.

Canonised 1323; Doctor of the Church 1567; Feast day 28 January.

BUTTERFLIES
A cloud of white butterflies accompanied the coffin of the dancer Emma Livry, and a similar cloud fluttered and swirled around the standard of Joan of Arc.
see also EMMA LIVRY

CATHERINE DE' MEDICI (1519–1589)
Catherine, born in Florence, was the granddaughter of Lorenzo the Magnificent. She married Henri II, King of France. When she was born her parents consulted astrologers, who predicted a life of sorrow, trouble and storms, and said that she would be the cause, if she lived, of very great calamities and finally the total ruin of the

house into which she married. It was suggested that she be put in a basket and hung from the city wall in the hope that a cannon-ball would kill her, or that she be placed in an enclosed order of nuns, or that she be put in a bordello. Instead, however, she was married to Henri, whose father was Francis I of France, as part of an elaborate bargain between the French and Catherine's uncle, Pope Clement VII. The pope assured the king that this marriage would strengthen the French and Italian alliance against Charles V, Holy Roman Emperor, while he promised Charles V that Catherine would weaken and even destroy the French state. Catherine's husband said she was the greatest trouble-maker in the world, and warned that she would wreak havoc if she ever got into government.

She lived at the French court first as princess, then as dauphine, as queen, and as regent to her son. The first ten years of her marriage were barren, but with the apparent help of drugs, astrology and sorcery, she later had children, among them three who became kings: Francis II, Charles IX, and Henri III. Her husband's most famous mistress was Diane de Poitiers, whose nose Catherine once considered having chopped off.

One of Catherine's nicknames was Jezabel.

The first step in Catherine's French political career was to arrange for the death by poisoning of her brother-in-law, François, heir to the throne, and she is noted for the use of poison as a device, administering lethal fish sauces and offering decorated apples full of poisonous vapours. She, unattractive, even ugly, surrounded herself with a flying squad of beautiful women who could trick and charm her enemies.

She became regent when Charles came to the throne at the age of eleven. This was the time of the Wars of Religion, and Catherine hatched plots in all directions, now against Protestants, now against Catholics. On the death of Charles, she realised her ultimate ambition of holding complete power. She is most vividly remembered as the force behind the Massacre of the Innocents on Saint Bartholomew's Day.

August in Paris is usually hot and sultry, and so it was on the eve of the 24th, 1572. Aristocratic leaders of every kind were gathered in Paris to celebrate the marriage, on the 18th of August, of Catherine's sister Marguerite to Henri, King of Navarre, a Protestant. People were relaxing with games such as tennis, and with tournaments, banquets and masked balls. Catherine's new palace at the Tuileries was now complete and contained a menagerie, an aviary, fishponds, an orangery and a warren for breeding game. On the eve of the massacre, all the visitors were invited to see a new kind of performance, a story–ballet, *Le Ballet Comique de la Reine*. This was presented at a banquet, and Catherine had written the story herself, assisted by the designer Beaujoyeulx. Part of the plot told how Henri, the bridegroom, was attacked and beaten to death by members of the French royal family, and how his soul was consigned to hell.

The surface story of the ballet was that of Circe the enchantress. The performance cost over three million francs, lasted six hours, and displayed brilliant costumes, fountains, airborne figures and a range of music and song, as well as dance and mine and masquerade. Queen Catherine, who was well known as a gifted dancer, and her women posed as naiads on golden steps, and there were chariots, magic gardens, sea horses, and a heaven from which Jupiter came down. The choreography was worked out on geometric principles.

Paris then was a city of 210 000 inhabitants, contained by gates and divided in two by the Seine. It could be used as a trap. And it was.

The key victim of the massacre was Admiral Gaspard de Coligny, the most powerful military and political Huguenot and a central enemy to Catherine's cause. Catherine had been trying to get rid of him for ten years, poison and assassination plots having failed during that time. Two days before the massacre, Catherine had arranged to have Coligny shot, but that too failed. The shot was fired in broad daylight when the admiral was walking with a group of Huguenots. He was studying a report and he suddenly stooped to adjust his slipper. The bullet hit his arm and hand.

On the eve of Saint Bartholomew the city gates were locked, boats were chained up to the riverbank, arms were assembled, and the attacking murderers tied white shirt sleeves to their left arms and decorated their hats with white crosses. The houses of Huguenots had been marked with a cross.

At around two in the morning, Catherine ordered the tocsin to be rung, beginning with the great bell of St Germain l'Auxerrois which had never before been sounded except for royal masses. Assassins stormed the house where Coligny was recovering, killed all in their way and broke into the admiral's room wielding swords, daggers, lances and muskets. When Coligny was dead they threw him out the window. The tocsin rang from all the belltowers of Paris, torches were lighted, and there began a night of murderous rampage, looting and burning all over the city. People were massacred in their beds, or else pursued to the tops of houses and hurled onto the cobbles; bodies were dragged along the streets by ropes to be dumped in the Seine by ferrymen who took them out mid-stream and tipped them in. Heaps of bodies were collected outside the Louvre Palace. On bridges victims were stabbed and then forced to walk the plank so that billowing streams of blood followed the bodies as they settled in the water. People who survived and began to swim were stoned to death. Little children were tipped from baskets into the water to drown, women dragged naked along the cobbles until they died.

A pack of hounds was loosed, thirsty for the blood that ran in the streets, and the king responded to the slaughter with gruesome and repulsive glee, revelling in seeing the corpses of Huguenot noblemen delivered to him at the Palace. Catherine and the flying squad and others at the Louvre ran from window to window enjoying the spectacle below.

It was not long before looting began in earnest, and before people were killing purely for the purpose of robbing the dead. Jewellers, lapidaries, money-changers, silversmiths and goldsmiths were slaughtered in this wave of killings. Then ordinary shopkeepers—shoemakers, hatters, silk merchants—and children were butchered with their parents. Valuable libraries were looted. A bookbinder was roasted alive on top of a pyre of his books. And of course personal vendettas were settled, members of families killed in hatred.

By midday the Palace had issued an official cease-fire, but the slaughter continued to some degree and spread to other cities of France, where it continued throughout September and October. Catherine had succeeded in her plan, which was to gain power over her son the king and to put in place mechanisms that would eventually overthrow the rival house of Guise. On 2 September a horseman arrived in Rome from Paris with the news of the success of the massacre. Pope Gregory XIII was delighted and gave the messenger a hundred crowns as a reward. A medal was struck bearing the pope's head on one side and on the other the angel of doom.

see also SAINT BARTHOLOMEW, SHOEMAKER, SLIPPER

CERITO, FANNY (1821–1909)

Fanny was born in Naples and made her ballet debut there in 1834 in *L'Oroscopo*, and by 1837 she was dancing in Milan. Her greatest successes were as the Daughter of Fire in *La Fille de Feu* (or *Alma*) and in *Ondine*, both of which she danced in London. She performed the *Pas de Quatre* with three other dancers, Marie Taglioni, Carlotta Grisi and Lucile Grahn, at the command of Queen Victoria. In 1847 she danced at the Paris Opera in *La Fille du Marbre*. She left Paris for Russia in 1855, and her dancing career came to an end when a piece of scenery caught fire and fell on her. Although she was not badly injured, the incident terrified her and caused a complete loss of confidence, so that she left the stage forever, spending the rest of her life as a shopkeeper in Paris.

see also ALMA, MARIE TAGLIONI

CHERRY

The cultivated cherry was brought to Rome by Lucullus in 89 BC from the south-west of the Black Sea, and was introduced into Britain by the Romans. The bright or dark red fruit is so sweet, sensual, delicious and attractive that the cherry is a symbol of virginity, and has been used in a sexual context throughout literature and art. It is called the fruit of paradise. Because the cherry tree bears its flowers before its leaves, it symbolises man born naked into the world without possessions, and foreshadows death whereby man returns naked and alone to the earth. In Japan the cherry stands for prosperity, and in China for hope, virility and feminine beauty.

CHRYSANTHEMUM

There are over two hundred species of chrysanthemum. In Greek the name means golden flower. The chrysanthemum became popular in China at the time of Confucius in about 500 BC, was known as the flower of life, and was introduced into Japan about eight hundred years later.

The chrysanthemum became the floral emblem of Japan, and its image is found throughout Japanese culture, in all art forms. The image on the Japanese flag was not strictly speaking a sun, but a chrysanthemum. A chrysanthemum festival was held annually on 9 November in the emperor's garden. It was a festival which had a severe, ceremonial and religious character, following strict rituals. The Order of the Chrysanthemum was the highest imperial honour. The last of the festivals was held in 1886 when an imperial edict abolished many ancient court rituals and forms of dress. After this the chrysanthemum festival became a more simple flower show.

Whole gardens in Japan are still devoted to the cultivation of chrysanthemums, and in 1911 the imperial garden contained examples of every known variety. The Japanese word for chrysanthemum is *kiku*.

The first chrysanthemums cultivated in Europe were imported into France from China in 1789, but were not particularly popular until one of Napoleon's soldiers, after the Battle of Waterloo, retired to Toulouse and began to grow them, giving them names such as Bonaparte, Austerlitz, Rivoli. The popularity of the flower grew, and in 1851 at the Great Exhibition in London there were millions of them in pots. In Italy and France today the chrysanthemum is used principally as a flower of death, and decorates graves on the feast of All Souls.

Chrysanthemums are used in folk medicine for coughs and insomnia, and kidney and gall bladder complaints, but are also poisonous and have often proved fatal to women when used to induce abortions. The petals can be used in cooking, and dried flowers can also be used to make a tea. Pyrethrin, found in some types, is a useful insecticide and is harmless to humans and pets.

CINDERELLA

If somebody asked me to say, in a couple of sentences, what 'Cinderella' was all about, I'd go for the slipper. It's one of the great old shoe stories, the great foot stories. There are as many versions of the story of Cinderella as there are seeds in a pomegranate. There are a lot of

Cinderella stories. I notice there's one in which the girl lost a slipper of red velvet braided with pearls.

In the imagination of everyone who has seen or somehow been touched by the Cinderella of Walt Disney, the story is crystalised into the elements and values and images set down by the studio. But the details of this story as they surface in different and ancient cultures are a source of fascination to me, and I imagine that these elements are somehow deep in the blood of all people (I don't know how else to express it) and are partly responsible for the grip the story had on Walt Disney himself, and for the grip he was able to get on his audience with his telling of the tale. The oldest version of Cinderella I know of is Chinese, written late in the ninth century:

Long, long ago, before the Ch'in dynasty, before the Han dynasty, there lived in the caves of South China a cave-master called Wu. (I like that man's name.) When his wife died he remarried, and his daughter Yeh-hsien was ill-treated by his new wife, who also had a daughter. The stepmother favoured her own daughter. (So there you have the beginning of the story with the death of the mother.)

Yeh-hsien had a pet fish which was two inches long when she caught it, but which had grown to be more than ten feet long, and this fish used to pillow its head on the riverbank where Yeh-hsien sat. (I imagine the fish was red. You don't need much imagination, really.)

One time the stepmother disguised herself as Yeh-hsien and when the fish put its head on the riverbank, she killed it and cooked it and ate it. As Yeh-hsien moaned with terrible grief, a strange man with long hair and rough, coarse garments descended from the sky to comfort her. He told her that the bones of her fish had been buried under a dunghill, and that if she gathered them up and kept them in her room she had only to pray to them and they would respond to her every wish.

It was festival time, and Yeh-hsien was left at home to tend to the fruit trees while her stepmother and stepsister went off to enjoy themselves. The girl prayed to the bones of the fish and she was granted a cloak made from the feathers of kingfishers, and a pair of golden shoes. She threw on the cloak and slipped on the shoes, which were a perfect fit, and arrived at the festival looking like a princess rather than the ragged waif who had been left in the orchard. But her stepmother looked at her suspiciously, and she feared she had been discovered. So she fled, and as she did so one of the golden slippers flew off and was left behind. A man collected the shoe and sold it to T'o-han, the ruler of an island kingdom.

T'o-han was entranced by the tiny shoe, and he wished to find its owner. He ordered that every woman in the district should try the shoe, confident that the foot that fit the slipper would match it in beauty, and that the owner of the foot would be suitable to be his bride. The golden shoe was light as down and made no sound, even when treading on stone. It was at least an inch too small for the smallest foot to be found. T'o-han sent his servants out far and wide beyond the island kingdom, and eventually Yeh-hsien was found. When she put on the shoe she was seen to be as beautiful as a heavenly being, and she and the king were wed.

Let it also be recorded that the stepmother and her daughter had been, in the meantime, killed by flying stones.

*

There now, that was nice, wasn't it? I love the phallic fish that embodies the spirit of the dead mother—so powerful and brilliant. I imagine the lovely Chinese girl in her awful old grey dress, lying on the riverbank talking to the great huge red fish that's got its head out of the water resting on the weeds. Have I seen that picture painted on a teacup? Possibly. Or maybe on a screen somewhere in my travels. I must say the image of the stepmother catching the fish and taking it home and cooking it and eating it is a terrible one. Bones are interesting, so talismanic. People keep their children's teeth, sometimes, or the ashes of their loved ones, or locks of hair, but you don't run into many people who treasure a bone. You'd have to ask the undertaker to arrange for the severing of a finger or something. It could catch on. I daresay if you can donate living parts to other people, you ought to be able to donate a bone to your nearest and dearest, if they want it. Perhaps this is a grisly idea. Why is a hare's foot lucky? Samuel Pepys, you know, kept the foot of a hare in his pocket as a cure for indigestion. And the animal is a great old symbol of fertility, and all symbols of fertility are symbols of good luck. Why the foot? Well, it's a handy little thing to chop off and neaten up and dangle from a pin. But it's also the part of the body that speeds the creature along, the part that has been in touch with the earth.

But to return to the thing that really fascinates people about Cinderella—the glass slipper. Not gold, not kid, not silk, not satin, not red velvet—glass.

This was the fabulous inspiration of Charles Perrault, who collected the story in 1697 and was the first writer we know of to speak of a 'little glass slipper'. I have of course heard the theory that the slipper was really made from fur, and that Perrault mistook the word for fur for the word for glass. Well, be that as it may, he was certainly onto a good thing.

It's such an incredibly romantic and dazzling idea, a tiny slipper of clear and sparkling glass. She must have had nice little toes, that Cinderella, smooth pink baby toes, or else nobody would want to look down at her glass footwear. Forgetting about gold shoes for the moment, consider the other materials I mentioned just now—kid, silk, satin, velvet—they are all so soft, so forgiving, so very flexible. But glass? It is a daring and absurd material from which to make a shoe. How could you walk, dance, run down the stairs in glass shoes? The reasons for the rightness and the attraction of the idea of the glass slipper are deep, but not really unexpected.

If the slipper is glass you will be able to see the foot through the shoe, the smallness and perfection of the foot. The shoe will attract you with its sparkle. And the brittle medium will symbolise the maidenhood of the wearer, will remind you that there is something here to be broken. The shoe, a glass vagina with a virginal hymen, seems to exert a strange and powerful attraction over the imagination. The fairytale slipper is accepted as a solution to the question of finding the right bride. When the girl puts her foot into the slipper, the gesture suggests the man slipping his penis into her vagina. When the prince finds that Cinderella's foot fits the glass slipper, he knows and a reader knows that his penis will fit her vagina. You would expect that Freud would have had something to say about this, and he did. In dreams the shoe represents the vagina, placed in the unconscious mind early in life partly because the child in the low cradle, the child playing on the floor, sees its mother's foot as the base for the centre of its world.

Petra's fairytales in the encyclopaedia were taken from the Brothers Grimm, and these versions of the stories, or the versions of Perrault, were the narratives written into the blood of the children of European countries and colonies for generations. Walt Disney has made a big difference to all this; he has extracted from both the Grimms and Perrault the elements that appealed to his moral and commercial sense and has, with his powerful images and songs, implanted his versions of the stories into the hearts of children all over the world.

If instead of sticking with the version of Cinderella's story that was made by Walt Disney, you read a translation of the version set down by Jacob and Wilhelm Grimm, you will get something like the following account. You will notice that the slipper is described as being golden, by which I take it to mean made from golden cloth:

The wife of a rich man was dying and she called to her bedside her only daughter, saying, 'Be good, my child, and when I am in heaven I will look down and be near you.'

Every day the girl went to her mother's grave and wept. Winter snow spread a white sheet over the earth, and by the time the spring sun had drawn it off, the man had taken another wife who had two daughters, beautiful to look at but black-hearted. (These girls are known to people these days as the ugly sisters, but the Grimms had them, externally at least, good-looking. Perrault said that

Cinderella was a hundred times more beautiful than they, but never actually called them ugly. From Perrault also came the fairy godmother and the pumpkin coach and the midnight curfew.)

These daughters and their mother forced the girl to wear an old grey dress and wooden shoes, and to work hard from morning till night, carrying wood, lighting the fires, cooking, washing and cleaning. She slept by the hearth among the cinders, and came to be called Cinderella.

One day, when the father was going to the fair, he asked all three daughters what gifts he might bring back for them. The two stepsisters asked for beautiful dresses and pearls, but Cinderella asked only for the first branch that might knock against her father's hat on his way home. When he brought her a branch from a hazel bush she planted the branch on her mother's grave and watered it with her tears. It grew, and a little white bird came always to perch on the tree, and whenever Cinderella asked for something, the bird would give her whatever she wanted.

By and by, the king organised a three-day festival to which all the beautiful women of the country were invited so that the prince could choose a wife. The three sisters were invited, but the stepmother forbade Cinderella to go, saying she was unworthy of such an honour. Cinderella begged to be allowed to go, and so the stepmother set her a task. She threw a dish of lentils into the ashes and said that if Cinderella could separate the lentils from the ashes in two hours, she could go to the ball that night.

Cinderella summoned the little white bird, who gathered the pigeons and turtledoves and all manner of birds beneath the sky, who descended and went pick, pick, pick until all the lentils were gathered in a dish. When the stepmother saw this she was amazed and furious, and said that Cinderella must now pick two dishes of lentils out of the ashes in one hour, before she could go. The birds once again came to Cinderella's aid, but the stepmother once again refused to honour her promise, saying this time that since Cinderella had no proper dress or shoes she would be a disgrace. And the mother and her two daughters set off for the ball, leaving Cinderella in tears by the ashes.

Then Cinderella hurried to her mother's grave beneath the hazel tree and she called for the white bird, who quickly clothed her in a gown of silver and gold and put on her feet tiny slippers of silk embroidered with silver thread.

She appeared at the ball where people, including her own family, believed she must be a foreign princess. As soon as the prince set eyes on her he asked her to dance. She danced with him all night and when she decided to go home the prince followed her, but she evaded him and ran first to the pigeon house and then to the hazel tree where she changed back into her ragged clothes and left the ball-gown on her mother's grave. The bird took the dress and shoes away.

The prince saw her enter the pigeon house and called to her father to chop it down. The father brought an axe and chopped it down, but the lovely girl was nowhere to be seen.

The next night Cinderella appeared at the ball in an even more beautiful gown and slippers, and the prince once again danced with her and once again she ran off, this time hiding in a beautiful tall tree from which hung the most magnificent pears. She clambered as nimbly as a squirrel and the prince could not see her among the leaves. The father brought the axe and chopped down his lovely pear tree, but there was no sign of the girl.

On the third day of the festival Cinderella went to her mother's grave again and the white bird dressed her in the most magnificent gown ever seen. Her slippers were golden. When the people at the palace saw her they were struck dumb with astonishment. In anticipation of her escaping from him forever, the prince had the staircase smeared with pitch so that when Cinderella rushed off into the night, her left slipper became stuck on the stair and she left it behind. The prince picked up the slipper and saw that it was small and dainty and all golden.

The prince said, 'No one shall be my wife but she whose foot this golden slipper fits.' He would search the kingdom for his bride.

When he came to Cinderella's father's house, the sisters were eager to try on the slipper. The eldest took the slipper into her room, where she discovered that the slipper was too small. Her mother handed her a knife saying, 'Cut off your toe. When you are queen you will have no need to go on foot.' So she cut off her toe and put on the slipper and the prince accepted her as his bride and rode away with her on his horse. (Such was his determination to match the slipper to the foot, he was prepared to overlook the discrepancy in the appearances of Cinderella and her stepsister. Weird.)

As they were passing the grave of Cinderella's mother, two pigeons appeared and began to sing.

Turn and peep, turn and peep.
There's blood within the shoe,
The shoe it is too small for her
The true bride waits for you.

So the prince looked at the blood that trickled from the shoe and took the girl home and asked her sister to try on the shoe. This sister cut off her heel and forced her foot into the shoe and rode off with the prince. However, once again the pigeons warned the prince and he saw the blood, and how it had stained the girl's stocking bright red.

(The golden slipper must have been in a terrible state by now. At least a glass slipper could be washed clean.)

So he took her home and asked if there were any other daughters in the house. He insisted that Cinderella must try the slipper. She washed her hands and face, sat on a stool, and removed her wooden clog. She put on the golden slipper which fitted like a glove on her tiny naked foot. And when she stood up the prince recognised her and hailed her as his true bride. He rode off with her, and when they passed the hazel tree the pigeons hailed her also and then they alighted on her shoulders.

At the wedding of Cinderella and the prince the pigeons flew down and pecked out the eyes of the two stepsisters, who were thus punished with blindness for their wickedness and falsehood.

see also FOOT, GLASS, TASK

COUCH

Freud's patients reclined on a *chaise longue* which was covered with an oriental rug, the designs on which formed

a complex series of mandalas. Freud sat in a squat green velvet armchair behind the patient's head, listening to the patient's story.
see also MANDALA

CYANE

When Pluto ran off in his chariot with Proserpine, more often known to us by her Greek name of Persephone, he came to the pool where the nymph Cyane lived. Cyane rose up from the water and recognised Proserpine, who had been drugged and abducted. She tried to block the way by stretching out her arms, but Pluto urged his horse on and flung his sceptre into the depths of Cyane's pool. It struck the bottom and opened up the earth so that Pluto was able to drive his chariot forward and down. Cyane, defeated, lamented for Proserpine and for the defiling of her pool. She nursed within herself a sorrow and a wound that nothing and nobody could heal. She wasted away with weeping and dissolved into the waters. Her limbs could be seen melting, her bones growing flexible, and the nails on her fingers and toes dissolving into nothing. Her hair, her fingers and her feet disappeared and she began to be transformed into clear, chill water. Her shoulders, her back, her sides and her breasts faded, until finally, instead of bright blood, water flowed through her softened veins, and nothing at all remained for anyone to hold but the running waters of the stream.

ELEUSINIAN MYSTERIES

These took place outside Athens in ancient times and were a dramatic reconstruction of the story of Persephone, who was drugged and abducted and taken to the underworld by Pluto, returning to earth later with a son conceived during her time with Pluto.

The people taking part in the mysteries underwent a long period of initiation during which they fasted and were celibate. Just before the performance of the drama, the people drank wine mixed with ergot from fungus on barley or rye. They went into trances and experienced hallucinations and crawling sensations of the skin, which were taken to be mystical experiences relating to the religious story of the drama.

As early as 600 BC the people of Assyria spoke of a 'noxious pustule in the ear of the grain', but the first well-documented record of the condition known as ergotism comes from the tenth century and refers to the 994 outbreak in France when 40 000 people died from this poison. The symptoms were twitching accompanied by numbness in hands and feet. There was intense pain, and there were burning sensations and epileptic seizures. Limbs became black and gangrenous, and victims believed that the heat they felt had burned them. Saint Anthony the Hermit, a saint with the power to protect people from fire, was invoked and the phenomenon became known as Saint Anthony's Fire. The outbreak of what was thought to be witchcraft in 1691 in Salem, Massachusetts, was probably in reality an outbreak of ergotism.
see also HALLUCINATION

FAITH, HOPE AND CHARITY
There is a Roman legend telling of how these daughters of Sophia were put to the sword during the reign of the

Emperor Hadrian in the first century AD. Their names are commonly given in the Greek: Agape, Elpis and Pistis. When they died they were twelve, ten and nine years old.

FERRAGAMO, SALVATORE (1898–1960)
Ferragamo was born into a peasant family in southern Italy. In 1927 he established his own shoemaking company in Florence, and rose to become one of the finest and most admired and beloved makers of shoes in the world.

As a child he was fascinated by the work of the village cobbler, and when his sisters were in need of proper white shoes to replace their wooden clogs for their first Communion, Salvatore borrowed all the tools and materials and made for the girls his first pairs of shoes.
see also SHOEMAKER

FOOT
The bound feet of Chinese women, thought to resemble the flowers of the golden lotus, were known as heavenly blossoms, the aim of binding the foot being to reduce its length to a third of its natural size. The ancient custom of foot-binding was carried out on girls of high-ranking families, small feet being more prized than any other mark of beauty. A pretty face was given by nature, but a small foot was the result of personal scarifice and effort. Poets exhorted men to take the heavenly blossoms in the palm of the hand and marvel at their exquisite and breathtaking beauty.

When a girl was about six years old she was tied to a chair by a female relative. Her feet were soaked, often in urine, in order to soften them and then her four smaller toes were bent under and tied to the soles of her feet. A bandage of silk or cotton ten feet long and two inches wide was wound over the four little toes, folding them right over, but leaving the big toe free. Next the bandage was wound around the heel in order to pull the toes together. Then the bandage was wrapped tightly round and round the foot so that the foot could not be opened. The arch of the foot would eventually break. Elaborately embroidered silken slippers were then slipped on over the bandages, and under the bandages the feet would gradually rot and give off a terrible smell. The slippers were of red, green or blue, the preferred colour being red. The slippers worn to bed were always red.

Girls were made to walk on their crushed feet. Every two weeks, a new and smaller pair of slippers was put on. Sometimes the little girls would crawl for years on their hands and knees to escape the pain of walking on their feet, and sleeping was difficult because of the pain. By the age of twelve, the feet were finished, and no longer painful. A great deal of care had to be lavished on the foot for the rest of the woman's life. Bathing, and paring of thickened skin and cutting of toenails had to be done regularly and with exceptional care. By the time the feet were finished the toes were turned right under and two fingers could be pushed into the cleft between the heel and the rest of the foot.

The foot was known as a lotus hook and became central to the sexual practices of Chinese men. There exists a nexus between the deformed foot and sexual desire.

The girls grew up to be crippled and unable to move naturally or do ordinary things. They had to shuffle and to walk with the aid of sticks. They were unable to leave home unless accompanied, and so they were completely dependent on their husbands, who also used the women's feet as sexual organs of great erotic value. Men could easily inflict pain by squeezing the bound feet; a man could take the whole foot into his mouth; and if the soles of the two feet were placed together, an orifice was formed. The woman's constant unnatural posture also altered the shape of her pelvis, and was believed to give her vagina wonderful extra folds, like gates and doors to a secret sanctuary. This belief is invalid but very widespread, and remains in the sexual–psychological fantasy of footbinding. Even today, long after footbinding has been abandoned (it died out completely by about the 1940s), there is a certain nostalgia for the return of the bound foot in China. A woman with bound feet is an inferior, an accessory to a man, and is a plaything, a toy, to be pitied and used. Very, very desirable, to some.

The six-year ritual of the binding of the feet was carried out by women on girls in order to prepare the girls for the pleasure of men. The mystery of the whole process of binding was part of its appeal, speaking always of the intimacy and inaccessibility of the boudoir. The tiny foot, just visible beneath the woman's trousers, tantalised a man's fancy and transferred his thoughts upward to the vulva, which was the forbidden Jade Gate. And the size and fragility of the feet aroused in men feelings of lust coupled with pity. The names given to women, particularly to concubines and palace dancers, reflected the attitudes men had to the women's feet. Names such as Moon Immortal, Golden Pearl, Golden Jade, Red Treasure and Jade Pavilion.

The origins of footbinding are variously described by different authorities, but the practice had begun by the tenth century during the Southern T'ang dynastic rule of Li Yu, who was a king and a poet and who controlled one region of China before the Sung dynasty brought about reunification. Li Yu had a theatrical golden lotus constructed, and in this his favourite concubine, Lovely Maiden, would dance. The lotus was as high as a tall man, with a bright carmine centre and decorated with pearls. Lovely Maiden wrapped her feet with white silk to resemble the hooves of a little deer, or the tips of the new moon, and then she danced in the centre of the golden flower, rising and whirling like a cloud.

This making of a golden lotus was a tradition brought from India and was based on an old legend of the Lady Deerfoot. A prince was once bathing in a pure stream when a female deer that had also come to drink at the water gave birth to a girl-child, who was beautiful beyond measure and who had the feet of a deer. The prince adopted her as his daughter, and then took her as his wife. Wherever the child walked she left impressions of lotus flowers on the ground beneath her. She bore a thousand sons, and each one was seated on a leaf of a thousand-leafed lotus flower.

see also LOTUS, URINE

GLASS

A translucent and transparent noncrystalline substance that behaves as a solid although some of its properties are liquid. It was known in the third millennium BC and there are in existence glass objects from the eighteenth Egyptian dynasty, which ruled from 1570 to 1320 BC. Glass was first used for windows in around 100 AD. All glass-making methods use sand and fire. Glass shatters easily, and the broken fragments are sharp and dangerous.

GREEN LANGUAGE

Birds are believed to be possessed of prophetic wisdom acquired in part from their presence in the air, from where they can see past and future and also the paradoxes of life. Green language and the ancient language of the birds are one and the same, and this is a tongue of riddle and paradox, employed in part in the poetry of the troubadours, a poetry which traces its inspiration to the wisdom of the Sufi in which the Beloved is symbolic and spiritual. In troubadour poetry the dame is both real *and* spiritual, an inspiring glorious creature and also a presence. The spiritual aspect of her guides the lover and protects him. She is what Jung calls the archetypal content, the anima, which will, in her positive aspect, lead the man on his inner journey of individuation.

HALLUCINATION

This is a vision brought on by the mental state induced by chemicals which, in non-toxic doses, produce changes in mood, perception and thought. Hallucinogens can elicit profound psychic changes in body image and personality while allowing the subject to retain consciousness. The subject is in a type of dream world where perceptions of space, time, colour, sound, touch, smell and taste appear to be altered, and where there is no dulling or clouding of the senses.

HOFFMANN, E.T.A. (1776–1822)
The author of the stories which inspired Offenbach's opera *The Tales of Hoffmann,* which is also well known as a movie made with Moira Shearer by Michael Powell and Emeric Pressburger in 1951. Hoffmann died when he was forty-six from a paralysing illness which caused him to die slowly from the feet up. Hoffmann wrote a great deal of music as well as stories, his tales prefiguring the work of Edgar Allan Poe and Guy de Maupassant in their use of creatures and situations born of a wild and dark imagination, deriving from hallucinations, fears and nightmares. The motifs of alcohol, fire and of the unknown, unconscious connections that exist between people run through his work. Some of the dreamlike, hallucinatory aspects of his stories suggest a link (this is completely imaginary on my part) with the work of Albert Hofmann.
see also ALBERT HOFMANN, MOIRA SHEARER

HOFMANN, ALBERT (1906–)
The author of several books on psychedelics, Hofmann synthesised LSD in 1943, and in the late 1950s recognised the close relationship between the structure of LSD and that of ololiuqui, from the seeds of the morning glory. He has studied the place of hallucinogens in religious ceremonies, including the Ancient Greek Eleusinian mysteries and Aztec and American Indian cults.

The images roused by the chemicals of Hofmann's research could easily belong in *Tales of Hoffmann.*
see also ELEUSINIAN MYSTERIES, E.T.A. HOFFMANN, LSD

HOOPOE

The hoopoe is the size of a thrush, has black wings striped with white. It has a crown of cinnamon feathers tipped with black, said to have been a reward from King Solomon. The story goes that when Solomon was walking in the desert the hoopoe hovered over him, casting a shadow and thus protecting him from the sun. The king gave the bird its heart's desire, which was a golden crown. However, the crown only had the effect of making the hoopoe the subject of jealous raids, and so the bird returned to Solomon who converted the crown into the feathered crest.

The hoopoe was a symbol in ancient Egypt of filial piety and appears on the sceptre of Horus, who waged war on his father's murderers. In Arabia the hoopoe also stood for medicine because its heart and head were believed in popular myth to possess therapeutic and aphrodisiac properties. It is also said to signify fornicators and adulterers.

There is a widespread but erroneous belief that the hoopoe builds its nest from its own excrement. The fact is that the adult birds don't remove from the nest the droppings of the chicks.

see also SOLOMON

LIVRY, EMMA (1842–1862)

French ballet dancer. See notes on Fanny Cerito and Marie Taglioni.

LOTUS

The sacred flower of Buddhism, the lotus is a symbol of purity because it develops beneath the mud of the pool and rises above the surface of the water to burst forth with pristine, unstained blooms.

Members of the Hill House Brethren regularly formed a magic circle in order to chant in English the Tibetan Buddhist mantra 'Hail to the jewel in the lotus'.

The blue lotus produces an hallucinogen.

LSD

> LSD? Nothing much happened, but I did get the distinct impression that some birds were trying to communicate with me.
>
> W.H. AUDEN

The lysergic acid amides are among the most potent producers of hallucination known. Lysergic acid was first synthesised in 1934, and in 1938 Albert Hofmann synthesised lysergic acid diethylamide when he was working on ergot. The hallucinations he experienced resembled those he had had when experimenting with ololiuqui from the seeds of the morning glory, as used by the Aztecs in religious ceremonies characterised by hilarity and hallucinations and unearthly visions and experiences.

One of the most infamous experiments with LSD took place at the Oklahoma City zoo. In August 1962 Dr L.J. West administered three grams of LSD to Tusko, a ten-year-old male elephant weighing 7000 pounds. Five minutes later, after collapsing in an episode resembling madness, Tusko choked to death, spasms closing his throat and causing anoxia. The purpose of the experiment had been to examine the effect of LSD on the brain of the elephant, which resembles a human brain but is much larger. Dr West warned doctors to take particular care in the administration of LSD to human subjects.

When Aldous Huxley was near death he took a dose of one gram of LSD and died quickly in a peaceful and possibly ecstatic state.

see also ALBERT HOFMANN, HALLUCINATION

MANDALA

This is the name given to a compact mystical and symbolic diagram, complex forms of which have appeared in art throughout human history, and which appear also in nature. It is based on the 8x8 squares which are the order of the celestial world expressed on earth, or on the 9x9 squares which lead to and enclose the universe. The forms discovered in the Mandelbrot sets, generated by computer to produce fractals, are also mandalas, suggesting that these forms occur so frequently in human expression because they are a fundamental shape of creation.

The concentric structure of the mandala is used an aid to meditation throughout the world's great religions. The design suggests the passage from state to state, from the material world to the spiritual world of perfection and eternal peace. Mandalas are to be seen in the ancient art of the native people of Australia; in Tibetan, Indian, Buddhist, Hindu, Christian, Arabic, Hebrew works; and in the drawings of children, psychics, and psychiatric patients. Carl Jung considered the mandala to be particularly revealing of the inner state of his patients, and to be very useful as an aid to integration of the spirit.

The mandala is also an image of the whole world, the enclosure of sacred space and penetration to the sacred centre. The alternating squares of the pattern depict the dual but complementary principles of the universe, and the whole diagram is an enactment of the cosmic drama, and a pilgrimage of the human soul. It is the centre of power and is a safe area, a temenos from hostile influences. The centre of the mandala is a sky door, giving access to heaven.

The rose windows in Christian churches frequently follow a mandala pattern, and in the Hindu religion the whole temple is built as a mandala, symbolising the universe and having gates or doors to the four cardinal points.

The lotus flower is frequently represented as part of a mandala, and is known as the eight-petalled lotus of Smashana-Kali, goddess of the cremation ground and of resurrection after death.

see also LOTUS

MANUAL

Each member of the Hill House Brethren had a loose-leaf volume called the Manual which contained the teachings of Irving and many quotations from other great spiritual writings, such as the Bhagavadgita and the Upanishads and the *Song of Songs* and the Book of Revelation, as well as words of poets and philosophers from many cultures and eras considered to be possessed of insight. Brethren were exhorted to imitate the obedience and poverty and manual labour of Saint Benedict and the Desert Fathers. Irving was particularly fond of Sufism, and liked to tell short Sufi anecdotes with a mysterious smile on his face. This smile was something both he and Petra had perfected to mask the fact that they were talking nonsense, and to suggest that their knowledge, insight and state of illumination were vastly superior to those of the other Brethren. It always amazed me that nobody saw through those eerie smiles, but nobody did. Brethren could add to their own Manuals by putting in more pages, and as Petra's teachings became more and more dominant, there were many pages devoted to her words.

A rich new element Petra brought to the Manual was the references to and quotations from folktales, which imparted to the lives of the Brethren a familiar yet deeply mysterious note of the good and evil values of ancient fairytale and folk wisdom.

MERMAID

The earliest recorded ancestor of the mermaid was Oannes the sea god, who was worshipped in Babylon around 5000 BC. The sea was the source of life, and Oannes rose from the waves at dawn and returned to the sea in the evening. He was a source of light and life, and instructed the people in the arts and the sciences. His whole body resembled that of a fish with the head of a man. Sometimes he was represented in art as a man wearing a fish cloak, but gradually he developed the form of a man with the tail of a fish. He symbolised the positive aspects of the ocean, whereas Atargatis (a female counterpart of Oannes), who was a goddess worshipped a bit later on in Syria and Israel, symbolised the destructive forces of the sea. Atargatis murdered her lover, abandoned her child, and threw herself into the sea from which she emerged as half-fish, half-woman.

Many of the traditional attributes of Aphrodite are fused in popular legends of mermaids. These include the long hair, which signifies fertility; the comb, meaning the female pudenda; and the mirror, suggesting her vanity and coldness. Added to these details was the seductive and fatal nature of the mermaid's song. The Greek sirens metamorphosed from bird-women to fish-women and became the prototype of the singers who lured men to their deaths. Before they were birds they were the women who failed to protect Persephone (Proserpine) from being abducted. The mermaid of twentieth-century imagination is the immediate descendant of the mediaeval temptress who symbolised the lusts of the flesh as delineated by the Christian church. They became emblems of vice, voluptuous harlots, representing the base desires which stand between a man and his chance of salvation.

Clement of Alexandria in his *Exhortation to the Heathen* said: 'Sail past the song for it works death. Exert your will, and you have overcome ruin. Bound to the wood of the Cross you shall be free from destruction. The Word of God will be your pilot, and the Holy Spirit will bring you to anchor in the haven of Heaven.'

The church sometimes attempted to reform stranded mermaids. And there was a mediaeval theory that the sea contained the counterpart of every creature living on the land. Once a mer-bishop was captured in Poland.

The mermaids had no souls. One way of acquiring a soul was to marry a mortal, as in the nineteenth-century story of Ondine, written by de la Motte Fouque, and told in the ballet which was first performed at the Royal Opera House, Covent Garden, in 1958. The man who married Ondine ended up living with her under the sea. The mermaid of Iona was unable to relinquish the sea for the promise of a soul and she wept for this fact so bitterly that her tears formed the green–grey pebbles on the Ionian seashore.

Sightings of mer-people have persisted throughout naval history, and in 1723 a royal commission was set up in Denmark to investigate the truth of such sightings. A merman was seen in the sea beside the very boat in which the commission was sailing. And there are people today who claim to be descended from the union of a mermaid and a man. A man in West Africa recently met a mermaid on a beach and was persuaded by her to rob his employer. She offered to double the money for ten percent commission, but he never saw the money again. In the nineteenth century there was a lot of interest in folk myth and heritage, and the systematic recording of traditional material gained a popularity which has continued to gather momentum.

In *Le Ballet Comique de la Reine* Catherine de' Medici used some of the mystery and drama of the sea-people by surrounding the queen in the ballet with sea-horses, tritons and mermaids. René Magritte and Paul Delvaux saw the possibilities of the mermaid figure in surrealist art. Post-Freudian theory delineates the mermaid as the personification of the concealed desires of the unconscious mind. She symbolises the urge to return to the womb, and demonstrates castration anxiety. J.K. Huysmans, John Keats, Oscar Wilde, H.G. Wells and

Matthew Arnold wrote literary versions of mermaid stories. And Hans Christian Andersen's tale 'The Little Mermaid' is perhaps the most well known of all mermaid stories today. It has, like most powerful folktales, been imported into the dream factory of Walt Disney where much of its meaning has been removed. Like Snow White and Cinderella, the Little Mermaid's legend has been defined for the people of the late twentieth century; the mermaid has been captured in the net of Hollywood and she may, consequently, have reached the end of her developmental swim.

Before I tell the story of 'The Little Mermaid' more or less as Hans Christian Andersen invented it, I think it is worth reflecting on Andersen's fascination with feet and crippling. The son of a cobbler, Andersen expressed some of his deepest fears and feelings with reference to the function of the feet. The castration image dominates in 'The Red Shoes', where the girl begs the woodsman to chop off her feet with his axe. She kisses the axe and watches her feet in her blood-red shoes dance away from her, leaving her a bleeding, footless beggar. The sexuality of women is represented by Andersen as thoroughly grotesque and terrifying. His Little Mermaid acquires human legs in order to follow her human prince, but the price of the cleaving of her tail is the cutting out of her tongue and the sensation, with every step, that she is walking on sharp swords. Both stories are inexorable tragedies, although Andersen gives them a sentimental overlay of a particularly weird kind of Christian redemption. Although the movie *The Red Shoes* is a far cry from the Andersen story, it retains the hideous sacrifice a woman has to make in order to follow her own truth. I have always found it strange and sinister that this movie was the inspiration for thousands and thousands of girls all over the world to take up ballet. Girls—such masochists, such willing victims, martyrs, lambs to the slaughter, mermaids ready to cleave their own tails, cut out their own tongues to follow the chimera of romance and desire. The stories should be morality tales, grim warnings, but they are apparently seductive scripts to be followed and obeyed. The masochist's thrill. Complex stuff.

Petra was, from an early age, transfixed by the story 'The Little Mermaid', which she read over and over from one of the old books in the junk room at the back of the house. She found the strains of cruelty and irony that run through this story exquisite; she would weep for the mermaid, and then return in fascination again and again to the images of cutting out the tongue, of walking on swords. The mermaid's age of fifteen became a key age in Petra's treatment of the children at New Haven, as if the idea of a fifteen-year-old girl had lodged itself in her imagination. Fifteen was the age when the girls at New Haven would be tested and tempted and shown to be either suitable or unsuitable for life in the adult community of Brethren.

The simple plot outline of the story is familiar to many readers: for the love of the prince the mermaid gives up her tail for legs, paying the price of her tongue so that she is rendered mute. Her sacrifice proves useless as she is unable to speak and identify herself to the prince, who will never know that she is the one who rescued him from the shipwreck and saved his life with her love. The plot is one thing, but the strange details in the telling give the story a compelling power which has gripped the imagination of readers since the story was first written.

'The Little Mermaid' was a story that Petra read frequently to the girls at New Haven, along with, among other European folktales, 'The Red Shoes'. The sexual pathology of mutilated and bleeding feet resonated within Petra, and the same pathology is found in Petra's interest in the bound feet of Chinese women and in the crippled, bloody feet of ballerinas.

I think that in the narrative of 'The Little Mermaid' Andersen's intense discomfort with sexuality is dramatised more vividly than in any other of his major works. This story is, in my view, particularly unsuitable for telling to small children, yet such is the blindness and perversity of people, the story is widely considered to have been composed for the entertainment of children alone, to have little relevance for adult readers. This is one of the key anti-feminist stories, yet girls in the 1990s apparently still identify with the sacrificial life of the mermaid. What I mean is, you couldn't get away with writing this story today, because of feminism. But there is something deep in the story, and some answering chime in girls. Even now. Like Cyane, the mermaid dissolves into the water. Why would girls get so hooked by this twisted stuff? I realise that Petra was hung up on stories about mutilated feet, and that she loved to feed this image to her young flock. But she is far from the only adult who presents this fare to a child, places it on a child's pillow as a bedtime story. Nightmare, more like. Look carefully; here is the story 'The Little Mermaid' by Hans Christian Andersen, as retold by me, Beau:

Far out in the wide sea where the water is blue as the loveliest cornflower and clear as the purest crystal, where it is so deep that very, very many church towers must be heaped one upon another in order to reach from the lowest depth to the surface above, dwell the mer-people.

Now, you must not imagine that there is nothing but sand below the water: no indeed, far from it. Trees and plants of wondrous beauty grow there with stems and leaves so light that they are waved to and fro by the slightest motion of the water, as if they were living beings. Fishes great and small glide in and out among the branches, just as birds fly about among our trees.

Where the water is deepest stands the palace of the mer-king. The walls of this palace are of coral and the high pointed windows are of amber; the roof is composed of mussel shells which, as the billows pass over them, continually open and shut. This looks exceedingly pretty, since each of these mussel shells contains a number of bright, glittering pearls, even just one of which would be the most costly ornament in the diadem of a king in the upper world.

The mer-king who lived in this palace had been for many years a widower; his old mother managed the household affairs for him. She was on the whole a sensible sort of a woman, although very proud of her high birth and station on which account she wore twelve oysters on her tail, whilst the other inhabitants of the sea, even those of distinction, were allowed only six. In every other respect she merited unlimited praise, especially for the affection she showed to the six little princesses, her granddaughters. These were all very beautiful children. The youngest was the most lovely; her skin was as soft and delicate as a rose leaf, her eyes were of as deep a blue as the sea. Like all other mermaids she had no feet, her body ended in a tail like that of a fish.

The whole day long the children used to play in the spacious apartments of the palace where flowers grew out of the walls on all sides. When the great amber windows were opened fishes would swim into these apartments as swallows fly into rooms on the earth; but the fishes were bolder than swallows, they swam right up to the little mermaids, ate from their hands and allowed themselves to be caressed.

In front of the palace there was a large garden full of fiery red and dark blue trees whose fruit glittered like gold and whose flowers resembled the burning sun. The sand that formed the soil of the garden was the bright blue of the flames of sulphur; and a strangely beautiful blue was spread over the whole, so that one might have fancied oneself raised very high in the air, with the sky at once above and below. When the waters were quite still the sun might be seen looking like a purple flower out of whose cup streamed forth the light of the world.

Each of the little princesses had her own plot in the garden. One chose hers to be made in the shape of a whale, another had the figure of a mermaid, but the youngest had hers quite round like the sun and she planted in it only those flowers that were as red as the sun. She was a singular child, very quiet and thoughtful. While her sisters adorned themselves with all sorts of things that came out of a shipwreck, she asked for nothing but a beautiful white marble statue of a boy which had been found in the wreck. She put the statue in her garden and planted a red weeping willow by its side. The tree grew up quickly and let its long boughs fall upon the bright blue ground, where ever-moving shadows played in violet hues as if boughs and root were embracing.

Nothing pleased the little mermaid more than to hear about the world of humans living above the sea. She made her grandmother tell her everything she knew about ships, cities, people and land animals, and she was particularly fascinated when she heard that the flowers of the upper world had a lovely fragrance. The flowers of the sea were without scent, and indeed the little mermaid could only imagine what a scent was, as she and her sisters had no sense of smell. She learned that the woods were green, and that the fishes fluttering among the branches of the trees were brightly coloured and could sing with a loud clear voice.

'When you have attained your fifteenth birthday,' the grandmother said, 'you will be permitted to rise to the surface of the sea where you will sit in the moonlight in the clefts of the rocks and see the ships sail by, and learn to distinguish the things in the world of men.'

And so as the sisters turned fifteen they rose to the surface and gazed out at the world above the water. None of the mermaids longed so ardently for this time as the little mermaid. She longed to be released from childish restraint. Many a night she stood by the open window looking up through the clear blue water while the fishes leapt and played around her. She could see the sun and the moon; their light was pale, but in size they appeared to be larger than they appear to humans. If a shadow passed over them, the little mermaid knew it must be caused by a ship sailing by full of human beings, and she stretched forth her white hands towards the keel of the ship.

Finally the day came for the eldest mermaid to rise to the surface of the sea.

When she returned to the palace she had a thousand things to relate. Her chief pleasure had been to sit on a sandbank in the moonlight looking at the large town which lay on the coast. The lights of the town beamed like stars and she could hear music and the distant noise of carriages. She saw church towers and she heard the ringing of the bells. She longed to visit the town.

Her youngest sister listened attentively to her stories. And when the little one next stood at her open window she fancied she could hear church bells ringing in the distance.

Year by year the sisters rose to the surface and came back with tales of the upper world. The sky was tinged with gold. The clouds changed from red to violet and glided through the heavens. A flock of white swans swiftly flew over the water as the sun disappeared with a bright rosy light into the sea. The green hills were covered with woods and vineyards from among which rose houses and castles. Birds sang and the sun shone so brightly that the mermaids had to plunge beneath the water to cool their burning skin. The mermaids met children bathing in the sea, but always the children ran away at the sight of them, and the dogs barked in alarm.

When one of the mermaids turned fifteen it was winter and the sea was green with great icebergs, larger than cathedrals, floating in the water. The mermaid sat on the pearly icebergs and let the cold wind play in her hair. Huge sailing ships sailed past her, the sailors gasping with astonishment and fear when they saw her. A storm blew up and the mountains of floating ice beamed with a deep red glow. Lightning flashed and thunder filled the air. The ships all furled their sails and panic reigned on board, but the mermaid sat on her iceberg watching the blue zigzag of the flashing lights with fascination. She returned to the deep where she described the storm to her sisters.

Sometimes in the early evening the older sisters would join hands and rise up to the surface where they would swim in front of the ships, even in storms, and they would sing sweetly of the lives they led at the bottom of the ocean, entreating the sailors to join them for a life of underwater bliss. The sailors could not understand the words, heard nothing of the hidden beauty of the seabed. All they knew was that if their ships were wrecked they would drown, and none but dead men would enter the mer-king's palace.

The little mermaid could not join her sisters in the evenings, but would remain motionless and alone in her father's palace, longing for her birthday so that she could rise to the surface. She would have wept, but mermaids cannot weep.

At last her time arrived. Her grandmother wound in her hair a wreath of white lilies whose every petal was half a pearl. Eight large oysters were fastened to the little mermaid's tail in token of her high rank. She said this was uncomfortable, but her grandmother explained that discomfort was usual if one wished to look one's best in public. Willingly the mermaid would have given up all the splendour, would have exchanged her heavy crown of pearls for a circlet of red flowers from her garden. She rose up through the waves and broke the surface, light as a flake of foam.

The sun was sinking and the evening star was shining in the western sky. The sea was as smooth as a looking-glass.

A large ship with three masts lay on the still waters, one sail unfurled. Music and song floated out from the vessel, and when darkness fell hundreds of lamps burst into light. The mermaid swam up to the captain's cabin and when the ship was raised by the gentle motion of the water she could see through the portholes many richly dressed people. Among them was a handsome young prince who was celebrating his sixteenth birthday.

When the prince appeared on the deck hundreds of rockets were sent up into the sky, turning the night into sudden and brilliant day. The little mermaid was terrified and plunged beneath the waters. It seemed that all the stars were falling down upon her in fiery showers. Large suns and bright fish swam in the air.

It grew late, and still the little mermaid gazed through the porthole at the young prince. She could hear the sound of thunder as a terrible storm approached. The sails were furled, and the ship was tossed on enormous waves until its masts bent and its timbers cracked and the violent waters rushed in. In what seemed like an instant the ship broke up and sank beneath the waves. The mermaid watched in horror, seeking for the prince. At last she found him, exhausted and half drowned, and she seized hold of him and held him above the water all night long.

In the morning there was no trace of the ship, save for a few floating timbers. The sun rose like fire out of the sea. As she held the prince's head above the water the mermaid could see the dry land and the mountains glittering with snow. A green wood extended along the coast and at the entrance to the wood stood a convent where orange and lemon trees grew in the garden, and where an avenue of tall palm trees led up to the door. The water in the bay was smooth and deep, and under the cliffs were dry, firm sands. The mermaid swam into the cove, bringing the prince to the warm sand where she took care to place his head high, and to turn his face towards the sun.

Bells began to ring in the tall white chapel, and girls came out to walk among the orange trees. Leaving the prince upon the sand, the mermaid swam away from the shore, covering her face with foam so that she could not be seen. Out behind some rocks she kept vigil over the prince. The girls came forward and found the prince and carried him into the chapel. Nobody knew that it was the little mermaid who had saved the prince's life. Feeling sad that he was gone, she returned to her father's palace.

When her sisters asked her what she had seen in the upper world, she made no reply.

Each evening she rose to the place where she had left the prince. She saw the snow on the mountains melt, the fruits in the garden ripen, but the prince she never saw. In her garden under the sea, she would sit and gaze at the marble statue which reminded her of the prince, but she cared no longer for her flowers which grew up in wild luxuriance, covered the steps, and entwined their long tendrils among the boughs of the trees. Her whole garden became a bower in which she sat and contemplated the statue, thought about the prince.

Finally, she revealed the source of her sorrow to her sisters, who took her by the hand and swam with her to the shore just by the prince's palace.

The palace was made from bright yellow stones, and a flight of white marble steps led from the terrace down to the sea. A gilded cupola crowned the building, and white marble figures of beautiful youths and girls surrounded it. Through the diamond panes of the high arched windows could be seen magnificent apartments hung with silken curtains. The walls were adorned with huge looking-glasses and exquisite paintings. Fountains played in the centre of the hallway, sunbeams from the glass ceiling fell on the water.

The little mermaid would go each evening alone to the palace, would swim in the channel flowing under the balcony and would watch the prince. At night she would hear the fishermen speaking of the prince's noble life, and she would recall how his head had rested on her bosom, how she had kissed him as he lay unconscious in her arms. The world of humans became more and more desirable to her, and she began to discuss with her grandmother the differences between humans and the people of the sea.

'Do men when they are not drowned live forever?' she asked. 'Or do they die as we die?'

'They must die as we do,' her grandmother said, 'and their lives are much shorter than ours. They live for less than a hundred years; we live to be three hundred. And when we die we become foam on the face of the sea and are nothing but foam. However, humans whose bodies become dust have a part known as the immortal soul, and this soul rises up from the body and ascends to glorious unknown dwellings in the sky.'

'I would willingly give up my three hundred years to be human for a day and to die and let my soul rise to the unknown dwelling in the sky. Tell me, Grandmother, how can I obtain an immortal soul?'

'That is impossible,' said the grandmother, 'because of your tail. I will explain. Humans think our beautiful tails are hideous, and they use, instead of tails, two clumsy props of legs with feet at the ends. No man would ever fall in love with you. Mind you, if a man *did* love you and make you his wife, then his soul would flow into you and you would be able when you died to partake of immortal human bliss.'

The little mermaid could never forget the prince. She realised that if she was ever going to see him again, ever going to know him, she would need somehow to abandon her beautiful tail and walk on human legs. She decided to consult the enchantress, who had dark and powerful knowledge of many strange and wonderful things.

The mermaid left her garden and went to the foaming whirlpool beyond which dwelt the enchantress. Neither flowers nor sea-grass bloomed along the way, and the sand was grey and forbidding as the mermaid approached the eddying waters that led into the great abyss below. All the trees and bushes around the house were polyps, and they resembled hundred-headed serpents, their branches like slimy arms with fingers of worms, every member, from root to uttermost tip, ceaselessly moving and extending on all sides. Whatever they seized they fastened upon with a firm and terrible grip. The mermaid's heart beat with fear. She saw that many of the polyps had something in their grasp, held as firmly by a thousand little arms as if enclosed by iron bands. The whitened skeletons of human beings who had drowned grinned out at her. She would have turned and fled, but she was conscious always of her longing to walk with the prince. She thought also of the immortal soul which she would gain when once the prince professed his love for her. Her thoughts gave her renewed courage, and she bound up her long hair, crossed her delicate arms across her bosom, and swifter than a fish can glide she dashed through the trees which stretched their eager arms after her in vain.

Eventually she arrived at a slimy clearing where immense fat snails crawled and where stood a house built from human bones. Here sat the enchantress, the sea-witch, caressing a toad while snails crawled about her.

She prepared for the mermaid a potion and she instructed her to swim to land, sit on the shore, and swallow the liquid. Thereupon the mermaid's tail would shrink and split and form legs and feet.

'The transformation will be painful; you will feel as if a sharp knife passed through your body. All who look on you will say you are the most beautiful girl they have ever seen. You will retain the undulating movements of a mermaid, but every step you take will feel as though you are walking on the sharp edges of swords. Blood will flow from you. Can you endure this suffering? You can never again become a mermaid when once you have received human form. Should the prince wed another instead of you, you will become foam on the sea. Besides all this, I require payment. A slight thing. You have the sweetest voice of all who dwell in the sea, and this voice is your most priceless possession. I will have to cut out your tongue in payment for the potion.'

'But how will I charm the prince if you take my voice from me?' the mermaid asked in horror.

'With your graceful form, your modest gait, and your eloquent eyes. Now, put out your little tongue that I may cut it off.'

The sea-witch rubbed the cauldron with a mixture of crushed toads and snails. Then she scratched her own bosom and let the black blood trickle into the pot. She threw in every horrible thing, and a smoke rose from the cauldron, assuming grotesque and terrifying forms in the air. A moaning and a groaning rose from the cauldron and sounded like the weeping of a thousand crocodiles in a swamp. The magic drink became at length as clear as spring water. It was ready to drink. As she handed it to the mermaid in a bright crystal phial, she swiftly removed the mermaid's tongue with one stroke of a fine, curved blade. The mermaid's mouth was filled with blood and she knew she would never speak again.

With the phial glittering in her hand like a star, the mermaid stole into the palace garden where she plucked from the flower-bed of each of her sisters a flower in remembrance. She kissed her hand again and again in sad farewell to her old life, and she rose through the dark blue waters to the world above.

The sun had not yet risen when she arrived at the prince's palace and went up the marble steps. The moon still shone in the sky when the little mermaid drank the liquid from the phial. She felt the liquid run through her like a sharp knife and she fell down in a swoon. When the sun rose she awoke, feeling a burning pain in all parts of her body. Close to her stood the prince, his coal-black eyes fixed upon her in wonder and surprise. She looked down at her legs and she tried to cover her nakedness with her long, long hair. The prince asked her who she was and how she had come there, but she could not speak. The prince then led her by the hand into the palace, and as she walked she felt beneath her feet the edges of a thousand sharp swords. She bore the pain willingly, and all who saw her marvelled at the lightness of her undulating movements.

When she entered the palace rich clothes of linen and silk were brought and the mermaid began to dance. She hovered gracefully about the room, every step costing her excruciating pain. The prince was entranced and said that she should always be with him. He had a couch of velvet cushions prepared for her and placed in the anteroom of his apartment.

The prince had his tailors make a suit of male apparel for the mermaid, in order that she might accompany him on his rides through his kingdom. Her feet bled continually, but she only smiled. During the night she would walk down the marble staircase, splashing the pavement with her blood, and she would cool her burning feet in the waters of the sea, thinking of her sisters who dwelt beneath the waves.

One night her sisters rose to the surface and discovered her, and after this they visited her every night, bringing tales of how her family missed her and mourned for her. She listened to them mutely and waved to them and smiled sadly.

The prince looked upon her as a sweet and gentle child, and the thought of making her his wife did not enter his head. All the time she knew that unless she became his wife she would in the end be changed into foam; until she became his wife she would not attain an immortal soul. The prince took her in his arms and told her she was dear to him, told her how she was a substitute for the beautiful girl who had saved him from the shipwreck. He explained that this girl was the only one he would ever truly love, and that she belonged to the convent and could never marry. He did not realise that it was the mermaid who had really saved his life, that it was she to whom his life was owed. The mermaid decided to devote her silent life to him, in spite of the fact that he would never marry her. She would not have a soul but she would never leave him.

His parents arranged for him to marry the beautiful daughter of the neighbouring king. Taking the little mermaid in his arms, kissing her lips and playing with her hair, he told her he would prefer to marry her, but was not able. He did not see the anguish in her silent smile. The prince had never seen the princess, but he said he knew he could not love her.

The season of the wedding came, and bells and trumpets sounded in the city, soldiers marched in procession waving banners and bearing gleaming bayonets. There were balls and entertainments and at last the princess arrived. As if by a miracle, she was the very girl who had come down from the convent when the prince lay unconscious on the shore. Enraptured, the prince pressed her to his fast-beating heart.

The little mermaid knew that on the wedding day her own heart would break and she would return to the water as foam.

Flames burned in silver candlesticks on the cathedral altar; the bride and bridegroom joined hands while priests intoned the holy words that united them forever. The little mermaid, clad in silk and cloth of gold, held the bridal train, but she was blind and deaf to the ceremony for her mind was filled with the knowledge that she had lost both this world and the next.

The bride and groom spent the night on the prince's ship where a pavilion of purple and gold had been fitted with the softest couches. A wind swelled the sails and the ship glided lightly over the waves. Coloured lamps were hung out and there was dancing on deck. The little mermaid had never danced so lightly, so gracefully as she did that night. Her feet bled and her heart broke. It was the last time she would ever see the prince for whom she had forsaken her home, her family, her voice. For him she was now doomed to eternal nothingness.

Then she saw her sisters rise out of the sea, their faces deathly pale. And she saw that their heads were shaven.

'We have given our hair to the sea-witch,' they said, 'in return for this knife. To save your life you must take this knife and plunge it into the heart of the prince. It is your life or his. Hasten, before the sun is up he must die.'

So the mermaid took the knife, and she parted the purple curtains of the bed on which the prince and his princess were sleeping. She kissed the prince's brow and then, unable to do the deed, she flung the knife far, far out to sea. The waves rose like bright blazing flames and the water where the knife fell was tinged with the colour of blood. With eyes fast becoming dim and fixed the little mermaid gazed one last time at her beloved prince, and then she plunged from the ship into the sea, feeling her body slowly but surely dissolving as she went.

The sun rose and as the mermaid dissolved she

looked up into the red clouds, and overhead there hovered a thousand beautiful transparent forms whose voices sang to her with a sweet and ghostly melody. They had no wings, but were borne along by their own lightness. The mermaid saw that she had a form as transparent as theirs, these daughters of the air, and she felt herself being lifted up, up and raised above the foam of the sea, up into the air.

For the first time since the sea-witch cut out her tongue she was able to speak. She asked the daughters of the air where they were taking her.

'We take you into the air on a new quest for an immortal soul. Because you are a mermaid, a daughter of the ocean, you have no soul. We, the daughters of the air, like you, have no soul. Mermaids can acquire a soul by union with a man; we can acquire a soul by performing a multitude of good deeds. We fly to hot countries where the children of earth are dying in the heat of pestilential breezes, and our cooling breath revives them. We diffuse ourselves through the atmosphere, spreading the fragrance of the flowers, bringing joy and health and delight. By doing good in this way for three hundred years we win immortality and receive a share of the eternal bliss of human beings. Come, little mermaid, join us in our acts of kindness and after three hundred years you will be immortal. Sometimes the quest is shorter than three hundred years. If we fly above a good child and we smile for joy, God shortens our time of probation by one day. But if we see a bad child and weep bitter tears a day is added to our time.'

The mermaid stretched her transparent arms to the

sun and for the first time in her life tears moistened her eyes.

Unseen she kissed the forehead of the prince, and then she soared high above the ship, to begin her three-hundred-year quest for a soul.

Well, that's the story of Hans Christian Andersen's Little Mermaid. I must say I can never work out if she wants a sex life or an eternal life. With the prince, of course, she would have had both. Hmmm. The final solution of the good and bad children deal is pretty unconvincing, and after all the poor damned mermaid has been through, I kind of wish she could have had a more interesting three hundred years coming up. Would you say this was a happy ending? I suppose we are to assume that after three hundred years, give or take a good and bad child, she makes it.

see also CATHERINE DE' MEDICI, CINDERELLA, SNOW WHITE, SWAN, CYANE, THE RED SHOES

NERVAL, GÉRARD DE (1808–1855)

Nerval was a French novelist and translator. The legends of Valois and the motifs of German Romanticism inform his stories, as do his travels through France, Italy, Germany and the East. It is by his strange story 'Sylvie' that he is best remembered, and in this story can be seen some of the inspiration for the better known work of Alain-Fournier, *Le Grand Meaulnes*. Nerval was schizophrenic, and he finally hanged himself with an apron string which he believed belonged to the Queen of Sheba.

ONEIDA

The utopian community of Oneida was founded in New York State in 1848 by John Humphrey Noyes, who was a charismatic Christian leader. Oneida was a socialist commune where a group of industrious believers lived and worked together, sharing equally in the fruits of their communal labours. Like many other communes in America in the nineteenth century, Oneida owed some of its theories and practices to the work of François Charles Fourier, a Frenchman who believed the world was approaching an age of harmony which would last for thirty-five thousand years. Fourier's information came to him in a divine revelation in which he saw that the peoples of the world were established in groups of between 1620 and 1820 members, there being 2 985 984 of these groups altogether. There would be a single language and a uniform way of living, the whole world being ruled by a supreme being in what was at the time of Fourier's writing Constantinople. The sea would lose its salt and turn to lemonade. Besides the wonders of these ideas were the principles of living in a commune and sharing tasks and produce and sex.

The impressive length of survival of Oneida was due to the charisma of John Noyes, who was a single-minded, persuasive and compelling patriarch, at the true centre of whose philosophy was his own belief in himself and his right to rule. He preached equality with such fervour that the inequality of his own position was seldom questioned, and when it was Noyes always emerged supreme. Members of the community aimed to please Noyes, believing that in so doing they were pleasing God.

This clear link between Noyes and God in the understanding of the people was one central element in the power Noyes had over his flock; the other element was his sexual authority—he had total control over the access the men had to the women. He would say who was permitted to bed whom, and he was the principal initiator of young girls into sexual acts. 'Complex marriage' meant that people had many different sexual partners, but always at the suggestion and with the permission of Noyes. A convention of public humiliation consisting of confession and criticism kept complex marriage public and possible. Because Noyes had the final say in which girls were available to which men, and because all the women were bound to him by his own sexual powers, he was able to reward or punish the men as he wished. In this way he was able to control his community. When he was no longer in charge, Oneida could no longer function and the community broke up.

Until 1869 having babies at Oneida was discouraged because the community was too poor and busy to raise children. This ban was able to be enforced because Noyes taught a form of contraception whereby the men were forbidden to ejaculate and were given training in how to control their orgasm. Women were allowed to achieve orgasm. But in 1869 Noyes began his experiment in scientifically controlled human breeding known as stirpiculture, a child being described as a stirpicult. Noyes said which men and women were permitted to produce a child, and then the child was raised communally, cut off from the world outside Oneida.

PAVLOVA, ANNA (1881–1931)
Anna Pavlova was born into a poor Russian family and suffered a lot from illness as a child. When she was eight she was taken to see the Imperial Russian Ballet in a performance of *The Sleeping Beauty* and she was so entranced and inspired by what she saw that she determined to become a dancer. She danced *The Dying Swan* (which was created for her by Michel Fokine using the swan music from *Carnaval des animaux* by Saint-Saëns) for the first time in 1905, and became a prima ballerina in 1906. She spent her life touring the world with ballet, bringing it to great cities and remote villages all over the globe, and died in Brussels.

People who saw Anna Pavlova dance *The Dying Swan* have said that the dancer seemed truly to become the swan before their eyes, as if by sorcery and metamorphosis, by a spiritual ecstasy radiating from the dancer to the audience, who were enraptured and transported. Anna Pavlova also danced in the ballet *Swan Lake*, a separate work from *The Dying Swan*.

Her last request when she was dying of pneumonia was for her swan costume to be prepared, and the show went on without her, her place being taken by a spotlight that danced where she would have danced. This strategy was used in the film *The Red Shoes*, when the ballerina has plunged to her death under the train, and the show goes on, the ghostly presence of the dancer being suggested by a light.

This same device was used in the chapel at Hill House. Sometimes Petra would stay away from the service at which she was expected; her music 'The Arrival Of The

Queen Of Sheba' would play and the company would rise from their knees in expectation, but instead of Petra, in would come a blue light that would slowly proceed down the centre aisle and hover at the podium. Then it would roam at will through the congregation, stopping every now and then to bless somebody before moving gently on. Tapes of Petra's sermons were played as the light made its majestic and mysterious progress round the room.

Another time the device was used at Hill House was when they held the memorial service for Celeste. *The Dying Swan*, which the Brethren had seen performed by Celeste on other occasions, was performed by a ball of light. A dance of the loneliness of death.

see also SWAN, THE RED SHOES

PERSEPHONE

See notes on Cyane and Eleusinian Mysteries.

PSILOCYBIN

All the sacred mushrooms of Mexico belong to the genus *Psilocybe*. After the *P. mexicana* was cultivated at the Natural History Museum in Paris, Albert Hofmann tested it by eating thirty-two dried mushrooms. His visions were full of Mexican images and colours, and he saw an Aztec priest. He found himself trapped in a whirlpool of changing shapes and colours, and he felt he would remain there until he dissolved.

Although psilocybin has only one percent of the potency of LSD, its effects mirror those of LSD.

The Mazatec shaman Maria Sabina described her experience with *Psilocybe* mushrooms (Teonanacatl or flesh of God): 'I saw our past and our future. I knew I saw God: an immense clock that ticks, the spheres that go slowly around, and inside the stars, the earth, the entire universe, the day and the night, the cry and the smile, the happiness and the pain.'

Aldous Huxley and Timothy Leary have written eloquently of the effects of the hallucinogens. And in 1896 Silas Weir Mitchell, inventor of the celebrated Rest Cure which was the forerunner of the Deep Sleep Therapy so famously used at the Mandala clinic by Ambrose Goddard, tried pure mescaline and reported seeing brilliant visions. There is a similarity between the visions of the subject of mescaline and the wonderful images storytellers describe in fairytales. The redcap mushroom is a ticket to the land of fairytales. And the motifs Weir Mitchell used to describe the Rest Cure were often in the language of the darker kind of folktale—his patients were 'fattened and reddened' the way Hansel was prepared by the witch for the oven. Weir Mitchell was of a very gothic and romantic turn of mind and could describe an hysterical woman as a vampire who sucked the blood of the healthy women around her. The trouble with many sick women, he believed, was that they desired knowledge, a code for the forbidden knowledge of sex. Knowledge would detract from the woman's appeal to men, since for 'most men, when she seizes the apple, she drops the rose'. The women had to be removed from their familiar surroundings, confined to their beds in a locked room, given a guardian or a jailer, and fed milky foods every two hours.

Ambrose Goddard was also given to putting a romantic gothic structure on his medical narrative, although he was much more open about it, describing the female patients he first sedated and then raped as Sleeping Beauties. And Ambrose named one of his dogs Silas in honour of Weir Mitchell.

see also ALBERT HOFMANN, REDCAPS

RED SHOES, THE

The folktale 'The Red Shoes' was a story that greatly appealed to Hans Christian Andersen, who retold it adding some details of his own. The heart of this story, with its powerful image of the scarlet shoes which dance and which are symbolic of the girl's passion as it gets out of control, was partly the inspiration for the ballet film *The Red Shoes*, made in 1948, and also for a ballet which played at the Alhambra Theatre in London in 1899. The story of the film is considerably different from the folktale and was danced as a ballet in Melbourne in 1996. In the film and in the subsequent ballet, the device used in Brussels after the death of Anna Pavlova is employed, having a light on stage to replace the absent ballerina. This device was also used religious ceremonies by the Hill House Brethren.

Here's the old story:

Once there was a poor motherless child who had no shoes. But the child saved cloth scraps whenever she found them and over time sewed herself a pair of red shoes. They were crude but she loved them. They made her feel rich, even though her days were spent gathering food in the woods until far past dark.

One day, as she trudged down the road in her rags and her red shoes, a gilded carriage pulled up beside her.

Inside was an old woman who told her she was going to take her home and treat her as her own little daughter. So to the wealthy old woman's house they went, and the child's hair was cleaned and combed. She was given pure white undergarments and a fine woollen dress and white stockings and shiny black shoes. When the child asked after her old clothes, and especially her red shoes, the old woman said the clothes were so filthy, and the shoes so ridiculous, that she had thrown them into the fire where they were burnt to ashes.

The child was very sad, for even with all the riches surrounding her, the humble red shoes made by her own hand had given her the greatest happiness. Now she was made to sit all the time, to walk without skipping, and to not speak unless spoken to. But a secret fire began to burn in her heart and she continued to yearn for her old red shoes more than anything.

As the child was old enough to be confirmed on the Day of the Innocents, the old woman took her to a crippled shoemaker to have a special pair of shoes made for the occasion. On the shoemaker's shelf there stood a pair of red shoes, made of the best leather that was finer than fine. The shoes glowed. So even though red shoes were scandalous for church, the child, who chose only with her hungry heart, picked them. The old lady's eyesight was so poor she could not see the colour of the shoes and so paid for them. The shoemaker winked at the child and wrapped the shoes up.

The next day, the church members were agog over the shoes on the child's feet. The red shoes shone like burnished apples, like hearts, like red-washed plums. Everyone stared; even the icons on the wall, even the statues stared disapprovingly at the red shoes. But the girl loved the shoes all the more. When the preacher intoned, the choir hummed, the organ pumped, the child thought nothing more beautiful than her red shoes.

By the end of the day the old woman had been informed about her ward's red shoes. 'Never, never wear those red shoes again!' she said. But the next Sunday, the child couldn't help but choose the red shoes over the black ones, and she and the old woman walked to church as usual.

At the door to the church was an old soldier with his arm in a sling. He wore a little jacket and had a red beard. He bowed and asked permission to brush the dust from the child's shoes. The child put out her foot, and he tapped the soles of her shoes with a little wig-a-jig-jig song that made the soles of her feet itch. 'Remember to stay for the dance,' he said, and winked at her.

Again everyone looked askance at the girl's red shoes. But she so loved the shoes that were bright like crimson, bright like raspberries, bright like pomegranates, that she could hardly think of anything else, hardly hear the service at all. So busy was she turning her feet this way and that, admiring her red shoes, that she forgot to sing.

As she and the old woman left the church, the soldier called out, 'What beautiful dancing shoes.' His words made the girl take a few little twirls right there and then. But once her feet had begun to move, they would not stop, and she danced through the flower beds and around the corner of the church until it seemed as though she had lost complete control of herself. She did a gavotte and then a csardas and then waltzed by herself through the fields across the way.

The old woman's coachman jumped up from his bench and ran after the girl, picked her up, and carried her back to the carriage, but the girl's feet in the red shoes were still dancing in the air as though they were on the ground. The woman and the coachman tugged and pulled, trying to pry the red shoes off. It was such a sight, all hats askew and kicking legs, but at last the child's feet were calmed.

Back home the old woman slammed the red shoes down high on a shelf and warned the girl never to touch them again. But the girl could not help looking up and longing for them. To her they were still the most beautiful things on the face of the earth.

Not long after, the woman became ill, and as soon as her doctors left, the girl crept into the room where the red shoes were kept. She glanced up at them so high on the shelf. Her glance became a gaze and her gaze became a powerful desire, so much so that the girl took the shoes from the shelf and fastened them on, feeling it would do no harm. But as soon as they touched her heels and toes, she was overcome by the urge to dance.

And so out the door she danced, and then down the steps, first in a gavotte, then a csardas, and then in big daring waltz turns in rapid succession. The girl was in her glory and did not realise she was in trouble until she wanted to dance to the left and the shoes insisted on dancing to the right. When she wanted to dance round, the shoes insisted on dancing straight ahead. And as the shoes danced the girl, they danced her right down the road, through the muddy fields, and out into the dark and gloomy forest.

There against a tree was the old soldier with the red beard, his arm in a sling. 'What beautiful dancing shoes,' he said. The girl was terrified and she tried to pull the shoes off, but as much as she tugged, the shoes stayed fast. She hopped on one foot and then the other, trying to take off the shoes, but her one foot on the ground kept dancing even so, and her other foot in her hand did its part of the dance also.

And so dance and dance and dance she did. Over highest hills and through the valleys, in the rain and in the snow and in the sunlight she danced. She danced in the darkest night and through sunrise and she was still dancing in twilight as well. But it was not good dancing, it was terrible dancing, and there was no rest for her.

She danced into a churchyard and there a spirit of dread would not allow her to enter. The spirit pronounced these words over her: 'You shall dance in your red shoes until you become a wraith, like a ghost, till your skin hangs from your bones, till there is nothing left of you but entrails dancing. You shall dance door to door through all the villages and you shall strike each door three times and when people peer out they will see you and fear your fate for themselves. Dance, red shoes, you shall dance.'

The girl begged for mercy, but the red shoes carried her away. Over the briars she danced, through the streams, over the hedgerows and on and on, dancing, still dancing, till she came to her old home and there were mourners. The old woman had died. Yet even so the girl danced on by, and dance she did as dance she must. In exhaustion and horror she danced into a forest where lived the town's executioner. And the axe on his wall began to tremble as soon as it sensed her coming near.

She begged the executioner as she danced by his door to cut off her shoes to free her from her fate. And the executioner cut through the straps of the red shoes with his axe. But the shoes stayed on her feet. And so she cried to him that her life was worth nothing and that he should cut off her feet. So he cut off her feet. And the girl kissed the hand that had guided the axe; she kissed the axe that had chopped off her feet, and she fell to the ground as her blood flowed bright as red shoe-leather across the pavement. And the red shoes with her feet in them kept on dancing through the forest and over the hill out of sight. And now the girl was a cripple, and had to find her way in the world as a servant to others. The cobbler made for her a pair of wooden feet, and as she travelled she could always see the red shoes in the distance, dancing in front of her. She never again wished for red shoes.

And the girl kissed the axe that had chopped off her feet.

see also ANNA PAVLOVA

REDCAPS

In the illustrations accompanying the fairytales and folktales of European people, you will often find pictures of the redcap mushroom. This use of the redcap reflects the fact that the hallucinogenic properties of the mushroom have the power to free the mind and spirit and send them into the realm of fantasy and magic. The redcap stands as a key or a cipher, a mark of the gateway between the mundane world and the world of the spirit where all is possible, where all good and all evil can be seen to operate in spectacular narratives and images.

The psychoactive constituents are muscimol and ibotenic acid.

The Latin name of the redcap is *Amanita muscaria*, and the mushroom is also known as 'fly agaric' because it is a useful insecticide when smeared on the walls of the house. These mushrooms are found throughout the world, as well as in Australia. The *Psilocybe* mushroom found in Australia is brown with a small blue or gold knob on top.

REFLEXOLOGY

This is a technique of alternative medicine where diagnosis and treatment are carried out by massage, particularly of the feet. It was used in ancient China and ancient Egypt. Dr William Fitzgerald introduced this form of therapy to the United States, describing ten zones or channels of the body along which flows the energy force, or the vital energy. The zones end at the hands and feet, and problems in all parts of the body can be relieved by attention to the ends of the zones.

REFRIGERATOR

Cooling in the refrigerator is produced by the evaporation of volatile liquids within a sealed tube, and the resulting gas is piped away to a compressor which condenses it back into liquid. This liquid then recirculates and evaporates again. James Harrison, who was an Australian, invented the refrigerator in 1850; his fridges were available commercially by 1860. His discovery was a boon to the brewing industry in Australia, as before the refrigerator it was not possible to brew beer in the summer months, except in the cooler climate of Tasmania. (An

American, James Perkins, patented the refrigerator in 1834, but did not develop the idea.)

SAINT BARTHOLOMEW

Bartholomew was one of the Apostles, sometimes known as Nathanael, and was martyred by being flayed alive and then beheaded. In the eleventh century Canterbury Cathedral acquired his arm, a very valuable relic. His emblem is the flaying knife, and he is the patron of tanners, taxidermists and plastic surgeons. His feast day is on 24 August.

SCARLET

Red dye was first used on leather in about 2300 BC by people in Syria. It was made from the dried bodies of the wingless females of the cochineal beetle.

SCHEHERAZADE

Scheherazade was the daughter of the Grand Vizier of the Indies, and she begged to become the wife of the Sultan Schahriah so that she could save the lives of other women whom the sultan was determined to murder. The reason for his killings was that he had discovered his sultana had been unfaithful, and he swore to take a fresh wife every night and have her put to the sword at daybreak so that she could never betray him. Scheherazade's plan was that she would become his wife, and would so entrance him with the stories she told him that he would be unable to resist letting her live in order to continue the tales. She sustained this ruse for a thousand and one nights and so saved the lives of a thousand women. After the thousand and one nights the sultan revoked the decree.

SERMON
This is the text of 'The Flower and Fruit Sermon' by the Reverend Mr Somerset Jones:

I take today two texts from Holy Scripture: 1 Kings 10: verse 13, 'And Solomon gave unto the Queen of Sheba all her desire;' and Matthew 6: verses 28–29, 'Consider the lilies of the field, how they grow; they toil not, neither do they spin: And yet I say unto you that even Solomon in all his glory was not arrayed like one of these.'

I place here before you on the Lord's table these roses from the church garden. Are they not lovely? They are as the lilies of the field. They are you and me.

And Solomon gave unto the Queen of Sheba all her desire. All her desire. *All* her desire. Wave after wave of legendary luxury. The horses of incomparable swiftness. The chariots of beaten gold. The drivers clothed in Tyrian purple, dust of gold sprinkled in their hair. A hundred and twenty talents of gold. Abundance. Harps, psalteries, singers, lions, cinnamon, silver, onyx, rubies. Almonds, apples, chestnuts, figs, lilies, mint, olives, pomegranates, grapes, anemones, amaryllis, roses.

The fruits of the earth and the flowers of the field.

Oh, the riches! The spices! Oh, the flowers! The golden roses and the cherry blossoms that sparkled in the sunlight. The downy peaches, dusky apricots.

The juice of the purple grape!

We are told that when the Queen of Sheba heard of the fame of Solomon she came to prove him with hard questions. Her camels bore spices and gold as gifts for the king, precious stones. And she communed with him of all that was in her heart. And his wisdom and prosperity exceeded all that she had heard.

I will share with you, my friends, one of the most touching and delicate stories of the queen's encounter with King Solomon. She presented him with two bouquets of white roses; one was made from fresh and dewy flowers, the other was a perfect and artful imitation of the other. Which of these two, the queen asked Solomon, which of these two is from nature?

And the king regarded the bouquets for a long time, careful to compose his answer. Then he said to his servants to open the lattice. And beyond the lattice lay a garden of beautiful flowers. Before very long, the bees flew in by the open window and they settled on the real flowers, avoiding the false.

Oh, Solomon, great is thy wisdom!

Great thy wealth, great thy power.

And yet Jesus comes to us with the greater glory, the greater wisdom, the greater power, and he indicates the lilies of the field and says to us that here in the natural world around us is the true and undetected glory of God. The scarlet anemone, the golden amaryllis which lie in the grasses at our very feet! The birds of the air, the flowers of the field—oh, they toil not, neither do they spin. Oh! Ho! The great King Solomon in all his glory was not arrayed like one of these. Consider, consider. The lilies of the field. The fruits of the trees. The beauties of the earth. The innocence of the flowers, the innocence of a little child. Solomon in all his glory had not the beauty and innocence—and, dare I say, wisdom—of a little child. Suffer the little children, Jesus says. Suffer the little children to come unto me.

And in that text from the Book of Matthew, in that self-same text, comes the greatest wisdom, the greatest prayer of all. Jesus exhorts us to pray to Our Father, and in that prayer we ask God for our daily bread, and we know that when we ask with open hearts and pure minds, we will be given our daily bread. We will be fed. We will be clothed. We will live in splendour as the lilies of the field, as the true flowers of the earth, as the fruits of the glory of God.

Our desire, all our desire, must be to do the will of God. Forget the chariots, the camels, the spices and the beaten gold and silver. Give us this day our daily bread, and forgive us our trespasses. God forgives. We need but ask. Take no thought for your life, what you shall eat or drink or wear. You are the lilies of the field. You are the roses of Sharon. We are God's people, his flock. We will reap what we sow.

I call upon you to know that you are birds of the air, to acknowledge your regal status as lilies of the field. And go forth into the world naked in spirit and innocent and unashamed. For the things of this world are as dross beside the wondrous beauty of Eternity. Eternity! Eternity! The great endless, timeless circle of Eternity. Give us this day our daily bread, and show us your face, Lord God, in Eternity.

see also ALMOND, SHEBA, SOLOMON

SHEARER, MOIRA (1926–)

A Scottish-born ballerina whose repertoire included the classical works *Swan Lake, Sleeping Beauty, Coppelia,* and *Giselle*. She starred in the Powell and Pressburger films *The Tales of Hoffmann* (1950) and *The Red Shoes* (1948), and is particularly celebrated for her role in the latter.

see also THE RED SHOES

SHEBA

There were many queens of the realm of Sheba, which was probably southern Arabia and was a place of great wealth and prosperity and beauty where matriarchy reigned. Priestesses there were known as holy harlots from the wilderness, wearing crowns and bracelets and rings and necklaces of unrivalled value and loveliness. The priests were called kindred of the moon, and were known in Hebrew as angels; in Arabic as close kindred, which is also a title of the Sufi mystics.

Sheba was a woman who sought wisdom, and was known in the Old Testament as well as in Asian and European folklore. Because she not only sought wisdom but told tales, she was a type of storyteller, the narrator of fairytales, one who stood ambiguously outside the action. She frequently threw a very personal, unusual and original light on things. She spoke in riddles, was practised in trickery. The knowledge, the wisdom, was ultimately sexual, and some stories have it that Sheba bore a son to Solomon.

The legend goes that King Solomon heard from the hoopoe that the rich and fabulous queen of the south was coming to visit him. Solomon rewarded the bird with a golden beetle to eat. This Solomon is as important in the Koran as he is in the Bible, and with the added zing of wizardry. In the bible story Sheba puts her questions to Solomon and is rewarded with the wisdom of his answers, and he and she exchange rich gifts. She in fact becomes the complement to the male principle of wisdom as it is shown in Solomon. And she conflates in the mind with Scheherazade, the wise dancing girl who told her stories to save lives. Christ invoked Sheba as one of the just who will rise up to condemn the unfaithful. She appears in much Christian literature as a prophet, the richest source of writing about her being in the *Golden Legend* of Jacobus from the thirteenth century.

Jacobus tells how Seth, son of Adam, takes a branch from the Tree of Knowledge in the Garden of Eden and plants it in the mouth of Adam's corpse, and a tree grows. Solomon, centuries later, has the tree cut down to be used in the building of the temple. However, the wood will not be worked, and so the builders throw it away and it falls into the stream of Kidron where it becomes a footbridge.

When the Queen of Sheba comes to the bridge on her way to visit King Solomon, she realises prophetically that the wood of the bridge will in future become the wood of the cross. She understands that she would defile it with her footstep. So instead of walking on the bridge, she steps into the water and wades across the stream. Prophetic vision collapses time, and the Queen of Sheba becomes a type of Christian of the future. Solomon hears of the power of the wood which will bring about the end of his kingdom, and believes he can cheat the future by throwing the wood into a pond. The pond develops, as a result, such magical properties that the waters could cure the sick—it was this place, the pool of Bethesda, into which an angel descended and moved the water, ensuring its virtues. And it was from this piece of wood that the cross of Christ was fashioned.

As represented in paintings, the Queen of Sheba, identified with the beloved in the *Song of Songs*, is black, with long golden hair. She is equal, in popular imagination, to all that is sensual and luxurious, voluptuous and desirable, to the mysteries, spices and drugs of the Orient. And some of the character and incident given to her in the Eastern legend is worth relating.

When Solomon heard from the hoopoe that Sheba was coming to visit him, he called up a mirror resembling a stream of water across the floor of the palace courtyard. Sheba bared her legs at the sight of the stream, but Solomon told her it was really a glass pavement. At this Sheba realised she had exposed the deformity of her legs and feet, and she said she was a sinner, her sinfulness shown in the cryptic allusion to her legs, and would henceforth submit to Allah. Solomon cured her deformity, sometimes recorded as hairiness, or reptilian scaliness, sometimes as ass's hooves, sometimes as webbed feet.

On the tessellated pavement of the cathedral at Otranto, among the stories of Adam and Eve, Noah, and King Arthur, is depicted the story of Solomon and Sheba. Sheba holds up her shoe, which is studded with fabulous blue stones matching her one visible earring. Her left foot is bare and there are no divisions for the toes, so that she has the foot of a waterbird. She is placed next to roundels where there are a double-tailed mermaid and an octopus, paralleling her deformed femininity with other monstrosities, underlining her otherness. Her asymetrical body emphasises her outlandish, outsider status.

She is like the bird-footed temptresses of Saint Anthony, and her deformity easily translates from the particular to the general, with the potential to embrace all women. The evil, ass-hoofed or brass-footed daughters of Hecate, who could disguise themselves as beautiful maidens, were not only bloodsuckers and succubi but were child-stealers. The news, as far as women and their feet are concerned, is generally bad, or at least very interesting, and the misshapen feet can be presumed to refer to the fact that men fear and at the same time desire what is beneath a woman's skirt.

The site of danger in Western culture is female sexuality, and when the Queen of Sheba's feet and legs were cured of their infirmity by Solomon, or perhaps by the waters of the stream, she was not only redeemed before God, but she was purified of the monstrosity and evil of her female nature.

She had been transformed.

It is transformation of one kind or another that is the stuff of fairytales. And feet are right in there—Bigfoot Bertha (actually the mother of Charlemagne) is one heroine, and dainty-footed Cinderella is another. So many stories of wronged girls who require transformation before they can take their place in the world. There was a shift of the web-footed heroine/storyteller along the way, a shift in which the Queen of Sheba figure, through the Bigfoot Bertha figure, became by twists and turns the storytelling web-footed figure of Mother Goose. Jacob Grimm records that in German folk tradition the name Bertha used to denote the old storytelling grandmother.

The power of wisdom and knowledge in fairytales is linked by history to the story of the Queen of Sheba and the wisdom of Solomon. The sexual elements in the story of Solomon and Sheba are carried into fairytales, where the mysteriousness of sex is translated into the wonderful and the magical, and where the magical always in truth leads back to the carnal and to the mystery of the enclosed garden of female sexuality invoked in the *Song of Songs*.

see also FOOT, HOOPOE, SOLOMON

SHOEMAKER

The tools of the shoemaker are the same as the torture tools of the devil—the rasp, pliers, nippers, hammer, pincers and awl. In very ancient times the shoemaker had the job of propitiating the animals whose bodies had been sacrificed for the making of shoes. An old Australian term for shoemaker was 'snob'. The patron saints of shoemakers are Crispin and Crispinian, poor Roman cobblers to whom angels brought each night the leather for their work.

SLIPPER

The slipper of the Chinese Cinderella was golden. When Frank L. Baum wrote *The Wizard of Oz* he gave Dorothy silver slippers, but when the book was produced as a movie the slippers became red, and are known as the famous ruby slippers.

see also CINDERELLA

SNOW QUEEN, THE

This story, which Hans Christian Andersen published in 1844 and which is retold here by me, follows the lives of a girl and a boy, Gerda and Kay, and tells how their happiness was first disrupted by the agency of an evil magic mirror, and then by Kay's capture by the Snow Queen. The loyalty of Gerda in her search for Kay is an example of love and fortitude in the face of great difficulty and despair:

A wicked magician constructed a mirror which distorted all things it reflected, making good evil. This mirror was carried from place to place, carried so high that it fragmented into millions of shards, and these fell to earth, each fragment, no matter how tiny, having the power to pervert and corrupt. A splinter in the heart, and the heart became as cold as ice.

Kay was playing with his friend Gerda when he received in the eye a splinter of the mirror, and also one in the heart. His character was utterly changed by this, and he became harsh and cruel. Then one day when he was playing in the frozen square, he decided to tie his sledge to the sledge of a stranger and be pulled along. But the strange sledge took Kay far out of the town, travelling faster and faster through the snow.

Finally the sledge stopped and the driver stood up to reveal herself as the Snow Queen, wearing a cap and coat entirely made from snow, and she was tall and slender and dazzlingly white. She sat him next to her under her bearskin, and he felt as if he were sinking into a drift of snow. She kissed him, and her kiss was as cold as ice and went straight to his heart. He thought he would die, but soon he lost all feeling of the cold and saw that the Snow Queen was the most beautiful woman he could ever imagine.

They flew into the sky, into a black stormcloud, over woods and lakes and sea and land; and beneath them the cold wind whistled, the wolves howled, the snow glittered, and the black crow flew cawing over the plain, while up above the moon shone, clear and tranquil.

Gerda set out in search of Kay, putting on her new red shoes and going down to the river.

'Is it true,' she said to the waves of the river, 'that you have taken Kay away from me? If you will only restore him to me, I will give you my new red shoes.' She stepped into a boat and tossed the shoes out into the water, and the waves received them, and Gerda floated away in the boat, the shoes floating behind her on the water. But the boat moved faster than the shoes, and soon the shoes were left far behind.

Gerda asked the flowers, the birds, the trees and the winds if they had seen Kay, and some thought they had, and some led her in false directions. She came to the palace of a prince and princess, who were kind to her, and fed her and dressed her in fine clothes of silk and velvet and sent her out on her search in a golden carriage. But robbers saw the gleaming carriage and they seized the horses, stabbed the coachman and the footmen to death, and dragged Gerda from the carriage.

The robber-woman was about to stab Gerda also, when her daughter jumped on her mother's back and bit her on the ear, saying she wished to have Gerda as a playmate. The robber maiden drove Gerda in the golden carriage to the robbers' half-ruined castle where they had supper of soup from a cauldron and hare from a spit. They slept in the maiden's bed, surrounded by a hundred woodpigeons and a reindeer. The robber-maiden kept a dagger by her side. Gerda talked to the woodpigeons, asking them for news of Kay, but the robber-maiden said if she would not be quiet she would feel the dagger in her heart.

Kay, said the woodpigeons, could be found in Lapland, and so the robber-maiden, who could be kind as well as cruel, gave Gerda her reindeer for transport, gave her some food, and sent her on her way to follow the red and blue of the Northern Lights. The Wise-woman at Finmark whispered to the reindeer that Kay was with the Snow Queen, and that the only power that could save him from her spell was the power of Gerda's innocent love.

Gerda lost her boots and her gloves, and the reindeer brought her finally to the gate of the Snow Queen's palace, where she would find Kay, and the reindeer returned to the bush of red berries where he would wait for Gerda.

The walls of the palace were formed of the driven snow; there were over a hundred halls, the largest of them many miles wide, all illuminated by the Northern Lights; all vast, empty, icily cold and dazzlingly white. No sounds of mirth ever resounded through these dreary spaces. In the midst of the empty, interminable snow-saloon lay a frozen lake, and when the Snow Queen was at home she sat in the centre of this lake. Kay played among the sharp fragments of ice, putting together a puzzle, trying to form the word Eternity from pieces of ice. For the Snow Queen had promised him that if he could form the word Eternity from slivers of ice, she would give him the whole world, and a new pair of skates as well. But he could not do it.

The Snow Queen had left her palace to visit other countries, and Kay was alone playing with his Eternity puzzle. Gerda entered the hall, saw Kay and ran to him and flung her arms around him. He sat cold and motionless, while Gerda wept hot tears which fell on his face and then upon his heart. He wept, and the splinter of evil glass floated from his eye and fell with his tears. And they laughed, and suddenly they were able to form the letters of Eternity with the sharp fragments of ice.

And they ran through the ice palace and out into the snow, and ran until they found the reindeer who took them back to the Wise-woman. Then, travelling now with Kay, Gerda retraced her journey and came finally to the town where they had lived, and where they would live in joy and happiness forever after.

(Something that has always worried me about this story is whatever happened when the Snow Queen came back home to her palace and found that Kay had not only solved the puzzle of Eternity, but had cleared out with Gerda? She stands there in the cold, staring at the word Eternity written in ice, and then what? Weird.)

SNOW WHITE

My own version:

Once in the middle of winter, when snowflakes were falling like feathers from the sky, a queen sat by her window and sewed. And as she sewed she pricked her finger and three drops of blood fell upon the snow. The queen then wished that she could have a child who would be as red as blood, as white as snow and as black as ebony.

The queen gave birth to a daughter whose lips were as red as blood, whose skin was as white as snow, and whose hair was as black as ebony. The child was named Snow White, and the day that she was born the queen died.

After a year had passed the king married another wife, a beautiful woman, proud and haughty. This queen had a magic looking-glass; she would stand before the glass and say:

Mirror, mirror on the wall,
Who is the fairest one of all?

And the glass would always reassure her that she was the most beautiful woman in all the land. Until, when Snow White was just seven years old, the glass changed its story and revealed to the queen that Snow White was in fact the loveliest in the land.

Envy and pride grew in the queen's heart until she had no peace. So she called a huntsman and instructed him to take Snow White away into the forest and kill her, bringing back for the queen to eat Snow White's lungs and liver. But the hunstman was unable to bring himself to kill the child, and he allowed Snow White to run away into the forest. He killed a deer and cut out its lungs and liver and brought them to the queen, who was pleased and who cooked them and ate them for her supper.

Snow White was all alone in the forest as night began to fall. In fear she began to run, over sharp stones, through bushes of thorns. She felt the presence of wild beasts in the darkness as she ran. She ran through the night, and the next morning she came to a clearing where there was a cottage. She knocked at the door but nobody replied, and so she pushed open the door and went in.

There she found the table set with seven places, and she was so tired and hungry that she took a little food and drink from each place. Then she found a bedroom with seven beds and she chose a bed and fell fast asleep.

As darkness descended, the owners of the cottage, seven little men, came home from their work in the silver mines. When they discovered Snow White asleep in the bed they were amazed. They let her sleep on undisturbed, and the seventh dwarf slept for an hour at a time in the bed of each of his companions. So the night passed.

The next day Snow White told the dwarfs her story and they promised to protect her from the queen. Snow White would keep house for the dwarfs, and would open the door to nobody, for fear that the queen may come to look for her.

Meanwhile, the queen had gone to her looking-glass hoping again to be told that she was the most beautiful woman in the land. However, the mirror explained to her that Snow White was still the fairest, and that she was now living with the dwarfs. So the queen devised a new method for disposing of Snow White; she disguised herself as an old pedlar woman, and set off for the cottage of the seven dwarfs.

She knocked on the door and said, 'Pretty things to sell, laces and ribbons!' and Snow White let her into the house and bought a set of bright red laces.

'Let me lace you, child,' the woman said to Snow White. She laced her stays so swiftly and so tightly that Snow White lost her breath and fell down as if dead. 'And now I am the fairest in the land,' the queen whispered.

But the dwarfs came home and they cut the laces, and they warned Snow White that the woman was the queen and that Snow White must simply never open the door.

Of course the mirror, which could speak only the truth, advised the queen that Snow White was still alive and more beautiful than ever. Whereupon the wicked woman made a poisonous comb and set off for the cottage. This time Snow White said to the woman through the window that she was unable to let anybody in, but the queen, appealing to the girl's vanity, handed her the comb through the window. Snow White combed her hair and fell down as if dead.

Again the dwarfs came home in time, and they took the comb from Snow White's hair and she was revived. And again the queen spoke to the mirror, and again the mirror told her that Snow White had survived.

Blood rushed to the queen's heart and she was white and shaking with rage.

She went to a secret lonely room where she made a poisonous apple. On the outside the apple looked ripe and beautiful, with one white cheek and one red, so that anyone who saw it would long for it; but whoever ate it would surely die. For the red side of the apple was deadly.

When the queen offered the apple to Snow White the princess declined it, but the queen cut the apple in half and she ate the white side herself. So Snow White took the red half of the apple and she bit it, and she fell down dead.

The queen looked at her in triumph, and laughed and said, 'Red as blood, white as snow, black as ebony! And now you are dead!' And when she returned to the mirror and questioned it, she heard that she, the queen, was now the fairest woman in the land.

The dwarfs were unable to revive Snow White, so they placed her on a bier and washed her with water and with wine, and combed her hair and sat by her and wept three days and three nights. And when the time came to put her in the cold dark ground, they saw that her cheeks were still so red and her white skin so sweet that they could not bear to bury her. So they fashioned a transparent casket all of glass, and then they carried the casket up onto the mountain and one of the dwarfs always kept watch. The birds of the forest also came to keep watch, first an owl, then a raven, then a dove.

For a long time Snow White lay in the coffin on the mountain top, and she did not change. As white as snow, as red as blood, as black as ebony.

Until one day a king's son came riding by and saw the coffin, and fell in love with the sleeping maiden. He offered to buy her from the dwarfs, but she was not for sale. Then he asked if he might have her for a gift, as he could no longer live without the sight of her. So the dwarfs gave him the casket containing their lovely Snow White.

As the prince's servants carried the casket down the mountainside, they jostled it, and suddenly the piece of apple which had stuck in Snow White's throat was dislodged, and Snow White's eyes flew open and she pushed back the glass lid. She was alive after all. The prince asked her to be his bride.

The wicked queen was bidden to the royal wedding feast, and when she was dressed in her finest garments, ready to set out, she went to her mirror and asked her question: Who is the fairest in the land? The looking-glass told her that the new young queen was the most beautiful woman in the land. The queen uttered a curse as she set off for the wedding in a rage.

When she recognised the young queen as Snow White she stood still with superstitious fear and rage, and was unable to stir. Then iron slippers were heated on the great fire, and they were brought in with tongs and set before her. She was forced to put on the red-hot shoes and dance until she dropped down dead.

(What a punishment! Hot-footing it to hell. But—why was the queen such an incompetent killer? Why was Snow White so ready to be tricked, and so disobedient? Weird.)

see also GLASS

SOLOMON

The reign of Solomon can best be interpreted through a collection of legends from Egypt, Phoenicia and Arabia, which is the land of Sheba, Solomon being not one specific man but a story-king fabricated from several sources. If you read the biblical fragment called *Song of Songs*, as you might read a song or a poem, without any reference to the Christian church, you will see that it is a wonderful erotic hymn. (Her stature was like a palm tree, her breasts like clusters of grapes, her mouth like honeycomb, her teeth like flocks of sheep, her belly like a heap of wheat decorated with lilies.) Bearing this in mind, you can follow the story of Solomon in much the same way as you might the legend of King Arthur—there are some facts and there are some fantasies and in the weave of these we are given the stories of people like Solomon.

Solomon was the son of David, King of Israel, and his wife Bathsheba. His reign was in the tenth century BC and was memorable for its fabulous grandeur. He grew to be wiser than all men, and the distilled wisdom of three thousand proverbs is attributed to him in the Book of Proverbs. His knowledge was encyclopaedic: 'And he spake of trees, from the cedar tree that *is* in Lebanon even unto the hyssop that springeth out of the wall. He spake also of beasts and of fowl, and of creeping things, and of fishes.' (1 Kings 4:33)

He also talked to the animals, and there is a legend that he possessed a magic ring which enabled him to converse in animal language. He spoke the language of the birds, known as green language.

According to the Koran, Solomon stole his throne from one of the queens of Sheba in the first place.

see also GREEN LANGUAGE

SWAN

Although the swan is not in fact a musical bird, it was associated with music by the ancient Egyptians and Greeks. Its voice is sweeter as its death approaches, and because of this fact the swan is believed to be able to foresee its own death, and to sing against death, demonstrating joy in tribulation. The last appearance of a singer or dancer is called a swan-song, the final and dearest performance.

Because the wings are dazzlingly white and the flesh is very dark, the swan is an emblem of hypocrisy; but it also stands for purity and love, being a symbol of Venus, Mary and Christ. The dying swan is a type of martyrdom. Because Zeus became a swan in order to rape Leda, the bird also stands for lust and is a phallic symbol. (After the rape, Leda gave birth to Castor and Pollux, Helen and Clytemnestra.)

Owing to its power and grace and beauty, the swan is a royal bird, and it was used in Greek heraldry from as early as the fourth century BC. Several mediaeval families in Europe claimed descent from the Knight of the Swan. In England the privilege of keeping swans was granted by the crown.

There are swan motifs in many ancient folktales, including those where royal children are changed into swans, and those such as 'Lohengrin' where the Knight of the Swan appears and disappears in a boat drawn by a mysterious white swan.

In Hindu legend the swan is the divine bird which laid the cosmic egg from which Brahma emerged, and two swans together are deities dwelling in the mind of the Great, and they subsist on the honey of the blooming lotus of knowledge.

The ballet *Swan Lake* was written by Tchaikovsky, and was first performed at the Imperial Bolshoi Theatre in Moscow in 1877. It tells the sad love story of Prince Siegfried who fell in love with Odette, the Queen of the Swans. Odette had been bewitched by an evil sorcerer in the form of an owl, and all her mother's tears, which filled the lake, could not undo the spell. She was therefore a swan, except between midnight and dawn when she regained human form. The swan-maidens who flew with her were under the same enchantment. But the spell could be broken if a man loved her, married her, and was forever faithful to her. Siegfried swore he would break the spell.

At Siegfried's birthday ball he was expected to choose a bride from among the princesses. However, a strange couple arrived and were presented to the prince. This was the sorcerer and his daughter Odile, and Siegfried, under the influence of the sorcerer, mistook Odile for his beloved Odette. Meanwhile, Odette was beating against the window panes of the ballroom. If Siegfried said he loved Odile, then Odette would be a swan forever. And Siegfried did it; he swore to love Odile forever.

But no sooner had he done so than he realised his mistake, and he saw Odette at the window and ran out into the darkness to find her. He discovered her at the lake among the swan-maidens, and as she began to sink beneath the waters in death, he threw himself into the lake beside her, and they carried their love into eternity.
see also LOTUS

SWANILDA
This is the name of the heroine of the ballet *Coppelia*, which was inspired by one of the stories of E.T.A. Hoffmann. The ballet tells of how Franz, Swanilda's fiancé, is fascinated by a beautiful girl who turns out to be a doll created by Dr Coppelius. The doctor drugs Franz in order to transfer his soul into the doll. However, Swanilda puts herself in the place of the doll and rescues Franz.

The ballet, also known as *La Fille aux Yeux d'Email*, was first performed in Paris in 1870.
see also E.T.A. HOFFMANN

TAGLIONI, MARIE (1804–1884)
Marie Taglioni was born in Stockholm, into an Italian family with a long tradition in ballet. She was the first ballerina to dance on point. She perfected the technique for the performance of *La Sylphide* at the Paris Opera in 1832. It was at this time that gaslight was introduced into theatres, so that the light of the lamp and the lightness of the dancers went hand in hand.

Taglioni, in drifting, diaphanous white, elevating herself on the tips of her toes, using darned but not blocked shoes, perfectly symbolised the romantic's flight from reality, turning in circles, and leaping and floating through the air. The ideal woman of romance had detached herself from the earth and become a creature of the air.

It was at this time also that the principal ballerina rose to complete dominance over her male counterpart in the dance. She had the power to lead the man on and to fly off like the capricious queen of the fairies, but her very lack of substance, her very wispiness placed her in the class of the doomed. This aspect of the ballet, an effect achieved by rigour and discipline and pain, endeared it to both men and women. There was a curious contract between the sexes where beauty and death and doom and glamour danced hand in hand. She was moth, she was also flame. She was purity, she was corruption. He worshipped her, he would kill her. She glowed with life, she would die. Woman at her most frail and pure was the embodiment of desire, and was deified in the ballerina as defined by Marie Taglioni.

Marie danced in many cities, and in St Petersburg the Czar left the box in order to be closer to her on the floor of the orchestra. As she was leaving Moscow, a group of followers acquired her used dancing slippers, boiled them and ate them. She danced in 1845 for Queen Victoria the *Pas de Quatre*, with Lucile Grahn, Fanny Cerito and Carlotta Grisi. (As a child, Queen Victoria had a Marie Taglioni doll.) This performance remains one of the most celebrated ballets of all time and is immortalised in a famous lithograph which etches on the mind an image of ballet as fairyland perfection.

One of the beloved pupils of Marie Taglioni, Emma Livry (1842–1862), died in a fire. Marie Taglioni designed the ballet *Le Papillon* for Emma, who first danced it in 1860. In 1862 during a rehearsal for *La Muette de Portici* Emma's costume caught fire and she burned to death. A crowd followed her funeral through the streets of Paris, and above the coffin flew an accompanying flock of white butterflies.

The poet Théophile Gautier described Marie as a 'happy angel'.

see also BUTTERFLIES, FANNY CERITO

TARTAR

Bitartrate of potash is present in grape juice and is deposited in the process of fermentation, adhering to the sides of wine casks in the form of a hard crust. When this crust is purified it forms white crystals which are then known as cream of tartar.

Tartar is also the name for the calcium phosphate which comes from saliva and concretes on the teeth.

Another name for tartar is argol, which is also the name for dried cow-dung used for fuel in Tartary, the central Asian region which is home to the Tartar people.

TASK

Petra sometimes enjoyed setting a child an impossible and useless task, rather like the tasks set for heroes and heroines in fairytales, with the promise of a reward. She had hundreds and hundreds of buttons, and she would give a child a certain time to find a hundred matching buttons and then sew them onto a towel in strict formation. The reward of course was nothing like going to a ball, more like being allowed to paint Petra's fingernails and toenails.

TOLSTOY, LEO (1828–1910)

Next to his study Tolstoy had a workshop where he took regular lessons in shoemaking. He made a pair of boots for one of his friends, Sukhotin, who is said to have stood the shoes in his bookcase next to the first twelve volumes of *War and Peace*, labelling the boots 'Volume 13'.

URINE

Apart from its use in the soaking of feet between bindings in footbinding, urine has a long history in Chinese medicine. A Chinese pharmaceutical text of the Ming dynasty lists the ways in which urine was used. The best urine, it says, comes from boys under the age of twelve, and is used neat, or mixed in soup. It cures headaches, chills, blood-poisoning, obstruction of the bowel, snake-bite, spider-bite and bee-sting. And has been known to cure incurable illnesses. It also has the effect, if taken daily, of preserving youth, and is very effective as an underarm deodorant.

see also FOOT

VIOLETS

In the language of flowers the violet stands for humility and love and death. Its secrecy and vulval shape have also made it a favourite flower among lovers, its scent awakening tender thoughts of love and pleasure and lust.

Along with lavender, violets are emblematic of sapphic love, and for this reason they were beloved by

Virginia Woolf. The perfume, after first thrilling the olfactory nerve, then has a soporific effect on that nerve, and induces a certain langour.

In Christian symbolism the flower stands for the humility of Christ, who deigned to take human form. And in art when violets are mingled with strawberries, which symbolise righteousness, the meaning meant to be conveyed is that the truly spiritual man is humble. The sensuality of both strawberries and violets is overlooked in this code.

White violets are one of the emblems of a thirteenth-century saint, Saint Fina. Her other emblem is a rat. She was a poor, paralysed young woman who spent her time lying on a board being attacked by rats against which she was unable to defend herself. After her death her board was discovered to be carpeted with powerfully sweet white violets.

There are several ancient references to violets. Persephone gathered poppies, narcissus and violets before she was carried off to the underworld. Violets grew on Calypso's island. The ancient Athenians wore crowns of violets, and the Romans placed violets on their banquet tables because the flower was believed to prevent drunkenness. The Romans also scattered violets on the graves of children to symbolise purity and modesty.

Napoleon loved violets and was known as Monsieur Violette after he said he would return from Elba when the violets bloomed in the woods.

In Roman mythology, when Jupiter, having raped Io, changed the girl into a heifer in order to protect her from the wrath of Juno, he gave her fields of violets on which to graze.

And in the ancient lore of Phrygia there was a vegetation god named Attis whose death and resurrection were mourned and celebrated each spring. Attis was born of a virgin who conceived the child by placing an almond in her cleavage. The death of Attis was one of violent self-sacrifice and suicide, as he castrated himself beneath a pine tree and bled to death. From his blood sprang violets.

The perfume of violets is sometimes said to emanate from the bodies, living or dead, of very holy people. The reality of extracting violet perfume from the flowers is as follows:

Lard is heated and fed daily with fresh blooms over a period of three months. Alcohol is then added to the lard, which releases the perfumed oil into the alcohol. The alcohol is heated, evaporated, condensed, and the violet oil can then be collected.

WATER LILIES

Fossils of water lilies have been found in material from as far back as the Upper Cenozoic period, so that water lilies are evolutionally one of the oldest type of plant. The *Victoria regia* is the largest tropical water lily, with gigantic leaves of up to six feet wide. These leaves can bear the weight of a child, and it was fashionable in Victorian India to photograph children seated on the leaves.

The lotus is the water lily of Egypt and Asia, and the images and symbolic meanings of these *Nymphaea* inform the stories of the religions of these regions. The lotus flower is a primary symbol of the vulva, and the lotus came to be seen as the gateway to all inner mysteries of creation. Sexual knowledge was seen as the way to spiritual knowledge, and with proper sexual exercises a sage might achieve the final flowering of revelation described as the thousand-petalled lotus of invisible light.

Giant water lilies such as the *Victoria regia* grow best in regions where there are long, hot summers. All the water lilies and lotuses are hearty feeders and need a good rich loam or clay soil enriched with cow manure which has been stored under cover for at least a year.

Most water lilies bloom on the surface of the water, supporting and feeding the flower at the top of the stalk which grows taller as the level of the water rises. However the fringed villarsia, which doesn't have the ability to lengthen the stalk, just lets the flowers go and they rise to the surface where they burst open like bubbles and can then be fertilised.

One of the most well known European stories in which the water lily is a motif is that of Thumbelina, the tiny girl who spends part of her adventurous life on a lily pad. And there is also the lovely old Buddhist legend of Deerfoot's thousand sons who each sat on a leaf of the thousand-leafed lotus.

*

I have a desire to stop here, with the thousand sons of Deerfoot, each on his leaf of the thousand-leafed lotus. It is obvious that The Footnote could go on forever and ever, with strands of meaning weaving more and more complicated webs, forming thicker and thicker carpets, designing mandalas of greater and greater intricacy. Nothing ever ends. They never got their holocaust, and when they do, that won't be the end. I have explained that my own attitude to time is that time is flat; I have said that the ideas of tense and of memory are tricky ones for me to grasp. Nothing ends. It's an Einstein thing. Nothing ever ends. Ever.

Be not afraid.

Bibliography

Attwater, Donald 1965, *The Penguin Dictionary of Saints*, Penguin, London.

Bachelard, Gaston 1987, *The Psychoanalysis of Fire*, trans. Alan C.M. Ross, Quartet, London.

Begg, Ean 1985, *The Cult of the Black Virgin*, Arkana, London.

Bettleheim, Bruno 1976, *The Uses of Enchantment*, Thames & Hudson, London.

Birch, Cyril (ed.) 1967, *Anthology of Chinese Literature*, Penguin, London.

Bredsdorff, Elias 1975, *Hans Christian Andersen*, Phaidon Press, London.

Brent, Peter 1972, *The Godmen of India*, Penguin, London.

Bronfen, Elisabeth 1992, *Over Her Dead Body: Death, Femininity and the Aesthetic*, Routledge, New York.

Cooper, J.C. 1978, *An Illustrated Encyclopaedia of Traditional Symbols*, Thames & Hudson, London.

Cornell, Judith 1994, *Mandala*, Quest Books, New York.

Drury, Nevill 1978, *Don Juan, Mescalito and Modern Magic*, Routledge and Kegan Paul, New York.

Eco, Umberto 1986, *Travels in Hyper-Reality*, Macmillan, London.

—— 1994, *Six Walks in the Fictional Woods*, Harvard University Press, Massachusetts.

Estes, Clarissa Pinkola 1992, *Women Who Run With the Wolves*, Random House, London.

Farmer, David Hugh 1978, *The Oxford Dictionary of Saints*, Oxford University Press, Oxford.

Feng, Jicai 1994, *The Three-inch Golden Lotus*, trans. David Wakefield, University of Hawaii Press, Hawaii.

Friday, Nancy 1996, *The Power of Beauty*, Hutchinson, London.

Gibbons, Monk 1951, *The Tales of Hoffmann*, Saturn Press, London.

Hamilton-Byrne, Sarah 1995, *Unseen Unheard Unknown*, Penguin, Melbourne.

Haskell, Arnold L. 1938, *Ballet Panorama*, B.T. Batesford, London.

Hollyer, Belinda 1995, *Stories From the Classical Ballet*, Macmillan, London.

Humphrey, Derek 1992, *Final Exit*, Penguin, Melbourne.

Johnson, Raynor C. 1963, *A Religious Outlook For Modern Man*, Hodder and Stoughton, London.

Jung, C.G. 1976, *Man and His Symbols*, Jupiter, New York.

Kaplan, David E. & Marshall, Andrew 1966, *The Cult at the End of the World*, Arrow, London.

Kingdom, Robert M. 1988, *Myths About the St Bartholomew's Day Massacres 1572–1576*, Harvard University Press, Massachusetts.

Klaw, Spencer 1993, *Without Sin*, Penguin, New York.

Levy, Howard S. 1992, *The Lotus Lovers*, Prometheus Books, New York.

Macfie, J.M. 1924, *Myths and Legends of India*, T. and T. Clark, Edinburgh.

Mackenzie, Donald A. 1994, *India,* Senate, London.

Maeterlinck, Maurice 1909, *The Bluebird*, trans. Alexander Teixeira de Mattos, Methuen, London.

Mann, John 1992, *Murder, Magic and Medicine*, Oxford University Press, Oxford.

Masson, Jeffery 1993, *My Father's Guru*, HarperCollins, London.

Mean, Carrillo 1975, *Sex and Shoe*, Bedrock Press, Woodpecker Point.

Morris, Desmond 1985, *Bodywatching*, Jonathan Cape, London.

Nerval, Gérard de 1965, *Les Filles du Feu*, Garnier-Flammarion, Paris.

Nogueres, Henri 1962, *The Massacre of Saint Bartholomew*, trans. Clair Elaine Engel, George Allen and Unwin, London.

Opie, Iona and Peter 1974, *The Classic Fairy Tales*, Oxford University Press, Oxford.

Ostwald, Peter 1991, *Vaslav Nijinsky: A Leap into Madness,* Robson Books, London.

Ovid, *Metamorphoses*, trans. Mary M. Innes, Penguin, London.

Parmelee, Alice 1960, *All the Birds of the Bible*, Lutterworth Press, London.

Philpotts, Beatrice 1980, *Mermaids*, Random House, New York.

Pizzetti & Cocker 1968, *Flowers: A Guide for Your Garden*, Harry N. Abrams, New York.

Prager, Emily 1983, *A Visit from the Footbinder*, Chatto and Windus, London.

Propp, Vladimir 1968, *The Morphology of the Folktale*, University of Texas Press, Texas.

Reyner, Ferdinand 1974, *Concise Encyclopaedia of Ballet*, trans. Andre Gateau, W. M. Collins, London.

Ricci, Stefania 1992, *Salvatore Ferragamo: The Art of the Shoe 1898–1960*, Rizzoli International Publications, New York.

Rowland, Beryl 1978, *Birds With Human Souls*, University of Tennessee Press, Knoxville.

Soman, Alfred (ed.) 1974, *The Massacre of Saint Bartholomew: Reappraisals and Documents*, Martinus Nijoff, The Hague.

Sutherland, N.M. 1973, *The Massacre of St Bartholomew and the European Conflict 1559–1572*, Macmillan, New York.

Shah, Idries 1968, *The Way of the Sufi*, Jonathan Cape, London.

Sister Nivedita (Margaret E. Noble) 1917, *Cradle Tales of Hinduism*, Longman, Green and Co., London.

Sorell, Walter 1967, *The Dance Through the Ages*, Thames & Hudson, London.

Stodola, Dr Jiri 1967, *Encyclopaedia of Water Plants*, T.F.H. Publications, New Jersey.

Storr, Anthony 1996, *Feet of Clay*, HarperCollins, London.

Terry, Walter 1954, *Star Performance*, Doubleday, New York.

von Franz, Marie-Louise 1978, *Time: Rhythm and Repose*, Thames & Hudson, London.

Walker, Barbara G. 1983, *The Woman's Encyclopaedia of Myths and Secrets*, Harper and Row, New York.

Warner, Marina 1981, *Joan of Arc*, Weidenfeld and Nicolson, London.

—— 1994, *From the Beast to the Blonde*, Chatto and Windus, London.

Wasson, R.G. 1968, *Soma: Divine Mushroom of Mortality*, Harcourt, Brace and World, New York.

Whistler, Rex 1959, *Hans Andersen*, The Bodley Head, London.

Zipes, Jack 1989, *The Brothers Grimm*, Routledge, New York.